W9-AUD-353

MISSING ISAAC

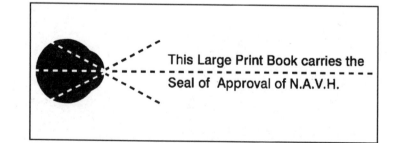
This Large Print Book carries the
Seal of Approval of N.A.V.H.

MISSING ISAAC

VALERIE FRASER LUESSE

THORNDIKE PRESS
A part of Gale, a Cengage Company

Farmington Hills, Mich • San Francisco • New York • Waterville, Maine
Meriden, Conn • Mason, Ohio • Chicago

**LIBRARY OF CONGRESS CIP DATA ON FILE.
CATALOGUING IN PUBLICATION FOR THIS BOOK
IS AVAILABLE FROM THE LIBRARY OF CONGRESS**

ISBN-13: 978-1-4328-4826-2 (hardcover)

Published in 2018 by arrangement with Revell Books, a division of Baker Publishing Group

Printed in the United States of America
1 2 3 4 5 6 7 22 21 20 19 18

For Dave and my parents

PART I

ONE

October 10, 1962

A sleepy purple twilight wrapped around the farmhouse, its tall windows glowing with warmth from somewhere inside. It was suppertime, and the cool October air smelled of cotton lint and field dust. Inside was an eleven-year-old boy playing checkers with his grandfather. As was his custom lately, he wore a flannel shirt many sizes too big for him.

"Pete, honey, you've got a closetful of clothes — why do you insist on wearing that old hand-me-down of your daddy's?" his mother asked.

"I don't know," he said with a shrug. " 'Cause he gave it to me, I guess."

There was more to it than that, of course. The truth was that Pete's father was both his hero and his best friend. There was no one he admired more than Jack McLean, no one he so longed to emulate. Not only that, but he thoroughly enjoyed his father's company — and Pete could tell the feeling was mutual.

So there he sat at his mother's kitchen table, wearing his daddy's shirt and holding a tentative finger on one of two red checkers still remaining on the board. "Okay, Daddy Ballard," he said to his grandfather as he lifted his finger and leaned back in his chair. "Your move." Their checkers game had become a weeknight ritual.

"You sure, son?" his grandfather said with a grin.

"Yes, sir."

Pete's mother peeled a colander of potatoes at the sink as a radio played in the windowsill.

Mrs. Kennedy attended a charity luncheon in Washington this afternoon. The First Lady wore an autumnal suit of red wool crepe . . .

Daddy Ballard made the only remaining move left to him. Pete's face lit up when he saw his opportunity — the long-awaited winning jump.

"I won! I finally won!" he cried as his grandfather laughed. "Wanna play again?"

His mother shook her head. "Now, Pete,

you know your daddy'll be home before too much long —"

She was interrupted by the blaring of a truck horn. It blew and blew all the way from the county blacktop, and you could hear the tires slinging gravel as they sped up the driveway and into the backyard. Pete looked at his mother, whose face had frozen in fear and dread.

All three of them had heard it — the split-second transformation of ordinary sounds into a cry of alarm. Truck horns, tires churning gravel, men yelling to be heard over machinery — these were everyday background noises on the farm. But when something went wrong, when someone got hurt, those very same sounds took on an urgent tenor. You could hear it. You could feel it in your bones.

"Y'all in there? Come quick!" It was Isaac, one of Daddy Ballard's field hands, who helped Pete's father work the cotton.

The adults bolted for Isaac's truck, with Pete leaping over the tailgate and crouching in back before they had time to tell him not to. Cold wind blasted his face as they raced down the narrow strip of pavement to a dirt road that divided two sprawling cotton fields. He had to hold on tight as Isaac drove straight through the cotton, bouncing

11

over furrows and tearing through tall, brittle stalks to get to a giant ball of light glowing in the distance.

So many trucks were beaming headlights onto the accident that it looked like a football stadium on Friday night. Chains rattled and clouds of red dust swirled everywhere as the field hands and Pete's uncles — summoned from their own family farm — made a frantic attempt at a rescue.

"Shut that engine off!"

"Get the slack out! I said get the slack out!"

"Back up, back up, back up!"

"Can you see him? I said can you *see* him!"

Daddy Ballard held Pete's mother back.

"Jack!" She screamed his name over and over and over.

At the center of it all was a massive red machine, his father's cotton picker, turned upside down in a sinkhole like a cork in a bottle. One of its back wheels was still spinning against the night sky, like it was trying to run over the moon. Pete could hear — or maybe he just imagined — clods of red clay splashing into the watery sinkhole far below the snowy clouds of cotton. And he knew, without anybody telling him, that his father was lost.

Spotting him standing beside the truck, wide-eyed and horrified, Isaac came to pick him up. But with nowhere to take him, Isaac just walked around and around the truck, Pete's legs dangling like a rag doll.

"You gonna be alright. You gonna be alright. We gonna make it alright." Isaac was shaking.

Pete heard a loud, booming crash as the trucks pulled the picker over onto its side to clear the hole.

"There he is! Lower me down! Hurry!" That was Uncle Danny, his father's oldest brother. Isaac had stopped in a spot that kept Pete's back to the accident. "Pull! Ever'body pull harder!"

There was a momentary silence before Pete heard the sound of water dripping off of something heavy. It reminded him of the sound his father's Sunday shirts made when his mother hand-washed them, plunging the saturated cloth up and down in the sink.

Soon the field hands began to moan. "Sweet Jesus. Mister Jack . . ."

Only then did Pete realize it — Isaac was soaking wet.

TWO

October 12, 1962

Pete stood next to his mother at the head of a long line of family just outside the First Baptist Church of Glory, with Daddy Ballard and Aunt Geneva, his mother's only sister, behind them. It felt oddly like Vacation Bible School, when the kids all lined up to march in and pledge their allegiance "to the Bible, God's Holy Word," before adjourning to their classrooms to memorize the names of the disciples and decorate bars of soap to give their mothers on commencement night.

Pete had tried hard to get all of his crying done last night — privately, in his room, sobbing into a pillow so his mother wouldn't hear. He couldn't bear the thought of making this day any harder for her than it already was. Grown men in the line were sniffling and dabbing at their eyes, but Pete remained stoic. Except for the sweat. He

14

could feel it soaking the dress shirt underneath his suit coat. And because he had forgotten all about the white handkerchief in his pocket, he wiped his damp brow with the sleeve of his coat. How could it be this hot in October? That didn't make any sense. And why wasn't everybody talking about it? Grown people usually went on and on about the slightest hiccup in the weather.

First Baptist was a pretty little church — red brick with double white doors, arched windows, and a big iron bell hanging beneath the steeple. Just last Wednesday, the church held a business meeting and voted to modernize by starting a central air fund, but for now the windows were slightly open to circulate the autumn air, and Pete could hear Miss Beulah Pryor finishing up "Heaven Will Surely Be Worth It All" on the organ. Soon she would play "Precious Memories," which was what she always played when families marched in to bury their dead.

As she began the opening strains, the undertaker opened the church door with one hand and summoned the family with the other. The sun shone so brightly in Pete's eyes that the man's face was just a featureless shadow. All he could see clearly was that spooky beckoning arm. His legs felt like they were turning to sand, and he didn't think he could move, but somehow he managed, one foot ahead of the other, up the steps and down the aisle.

Pete could feel the old wooden floor give a little with the weight of his family marching in, but he knew it would hold, as it had for so many other families before. He took his seat on the front pew between his mother and Daddy Ballard. Ordinarily Aunt Geneva would be playing the piano for the service. But not today. She and her family sat right behind them.

His mother kept still, her eyes fixed on the white dove that hung on the back wall of the baptistery. Hers was not a calm stillness but a constrained one, as if the slightest move might send her flying all to pieces. Miss Beulah's sister began to sing.

Precious mem'ries, how they linger.
How they ever flood my soul.

Pete ran his fingers through his sandy-brown hair, thick and wavy like his father's. His mother had tried for the longest time to subdue it with Brylcreem. But then out of the blue one Sunday morning, she pitched the Brylcreem in the trash, shrugged, and said, "Well, I guess the Lord blessed you and your daddy with untamable hair. Who am I to question it?"

Pete couldn't remember which had brought him more pleasure — emancipation from hair potion or the comparison to his father.

The family had congregated at his parents' rambling white farmhouse that morning so they could travel to the church together. All morning long, Pete had marveled at the adults' ability to talk about anything and everything except the terrible thing that had brought them together.

"Has everybody got coffee that wants some?"

"It's so good to see y'all. 'Course, we wish it was under happier circumstances . . ."

The aunts especially liked to talk about those "happier circumstances." With the exception of "some things we just can't understand," it was their very favorite thing to say.

A few minutes before eleven, Uncle Danny had called the family together in the living room. "Let's have a word of prayer before we go. And on the way to the church, y'all remember to burn your brights."

The whole family traveled in one long caravan with their headlights on high beam. All along the three-mile drive, every car and truck that they met pulled over to the side of the road in a silent show of respect. Ever since he was a little boy, Pete had known that burning headlights in a procession meant, "We're burying somebody we love," and the cars idling on the shoulder were answering, "We're just as sorry as we can be." Nobody had to say a word. They didn't even have to know each other. Their vehicles did the talking.

The preacher's voice brought Pete back to the church and the unthinkable thing that was happening.

"To everything there is a season. A time to live and a time to die. A time to plant and a time — like right now, as all you farmers know — to pluck up that which was planted. There is a time to mourn and a time to dance. Folks, don't nobody in this church feel like dancing today. Because for reasons we can't understand, it was Brother Jack's time to die — just as he was plucking up that which he had planted."

There was a logical reason for sinkholes. Daddy Ballard had once explained it. Some parts of Alabama have layers of limestone beneath the soil, and there are places where water flows beneath the rock. The water can wear away such a big section of limestone that the cotton field is like a rug covering up a hole in the floor. Anything heavy that runs over it will fall straight through. Pete's father had fallen through a rug of red clay and landed in a deep, dark hole. He had gone to the field that morning just as he had done his whole life. But this time, his field devoured him.

Pete rejoined the sermon just as the congregation stood for the closing prayer. He had no idea what the preacher had said. All he knew was that the pallbearers were about to carry his father away. Forever.

"Almighty God, we humbly come before you seeking that peace that passeth all understanding . . ."

After the funeral, the entire community descended on Pete's house, but the crowd was a blur to him, like a swarm of gnats swirling around the only person he really wanted to talk to right now, his mother. She had taken his father's worn leather recliner as her post and wouldn't leave it. She must've sat there for hours. As neighbors and church members filed in, they would lean down to hug her or reach out to squeeze her hand. Somehow she would smile and thank them "so much for everything." But Pete could see that she wasn't really there. His mother had hidden herself away somewhere deep down in that shell of politeness. He couldn't reach her. Nobody could. But he knew that wherever she was, she was still screaming his father's name.

He wandered into the dining room, where his Aunt Virgie was rearranging the already crowded buffet to make room for still more food just delivered by the Methodist ladies, who didn't see him at first. In hushed voices, they discussed his father's accident.

"Can you believe it? Before the family could get there, that colored boy found him an opening and jumped in that sinkhole tryin' to save Jack. They say he didn't have nothin' but a flimsy hay rope tied around him. It's a thousand wonders they're not layin' him in the ground at Morning Star Baptist this very minute."

Before Pete could hear any more, Aunt Virgie glanced up from the pound cake she was slicing and saw him standing there. She was actually his great-aunt, Daddy Ballard's sister. She was at least six feet tall and stout as a field hand.

"Pete, honey," she said, "c'mere and let your Aunt Virgie fix you a plate."

The Methodist ladies scattered.

"I'm not hungry," Pete said, "but thank you." The truth was that he didn't think he could swallow anything without throwing up.

"Well, you just let Aunt Virgie know if you change your mind, punkin'."

He knew she meant well, but she was talking to him like he was four, and that made him want to kick her in the shins, which was a mean and spiteful way to feel. "Don't be like that," his mother would say.

If food like this had appeared on a normal day, he wouldn't be able to fill his plate fast enough. The table, buffet, and kitchen counters were covered with platters of fried chicken, casseroles, and heaping bowls of potato salad, along with black-eyed peas, butter beans, creamed corn, green beans, candied sweet potatoes, and mountains of dinner rolls. Pete counted five plates of deviled eggs, three chocolate layer cakes, a red velvet cake, four pecan pies, a ham from Aunt Virgie's smokehouse, a big Mason jar of her homemade mustard, and a disturbing number of congealed salads made from Jell-O. Why couldn't people just bring Jell-O instead of mixing it with heaven knows what and covering it with marshmallows and nuts? Miss Beulah was forever bringing that awful lime-green one that Pete hated most of all.

In desperate need of escape, he slipped upstairs. There, in the blessed quiet of his room, he spotted something small, about the size of a pocketknife, on his bed. He smiled, even on this awful day, because he immediately recognized it — the rabbit's foot Isaac had often let him see but never let him touch.

"You let somebody touch your rabbit's foot," Isaac had told him, "and you got to give it to him. Otherwise, it's gonna bring you bad luck, the kinda bad luck usually 'sociated with a black cat crossin' your path. And that there's some serious bad luck."

Isaac had been a fixture on the farm ever since he was old enough to handle a hoe. When Pete was very small and would beg to go to the fields, he would sometimes get so tired that he fell asleep riding on the tractor in his father's lap. It was Isaac who would carry him to the truck and drive him home.

Now, Isaac was one of only ten or so field hands working for Daddy Ballard. Pete had heard the older men at church talk about times back in the thirties and forties when all the cotton had to be chopped, hoed, and picked by hand, and his grandfather had employed at least fifty hands — men and women, black and white. But machines had made it harder for poor people like Isaac to find work in the fields. He had been helping the Ballard family raise cotton since he was a boy and was like a right arm to Pete's father, who had been running the whole farm since Daddy Ballard retired. Isaac was likely around thirty, though Pete had a hard time guessing grown people's ages.

As he opened the window by his bed and looked out, Isaac waved to him from the barn, holding up two cane fishing poles.

"Gimme a minute to get outta my church clothes!" Pete called out.

Isaac pointed to the ladder he had propped against the house beneath the window and sat down to wait on a concrete table underneath the pecan trees. That was where Pete's father always cleaned the fish he caught.

Isaac was over six feet tall and broad-shouldered, with the kind of muscles you get from working hard, not from playing football. His skin was the color of strong coffee, and he had a kind face, one that looked like he would be glad to help you if there was any way he could. His work pants and cotton shirts were patched and worn but always neatly pressed. That was his mother's doing. Hattie hated wrinkles. She said they made a person look "no-account." Isaac was never without a wide-brimmed black fedora to keep the sun off his face and a black leather belt with a silver buckle that had a four-leaf clover stamped into it.

Colored girls thought he was handsome, Pete could tell. Once, and only once, he and his father had secretly accompanied Isaac to Tandy's, a barbecue joint that white people didn't go to — didn't even know about since Tandy ran it out of her tiny backyard, where everybody sat on five-gallon buckets turned upside down. Isaac knew how much Pete's father loved good ribs and had cleared it with Tandy to bring the two of them just that one time. When Isaac walked by a bunch of colored girls, they started giggling and whispering to each other. A new girl in the crowd had spotted him and "prissed up," as Isaac called it.

"What's this here?" she asked with a grin.

He answered, "M'name's Isaac — but you can call me Lucky." He winked when he said that last part. Isaac believed in luck. That's why he had carried the same rabbit's foot all these years.

Pete scrambled to get out of his suit and into his jeans and a T-shirt. He took time, though, to hang up his church clothes. No need to upset his mother today. He wanted to get a message to her. Opening his bedroom door to see who might be milling around in the hallway, he spotted his aunt coming out of the upstairs bathroom. "Aunt

24

Geneva," he said, "do you think it would be okay if I went with Isaac for a little while?"

She gave a sad smile and laid her hand against his cheek. "I think that would be fine, sweetheart," she said. "Want me to let your mama know?"

"Yes, ma'am."

"I'll tell her." Aunt Geneva slowly walked down the stairs, sinking into the great swell of conversation as Pete went back to his room. Slipping the rabbit's foot into his pocket, he pulled the flimsy screen off two bottom nails that barely held it to the window, climbed down the ladder, and ran across the backyard just as Mr. and Mrs. Highland were getting out of their car. The Highlands were from Birmingham and liked to tell everybody how things were done "in town." Pete wondered why they'd ever moved to a little dot on the map like Glory if they liked the city so much.

As she crossed the yard, Mrs. Highland pulled a mirror out of her purse and fussed with her hair. She was so busy studying herself that she didn't see Isaac standing there with his fishing poles, and bumped right into him.

"Beg pardon, ma'am," Isaac said, backing away from her the way you'd back away from a dog that might bite.

"Don't you people ever look where you're going?" she snapped as she kept walking.

"But Isaac didn't —" Pete stopped himself when Isaac put a hand on his shoulder.

"C'mon, Pete," he whispered. "Ain't no good come o' stirrin' that one up."

Isaac loaded the cane poles into his green pickup, and the two of them headed for Copper Creek — Pete's favorite. Right beneath the bridge, the creek was shallow, with cold, clear water gurgling over big rocks so smooth they looked like they had been hand-sanded and spit-shined. The water deepened just beyond a bend that you could barely make out from the road.

Isaac pulled over once they cleared the bridge, taking the cane poles, a stringer, and a box of worms out of his truck. "I can carry something," Pete said, and Isaac handed him one of the poles. They made their way down the bank and into the woods to a prime spot underneath a big cottonwood tree and plopped their corks in the water.

Once they got situated, Isaac sat quietly, looking out over the creek in the direction of his cork. Pete had always appreciated the way Isaac never rushed him into a conversation. He had a way of knowing when you were ready to talk and leaving you be till you got there.

"Isaac," Pete finally said, "did you really jump in and try to save Daddy before Uncle Danny and them got there?"

Isaac gave a weary sigh as he stared at the creek. "You don't need no pictures like that cloudin' up your mind," he said.

"But did you?"

Isaac hesitated. "Yeah," he finally said, without embellishing.

"Were you scared?"

"Yeah."

"But you did it anyways?"

"Mm-hmm."

"How come?"

Isaac's cork bobbed on the water and he gave his line a little tug. But the cork popped back up and steadied itself. "I reckon I done it 'cause I knew your daddy woulda jumped in there for me. Ain't many people I can say that about. Sho' ain't no white men I can say it about." As Pete's cork went underwater, Isaac said, "Looka yonder — you need to quit pesterin' me and look after your fish."

Pete gave the pole a tug and then stood up on the bank to pull in a small bream not big enough to fry. "I reckon I'll let 'im go," he said, freeing the fish and tossing it back in the creek. He put another worm on his hook, dropped his line in the water, and sat back down next to Isaac. They were silent for a while before Pete quietly said, "Thank you for tryin'."

"You welcome," Isaac answered. For a time, the two of them watched their corks and listened to the peaceful sound of the creek moving through the woods. But Pete had more questions.

"Isaac, how old were you when your daddy died?"

"Little older'n you — thirteen or so."

"Was it scary?"

"Whoo, yeah. But I didn't have time to be scared long 'cause they was people to feed — Mavis and Letha and Junie and Iris and Mama and me. Life throw you a hairpin turn sometimes — ain't nothin' you can do but keep drivin' and try to keep it in the road."

"Is that how come you didn't finish school?"

"Yeah, but our school wasn't much noways. B'lieve I taught myself more with all them books Mama brings me than I ever woulda learned at that little school."

"Where'd you get all your books — without going to school, I mean?" Now that Pete thought about it, he had never seen any colored people in the county library.

Isaac smiled. "Mama," he said. "She got it

all figured out. See, while she dusts all them white people's bookshelves, she keeps her eye out for anything she thinks I might like. She knows I love to read them history books and anything 'bout the ocean. When one o' them white ladies is feelin' 'specially worrisome about some get-together, Mama mentions to 'em — kinda casual like — how she sure would 'preciate any old books they weren't readin' no more, like maybe that *Treasure Island* and *History of Alabama.* And then she makes a point of lookin' at that watch Iris give her, like she might have to leave soon."

"And all those ladies give her books?" Pete asked.

"You kiddin' me, Pete? Mama's such good help that once word got out 'bout the books, some of them white women went out and bought some they thought she might want. She got 'em baitin' their bookshelves, tryin' to hook her into workin' for 'em. Mama's a sight. Now that she don't have to work for nobody but your granddaddy, he goes to the county liberry for her. Even gives her his *Birmin'ham News* after he's done with it, on accounta I told her I kinda like to know what's goin' on in the world."

"You got a favorite book?"

"Now, that there's hard to say." Isaac

paused for a moment to think it over. "I reckon if I had to pick one, it'd be *Treasure Island.* That boy Jim sure gets into some scrapes with all them pirates, but he makes it through alright."

"Ever wish you was a pirate?" Pete asked, tugging at his fishing line.

"Naw, I don't wanna be no pirate. Sure would like to be a sailor, though, out there on that big water, lookin' up at the sky from the deck of a ship bound for somewhere that don't look like no place I ever been. That'd be fine. It surely would."

"You could join the navy," Pete suggested.

"Naw," Isaac said. "Done got too old. They don't want the likes o' me. Plus the paper says we headed for war over in Vietnam, and that don't sound like no place I wanna go."

"How come you didn't join up when you were younger?"

"Mama needed me here," Isaac said. "Even missed the draft on accounta what they call a hardship exemption. Mighta been nice to ship out for some place across the ocean — back when there wasn't no war, I mean."

Pete felt a whole new wave of sadness. It had never occurred to him that Isaac might want to be anything different from what he was. The thought of his friend plowing cotton when he longed to sail the sea left a weight on Pete that he didn't know how to carry.

It was made even heavier by a sudden memory of his father — of the three of them — from last summer. Pete had ridden with the men to haul a new tractor tire from a dealership in Childersburg, and they had stopped at the Dairy Queen for foot-longs and milkshakes on the way back. While he and his father ordered at the window, Isaac waited in the truck. As they were bringing the food back, a wiry white teenager with greasy hair and a dirty T-shirt passed by and spotted Isaac.

"Boy, you ain't got no business here." He angrily jabbed his finger at Isaac's open window as he said it. Pete's father hurried him into the truck and set the food on the driver's seat. Then he stepped around to face the white boy.

"I'm not in the habit of askin' *children* where I can and can't go — or who I can bring with me," he said. "You need to move along."

The teenager had puffed out his chest the way boys do when they think they want to fight. He took a menacing step toward Pete's father, who didn't budge or flinch as he repeated, "Move along."

Jack McLean was at least a head taller than his adversary and clearly twice as strong. He had a look on his face that Pete had never seen before. Apparently the teenager saw it too. He moved along. When Pete's father got back in the truck and started handing out the foot-longs and milkshakes, Pete expected Isaac to thank his daddy for running that boy off. But he didn't. Isaac had a strange expression of his own — part angry and part sad, but mostly just far away, like he had suddenly gone to a place Pete couldn't get to.

"Pete, hold my milkshake for me while I get us down the road," was all his father said. The three of them ate their lunch on the highway, wasting no time getting away from whatever it was that just happened. Pete had never asked his father about it. He couldn't exactly say why.

"Where's your mind, Pete?" Isaac was saying, casting his line into the creek. "You look like you a million miles away."

Pete just smiled at him. "Hey, what book you readin' now?" he asked, searching for something happy to talk about.

"It's a real excitin' one 'bout the Gulf of Mexico," Isaac said. "You ever hear tell of a hurricane, Pete?"

"Ain't it some kinda big storm?"

"That's right. Only it's a storm like we ain't never seen. It starts way out in the ocean, and when it's out there in the water, they call it a tropical de-pression. Then it goes to headin' for land, and it gets bigger and bigger till it turns into a mighty wheel o' wind. And that wheel gets to goin' faster and faster the closer it gets to land, till by the time it hits, it's so powerful it goes to rippin' up trees and pushin' up waves the size of a barn and spinnin' off tornadoes and all such as that. They was one down in Texas a year or so ago that had 175-mile-a-hour winds. Can you b'lieve that? Ain't no car 'round here go no 175. And you know what else? They name them hurricanes after *women.* That one what tore up Texas go by the name o' Carla. Sho' is a pretty name for such a mean piece of weather. Then again, I reckon I met up with lots o' pretty women that was mean pieces of weather."

Pete giggled, pleased with himself for getting a grown-up joke. "Isaac, I think I'd like to see one o' them hurricanes."

"You crazy, Pete? Hurricane'll kill you. Don't you lemme catch you chasin' after no hurricane."

"Oh, I don't mean get *in* one. I just wonder what it looks like comin' in, you know? The people on the shore — what do they see when that mighty wheel o' wind is pushin' all that ocean straight for 'em?"

"I reckon they too busy runnin' from it to study it much," Isaac said. "But I know what you mean. Sometimes you just wanna see things you ain't used to seein'. Nothin' wrong with that."

Pete leaned out so he could see his reflection in the water. This little creek would ramble south to the Coosa River, which would eventually hook up with the Alabama and head down to the gulf. He wondered if the flowing water could somehow carry his image all the way down, from creek to river to sea.

"You said something 'bout bein' scared a while ago," Isaac said. "You scared o' the world without your daddy?"

Pete nodded.

"That's alright. Ain't nothin' to be 'shamed of. You lucky on accounta you got lotsa folks gonna look out for you. But one of these days, we all got to learn how to look out for ourselfs. And you can do it, Pete. I got faith in you."

Pete smiled. "Hey, thanks for the rabbit's foot."

"You welcome. Don't you be lettin' nobody touch it, now."

"I won't. How'd you get it in the house?"

"Climbed up to the window and pitched it in while y'all was at the church. Remind me to fix that ol' window screen for your mama so the mosquitoes won't carry you off."

"I saw you at the cemetery. 'Preciate you comin'."

All the field hands — black and white — had come to the graveside service. But Isaac wouldn't think of setting foot in a white church, and Pete knew that.

"Hey, when's your church homecoming?" Pete asked.

"First week in May, remember?"

"Can I come again?"

Isaac smiled. "If it's alright with *your* mama, I reckon *my* mama could make room for you on her pew and fry a little extra chicken."

Pete would go to Isaac's church every Sunday if his mother would let him, but instead he only got to go on special occasions. He loved the singsong back and forth between the preacher and the congregation. And the food — have mercy, it was good.

"You still in the choir?" Pete asked him.

"Mm-hmm." Isaac pulled in his line and put another worm on the hook, then plopped his cork into a promising spot

35

under some low-hanging branches.

"When did you and Daddy start singin' together?" Pete asked.

"Hard to say. I just remember I was singin' 'Guide My Feet' — that's prob'ly my favorite — while we loaded the planter one spring, and he started hummin' along. I told him if he meant to jump onto my song like that, he oughta learn the words and sing it proper. So I taught 'em to him. And then we started harmonizin' — your daddy liked to practice his tenor against me on accounta I'm a baritone. Worked out real nice."

"Did he ever teach you any songs?"

"Aw, yeah. Let's see . . . 'Sunset Is Coming but the Sunrise We'll See,' 'Just a Little Talk with Jesus' . . . bunch of them quartet songs. But his very favorite was —"

" 'Amazing Grace.' "

"That's right. 'Amazing Grace.' Most 'specially that last verse. And that's important, Pete. You got to always remember your daddy's favorite hymn. You got to honor him by rememberin' that."

Pete had heard them sing it together a million times. Not only would he remember the song, but he would remember their voices singing it together — forever.

When we've been there ten thousand
    years,
Bright shining as the sun,
We've no less days to sing God's praise
Than when we first begun.

THREE

August 3, 1963

Almost a year had passed since the accident. Pete understood now that his father had been more than just a boss to Isaac. He remembered the sound of the two men laughing together in the fields and the perfect harmony of their voices singing as they hosed down the pickers at night or fueled up tractors in the morning.

One morning they didn't notice Pete playing with his toy trucks nearby, and he heard his father say, "Don't you reckon we could drop that 'mister' business?"

Pete looked up to see Isaac shaking his head. "Naw," he said. "My folks wouldn't like that no more'n yours. Both sides go to sayin' I'm gettin' uppity."

The two men liked to go fishing together whenever a hard rain made the fields too wet to farm. Looking back on it, Pete thought his father might've been more at ease with Isaac than with Daddy Ballard. Many times he had seen his daddy slip Isaac some cash when it wasn't payday, and when Pete asked him why he did that, he said, "Because I know what it's like to want things you can't have."

It was true. Pete's mother's family owned more land than anybody around, but his father came from a hardworking household with six children. Pete had heard him joke about all the hand-me-downs he wore growing up: "By the time those shirts got to me, you could read the phone book through 'em!"

After the accident, Daddy Ballard had hired a manager to oversee things. So now, instead of going to the field with a friend, Isaac was working for a stranger. Pete wondered what that was like — and how Isaac was getting by without the extra cash his father used to provide.

When spring came, Isaac let Pete hang around while he readied tractors for the field, and they went for rides whenever they were sure the farm manager — or worse, Pete's mother — wouldn't catch them. She never used to mind when he rode in the fields with his father, but now she wouldn't hear of letting him near machinery. He and Isaac had to slip around.

In between tractor rides, Isaac had taught Pete how to whistle through his fingers, how to clean the fish he caught so his mother wouldn't have to trouble with it, and how to do a special walk that was supposed to make the girls look at you. Pete wasn't sure he wanted a bunch of girls looking at him, but Isaac said it was important. So every night in his room, he practiced the walk.

In September, Pete would have to go back to school and Isaac would be busy with the harvest, so they were making the most of a waning summer. It was late afternoon, and they were about to sneak over to Tandy's for some barbecue. Pete's mother thought they were going fishing.

"Psst!" Isaac got his attention and nodded toward the fishing pole propped against the barn. He knew Pete's mother was watching them out the kitchen window.

Pete immediately realized his mistake and dramatically smacked himself on the forehead. "Well, would ya look at me!" he said loudly. "About to go *fishin'* without my *fishin'* pole!" He grabbed it from the barn and laid it in the back of the truck. "And we've only got a coupla hours to *fish* before it starts to get dark!"

As Isaac drove them away, Pete asked him, "Did I cover okay?"

Isaac glanced at him and chuckled. "Lemme put it this way, Pete. You best learn how to grow cotton, 'cause you ain't never gonna be no movie actor."

Isaac drove about five miles down the main highway — the Florida Short Route — to a narrow county blacktop that led to his neighborhood. It was almost four when they pulled into Tandy's narrow driveway, and already they could hear laughter and loud conversation coming from the back-yard. Field hands weren't needed much right now, so they got off early on Fridays and Saturdays. (Nobody farmed on Sundays. The ladies of every church in town saw to that.) Since most everybody who came to Tandy's lived in her neighborhood, they could just walk over — a good thing since many of them were too poor to own a car. You'd never know something like this was going on if you didn't have Isaac to show you.

The two of them had been here so many times that Pete now had his own special bucket to sit on as everybody gathered to eat their spare ribs and sip ice-cold beer. Tandy's was a grown-up place, where she and her neighbors came to forget the fields they plowed and the houses they cleaned and have a good time together. They would

41

take barbecue home to their families, but they didn't bring their kids here. Tandy despised children and wasn't shy about saying so, but she had made an exception in Pete's case. There was just something about "them big blue eyes and that sweet smile," she had said the first time Isaac brought him there. Tandy had even taken to slipping a few Co-Colas and Grapicos into the galvanized washtub where she iced down the beer so Pete could have a cold drink.

"Well, look what the cat drug in," she said as the two of them came through the little gate that led into her backyard.

"Hey, Miss Tandy," Pete said. Without thinking much about it, he had added "Miss" and "Mister" to everybody's name here. When he did that for white people, it was a sign of affection or familiarity. Here it was a sign of respect that he felt Isaac would want him to show.

Tandy grinned. "Hey, y'self."

She was turning ribs on a grill made from a metal barrel that had been cut in half. A sauce-smeared apron protected her overalls. She was wearing pink scuff slippers and had a pink kerchief tied around her head. Tandy looked older than Isaac — maybe in her forties. She was tiny but fiery. Pete had seen her run big, strapping men out of her yard when they had guzzled too much beer and started getting on her nerves. That was one thing you *never* wanted to do — get on Tandy's nerves. Just to make sure he didn't get in the way, Pete left Isaac and Tandy alone and went to find his bucket.

Isaac handed Tandy some money from his pocket. "That's for last time and today," he said. "Sorry 'bout the wait."

"Somebody musta had a good night at the poker shed," she said. "You know that's a sorry bunch you runnin' with out there."

"Yeah. But I just got to have some kinda break in the days, even when I know I got a losin' hand. Ain't got much else."

"You got him," Tandy said, nodding toward Pete settling in at his usual spot in her backyard.

Isaac glanced across the yard at his young charge, who was using his shirttail to wipe some dust off Isaac's bucket.

"That boy looks up to me 'cause he don't know no better," Isaac said. "I ain't the man his daddy was."

"I 'magine his daddy would disagree, seein' as how you jumped down in that hole and like to died tryin' to save him."

Isaac shrugged. "Maybe I'm sorry as anybody at that card table."

"Naw, y'ain't," Tandy said, turning a row of ribs and closing the lid on her grill. She looked up from the smoke, tilted her head a little, and studied Isaac. "That white boy sees you better'n you see y'self. And I'm fixin' to tell you what he's lookin' at. He's lookin' at a butterfly what done flew through a tear in the screen door and now can't find his way back out the house. So he just light there at the kitchen window, flutterin' his wings and wishin' for the clear, blue sky." She shook her head and sighed. "I'd shoo you to the door m'self if I could find it. Go on and get y'self comf'table. I'll bring you some ribs directly."

Pete and Isaac were just digging into their barbecue, which Tandy served on brown paper, when the gate opened and a shout went up.

"Gap Tooth! Great day in the mornin', it's really him! Tandy, looka here — Gap Tooth's back!"

Tandy sauntered up to the tall, lanky black man with a guitar strapped to his back. He was wearing a suit of peacock blue, with a fedora and shoes to match. He looked like an exotic bird. "What make you think I'm gonna waste a single one o' my ribs on the likes o' you?" she said.

44

Pete thought the peacock man was about to be tossed out. But then he picked Tandy up and twirled her around as he said, "You gonna feed me 'cause you my big sister, and I *love* you!" He kept twirling her around as the two of them laughed and hugged each other. Pete had never heard Tandy laugh — and certainly had never seen her hug anybody.

"Who is *that*?" Pete whispered to Isaac.

"Tandy's brother, Tommy — nickname o' Gap Tooth," Isaac said. "He's a blues man. Travels all over the place — been up in Chicago for the last year or so."

Pete was lost. "What's a blues man?"

"He plays this music come outta Mississippi — or Georgia or Alabama, dependin' on who you b'lieve. Hard to explain. But after you hear it, you ain't never gonna forget it. I call it low-down music. Gap Tooth, he's been playin' it since he was old as you. He's *good.* He's *real* good."

"You reckon he might play something — since he brought his guitar with him, I mean?" Pete knew it was rude to stare, but he couldn't stop watching the peacock man.

"I reckon he might — after he gets him some ribs," Isaac said. "How 'bout you? Want some more?"

"Naw, I'm full."

45

"I see that." Isaac grinned, wiping a smear of barbecue sauce off Pete's chin with his napkin.

They were still laughing about the barbecue smear and talking about the blues when a tall shadow fell over Pete. He looked up to see the peacock man standing right in front of him, holding a half-eaten rib in one hand.

"Who in the Sam Hill is this?" Gap Tooth demanded.

"This here's Pete — Mister Jack's boy." Isaac stood up and shook hands. "Welcome home, Tommy."

"Thank you, brother. Good to see you."

"We slip Pete in now and again — just to get him out the house," Isaac explained. "But his mama thinks we fishin' — 'preciate it if you keep this little visit to y'self."

"Ain't nobody gonna hear it from me," Gap Tooth said, finishing off his rib.

Pete hopped up from his bucket and wiped his hands on his jeans to make sure he didn't get any barbecue sauce on that fancy suit. "I'm very pleased to meet you, Mister Gap Tooth — uh, Mr. Tommy." He held out his hand the way his father taught him.

At first the blues man just stared at him, but then he slowly broke into a gap-toothed grin and shook Pete's hand. "Well, shoot me in the head and bury me at Mornin' Star, 'cause now I done seen it *all*!"

The whole backyard roared with laughter.

"How come Tandy ain't done killed you and hid the body?" he asked Pete.

"I don't rightly know, sir," Pete answered. "I just try real hard not to get on her nerves."

The crowd roared again as Gap Tooth threw back his head and laughed. "You wise, boy — you wise. Tandy done had two husbands never figured that out."

"I see you got you some ribs," Pete said.

"I surely did," Gap Tooth replied. "I'm gonna get me some more later on, but I like to start slow and have me a beer after my first couple."

"I was just wonderin' . . ." Pete stared at the ground as he scraped at the dirt with the toe of his sneaker.

"Wonderin' what?"

"Well, sir, I was just wonderin' if you might play some of that blues music on your guitar. Isaac says you're real good. He says once I hear the blues, I'll never forget it, but I ain't never heard it. It's gonna get dark soon, and I'll have to go home. Reckon you might play just one song before I have to leave?"

The crowd egged him on. "C'mon, Gap Tooth! Play one for the boy! Sang that white baby to sleep, Gap Tooth!"

Gap Tooth laughed. "Y'all are full of it!" But he took the guitar off his back and pulled up a bucket to sit on. The crowd hushed and circled around as he started to play, like a congregation preparing to receive a great message.

Pete drifted over to the blues man's bucket and sat at his feet, captivated by the raspy baritone and fiery guitar licks. After every line or two, the crowd answered Gap Tooth, just like they answered the preacher in church.

When you love a no-good woman,
You gonna hang yo' head and cry.

"Tell it, brother!"

When you love a no-good woman,
You gonna hang yo' head and cry.

"I know that's right."

She told me that she loved me,
But I believe that woman lied.

"You know she did!"

Got to pack that old blue suitcase,
I'm gonna leave this town for good.

Pete listened in stunned silence. When the song ended and the crowd cheered, he just sat there with his mouth hanging open.

"Well?" Gap Tooth said, looking down at him.

"Isaac was right," Pete said. "I ain't *never* gonna forget *that*!"

Gap Tooth grinned at him. "Now get over to that grill and fetch me some more ribs. I ain't workin' for free."

When Pete came back with the ribs, Isaac was waiting for him. "Pete, we gotta hit the road."

"I know," Pete said, looking up at the dusky sky. They had a solemn agreement. Isaac would try to slip him away for these adventures now and again, but Pete had to promise never to breathe a word of it, never to tell his family anything he heard Isaac and his neighbors talk about because you just didn't know what might get somebody fired, and never to put up a fuss when it was time to go. Until now, Pete hadn't found it difficult to hold up his end of the bargain, but this time it was tough. He wanted to stay till midnight, and he wanted to tell everybody in town what the blues sounded like. He wouldn't, though. Isaac was counting on him.

"Hey, Gap Tooth!" someone in the crowd called. "Play 'Dust My Broom'!"

Pete looked up at Isaac to see if they might be able to stay for that one, but Isaac shook his head. So they said their goodbyes. Tandy followed them out and stood at the gate.

"You comin' back?" she asked Isaac as Pete climbed into the truck.

Isaac smiled. "Don't I always?"

"Alright. I save you some ribs."

"You not gettin' sweet on me, now are ya, Tandy?" Isaac gave her a mischievous wink.

"Shut yo' mouth!" she said. But Pete knew she wasn't really mad because she was smiling as Isaac got in the truck and drove away.

When they reached the fork in the road that led out of Isaac's neighborhood, Pete said, "Can I ask you a question?"

"Since when you got to ask me can you ask me?" Isaac looked puzzled.

"Well . . . this one's kinda personal," Pete said.

"Don't know 'bout that, but go on and ask."

"Do you and Tandy like each other?"

" 'Course we do."

"No, I mean do y'all *like*-like each other?"

50

"I reckon we do. Sorta. Sometimes. When you get older, Pete, you gonna find out this *like*-like business, as you call it, can get confusin'."

"Can I be your best man if you and Tandy get married?"

"Time me and her figures that out, I reckon you gonna be plenty old enough to stand up wi' me." Isaac smiled. "Now that you got me married off, you gonna remember our story this time?"

Pete nodded. "We wasn't catchin' nothin' worth keepin', so we threw 'em all back."

"That's right," Isaac said. "You stick to that now, you hear?"

"I hear. Isaac, that song they wanted Gap Tooth to play — about dustin' your broom — what does that mean?"

"Means you gonna leave and never come back."

"Oh. I don't wanna dust my broom. Do you?"

Isaac sighed. "Naw, Pete. Ain't no broom dustin' gonna happen for me."

FOUR

March 28, 1964

"Reckon when you and Tandy might get married?" Pete asked one spring afternoon on the creek bank. Isaac had just helped him figure out some problem or other — there was nothing the two of them couldn't work out together — and it made Pete wonder if his friend ever thought about having kids of his own.

Isaac laughed. "You bound and determined to get me hog-tied?"

"Naw!" Pete giggled. "I just think you'd make a real good daddy."

Isaac stopped laughing and looked away from Pete for the longest time. "You a good young'un, Pete," he finally said. "You stay like you are so you'll grow up to be like your daddy, okay?"

"Okay."

That was about two weeks ago on one of their first fishing trips of the spring. The fall harvest had come and gone, and now the dogwoods were blooming. Summer wasn't far away. Pete had visions of many afternoons on the creek bank once school let out and the cotton was in the ground.

Maybe it came from being an only child, with no brothers or sisters to play with and all of his cousins several years older, but Pete had always been more comfortable with adults than with children his own age. He didn't like the way kids could turn on you. One minute you could be on the playground, happily pitching a baseball back and forth with a schoolmate, and then out of the blue a cooler kid could come along and the two of them would run off together, leaving you all alone with an empty glove. Grown people didn't throw you away like that — Isaac especially.

It was the Saturday before Easter, and he hadn't seen his friend for a week. The fields had been too rain-soaked to plant, so he couldn't figure out why they weren't fishing every day. His mother told him Isaac was likely helping get ready for the Easter service, which was an all-day affair at Morning Star Baptist. That made sense. But Easter was tomorrow, so surely everything was done by now. And today was the best fishing day you could imagine — warm and sunny with a clear blue sky. Church or no church, Isaac would come for him. Pete was gathering up his cane pole and tackle box when he heard the barn door creak open behind him, and Daddy Ballard walked in.

"Son," he said, "I need to talk to you. I'm afraid I've got some bad news about Isaac."

His grandfather's somber expression carried Pete back to the night of his father's accident. He could hear a truck horn blaring in his head as the cane pole slipped through his fingers and fell to the ground.

"Sweetheart, won't you eat just a little something?" Pete's mother sat on the edge of his bed and stroked his hair. He had been in his room ever since Daddy Ballard left.

"No, ma'am," he said.

"You'll let me know if I can fix you anything — anything at all?"

"Yes, ma'am."

She got up and walked over to the window — the same one Pete had climbed through to meet Isaac the day of his father's funeral. He stared at her back, framed in late afternoon light. He had always thought he had the most beautiful mother in the whole world. But ever since his father died, something about her looked so tired — even now, when he couldn't see her face.

"Mama," Pete said, "do you think there's any way Isaac could be alright?"

Her eyes were teary when she came back to sit beside him. "I wish I could say yes, honey. I wish to goodness I could. But nobody's seen him since that card game last week. I think you know there are some pretty tough customers in that bunch. And when men go to gambling, they're usually drinking too."

"But they found his truck in the hollow," Pete said, sitting up. "If he made it to there, he musta got away from the card game okay. Maybe he ran off the road and hit his head. Maybe he's wanderin' around in the woods and doesn't know who he is. Maybe he's got that — that — amnesia, like on TV."

"Honey, about the truck . . . it wasn't wrecked. It didn't look like he'd lost control of it and run off the road. Your granddaddy said . . . well, he said it looked like somebody had pushed the truck off the road and into some bushes. There were limbs piled onto it, like somebody was trying to hide it. They're just not sure, sweetheart . . . if he actually drove it there."

Still, Pete couldn't give up. Searching for the tiniest flicker of hope, he blurted out, "Maybe he dusted his broom!"

"What?" his mother exclaimed. "Where

did you hear that?"

Pete struggled to recover. "Me and Isaac — we heard this song . . . on the colored radio station one time," he said. It was only a white lie to protect Isaac and the crowd at Tandy's. "Isaac said it was about leavin' and never comin' back — dustin' your broom."

"Well . . . I'm not sure you've got any business listening to blues music —"

"*You* know about the *blues?*" Pete couldn't believe it.

"Never mind that —"

"What if he did, though?" Pete asked excitedly. "What if he just didn't want to plow cotton no more and left to go get a job on a ship or something?"

His mother gently took his face in her hands and asked, "Honey, you know Isaac as well as anybody. Do you really think he's the kind of person who would abandon his family like that?"

Pete hated to cry, especially in front of his mother, but he couldn't help it. She put her arms around him and held him tight as the sorrows of the day poured down like rain.

FIVE

April 30, 1964

"Anything?" Pete's grandfather was on the telephone with Agent Davenport. Daddy Ballard had gone down to the sheriff's office and told him straight-out that if he wanted to keep his job he had better get on the phone with the FBI and get some help with this sorry excuse for an investigation.

Pete stood quietly and listened from the doorway of the living room. His grandfather was frowning, and Pete could see him clenching his jaw the way he always did when he was working hard not to lose his temper.

"So of all the fingerprints your men lifted from that truck, the only clear ones belonged to the sheriff?" There was a pause while Daddy Ballard listened and nodded. "And that red smear by the hood that appeared to be —" He looked up to see Pete staring and hanging on every word. "Now,

57

son, you go on outside while I talk to Agent Davenport. Soon as Roy and Lamar get here, we'll go fishing. I'll let you know if I find out anything. I promise."

Feeling a little sick, Pete slowly backed out of the doorway, went to the barn, and climbed the ladder to the hayloft. He sat down near the big opening where bales were pitched into trucks below and hauled to Daddy Ballard's cows and horses in the wintertime. Aunt Geneva's twin boys were walking toward the barn, but they didn't notice him high above.

Pete heard the barn door open and the sound of fishing rods rattling as they made their selections.

"What was it them Callahan boys was tellin' you while I filled up the truck?" Lamar said.

"They heard some stuff about Isaac, but I don't know that there's anything to it," Roy answered.

Pete froze and didn't make a sound.

"They said they heard the sheriff found a bloody hammer in the grass by Isaac's truck, but he ain't told it 'cause he's hopin' the killer'll trip up somehow and give hisself away."

"That sheriff's a piece o' work," Lamar said. "Never woulda called the FBI if Daddy

Ballard hadn't made him."

"Since they found Isaac's truck on Hollow Road, the Callahans think somebody killed him and dumped him in them pig wells way back in there," Roy said. "Man, if that's what happened, ain't nobody ever gonna find him. Ain't no sheriff's deputy 'round here gonna mess with them crazy hollow people. I heard that way back before the Depression, they kidnapped a deputy that come snoopin' around — locked him up in a old shed for about a week before they turned him a-loose. They say he run all the way back to the highway and was bawlin' like a baby when somebody stopped to pick him up."

"That's just a old tale," Lamar said. "Them people's odd, though, I'll grant you that. I don't know what Isaac woulda done to get hisself killed back in there. Then again, he wasn't no saint — likable fella and all, but some of them card players . . . well, they ain't choirboys, that's for sure."

"Sorry to say it, but if the boy's dead, he's dead," Roy said. "I guess it don't much matter where his body is — pig wells or not, it don't change nothin'. Hate it for Hattie and Aunt Babe, though. C'mon. Let's go in the kitchen and get us a Co-Cola for the road."

For a few minutes after they left, Pete

didn't move. He had forgotten all about the pig wells, but they had been there forever. They were part of a sawmill that Hinkey Pickett used to run. Hinkey's business had dried up during the Depression, and so did the wells. Then years later, a cholera epidemic hit the hollow, but this time it was after pigs, not people. Every single pig in the hollow caught the cholera and died. Miss Paul — short for Pauline, but nobody ever called her that — was Hinkey's wife and the undisputed queen of the backwoods. She had commanded her kin to cast their dead swine into the dry wells to prevent the cholera from spreading. It all happened before Pete was even born, but the grown folks still talked about it. And you could tell those wells and the cholera spooked them even now.

He stood up and looked out from the loft, calculating how long it would take him to hike from his house — which was just a little farther away than Daddy Ballard's — to the sawmill. He knew what he had to do. He would find a way to go. He would tell no one, but he would go.

Six

May 9, 1964
From the threshold of his mother's kitchen, Pete peered into the cool darkness outside. It was less than a half hour before dawn. All that stood between him and his mission was the rickety screen door that had whapped shut so many times it was hanging a little sideways. It opened with a creak as he stepped outside.

He was out of the house long before his mother could make it downstairs and tell him he couldn't go. Still, he hated the thought of making her worry, so he had left her a note on the kitchen table.

Patting his pocket, he made sure he had the rabbit's foot — a little luck would come in handy today — and then tugged at the slim leather holster attached to his belt to see if it was secure. It held a bone-handled hunting knife that he had gotten for his thirteenth birthday earlier in the spring. At the pump house, he filled his father's old canteen and looped the long strap around his neck, along with a frayed khaki knapsack that carried his food and a flashlight. With one last look over his shoulder, he took off running as hard as he could across the cotton field that began just a few yards behind his mother's clothesline.

By the time Pete stopped to catch his breath, the dark morning sky was streaked with sunrise. He sat down and scratched his back against a fence post while he waited for daylight. Slowly the faint rays of light widened and brightened till the whole sky turned pale blue like a robin's egg, lit with glowing feathers of cotton-candy pink.

Taking the rabbit's foot out of his pocket, he turned it over in his hand. There was a little chunk of fur missing right at the tip. Once, he guessed, it had been snow white, but years of being clutched for good luck had yellowed it. He thought about all the early mornings just like this one, when Isaac would've stuffed the rabbit's foot into his own pocket before heading out to the fields to meet Pete's father.

Daddy Ballard wasn't crazy about Isaac — said he did "too much carryin' on." But Isaac was Hattie's son, and Daddy Ballard would tell anybody that Hattie was as fine a

Christian as any white woman in the Baptist church. She had cooked and kept house for him ever since Ma Ballard died. Pete spent enough time at his grandfather's house to know that on those afternoons when Daddy Ballard was feeling especially lonesome, even if it was her usual time to go home, Hattie would find something to dust in the living room, where he liked to read his *Birmingham News.* As she flicked her feather duster over a lamp or a rocking chair, she would casually ask, "Mister Ned, anything of interest in that newspaper?" This would give him an excuse to discuss the affairs of the day with her, which never failed to cheer him up.

She was the only living soul he'd allow behind the wheel of the Cadillac that had belonged to his beloved wife. Hattie drove it to the Winn-Dixie every Monday morning to buy his groceries — the only time she ever wore her maid's uniform. Daddy Ballard told her she could wear whatever she wanted while she worked for him, but she thought it best to make it clear to anybody looking that she was on a white man's errand when she went to the grocery store. And he would always tell her to go on and get her groceries too, while she had the car. They could put it on his bill and settle up later, he used to say. But Pete knew every time she tried to pay him, he'd put her off: "Aw, Hattie, I ain't got time to fool with that right now."

Pete was there the day she tried to put her foot down and pay him back. Daddy Ballard had let her say her piece, and then, peering up at her from his newspaper, he countered, "Hattie, you scrub my floors, you wash my clothes, you cook my food, you look after me when I'm sick, and you generally put up with me day in and day out. Don't you reckon you earned them groceries?" She had thought about it for a minute before giving him a quick nod and heading back to the kitchen. From then on, they were fine about the Winn-Dixie.

Of all the white people she had worked for, he was the only one she invited to her three older daughters' weddings. He went too. And when her youngest, Iris, got accepted to Spelman but didn't have the money to go, Daddy Ballard paid her tuition and drove her to Atlanta himself. In their way, he and Hattie were friends. Pete had never thought about it before, but now he had to wonder — if Daddy Ballard could help Iris go someplace she had dreamed about, why couldn't he help Isaac get out of the fields and onto that ship he so wanted to sail?

Pete stood up and dusted off his jeans, then squeezed through a barbed-wire fence and trotted across the pasture. Weaving through a little band of woods, he made his way to Hollow Road and followed it to Copper Creek. By the time he got there, the sun was already hot enough to prickle his arms. He sat down on the old wooden bridge and dangled his feet over the water while he hurriedly ate two cold biscuits with ham left over from supper. Then he refilled the canteen with ice-cold creek water and made his way down the road, kicking an empty Campbell's soup can somebody had tossed out.

Before long, he had kicked the can all the way to the crossroads, which led east to the main highway or west through the hollow and down to the river. Right behind the split was an old shotgun house flanked by two ancient pecan trees. The front porch was warped, and there were concrete blocks where the steps should've been. He had always thought this old house looked sort of perched, like it might fly off at any moment. It was the home of Aunt Babe, Hattie's mother.

When Ma Ballard was growing up, Aunt

Babe had cooked for her family, the Jacksons. Aunt Babe had worked for them since she was a girl, and she could name every knot on every limb of their family tree. But everybody knew that Ma Ballard — "Sweet Ginia," Aunt Babe called her — was by far her favorite.

Pete jumped at the sound of Aunt Babe's rocking chair slamming against the front wall of the house when she stood up. He hadn't seen her sitting there on the porch, but she had seen him. Unlike Hattie, who was tall and lean, Aunt Babe was five feet tall and about that wide. Now that she was a little feeble, she sometimes walked with a red cane that Isaac had made for her. Aunt Babe loved red. Even the walls of her tiny kitchen were covered with old newspapers and the lids of Prince Albert tobacco cans spray-painted bright crimson.

She took her time coming down the wobbly stack of blocks and then marched across her front yard like she was about to get to the bottom of something. "Pete McLean, what you doin' way out here without no grown folks?"

"Nothin', Aunt Babe — just on my way to the creek to go wadin'."

"You ain't never set foot on no creek bank I know of without a fishin' pole."

Pete rolled his foot back and forth over the soup can and fingered the rabbit's foot in his pocket while he tried to think up a lie the old woman might believe. "Well, I'm — I'm lookin' for a spot to build me a fort."

"Naw y'ain't."

"No, really, Aunt Babe —"

"Lyin's a sin, Pete McLean. Yo' mama got Jackson blood. You gonna stand there in front o' my house and tell me Miss Lila, what got *Jackson* blood, done raised herself a hell-bound liar?"

"No, ma'am."

"The truth then — speak it now or we fixin' to get down on our knees right here in this yard and pray you don't bust the gates o' hell wide open."

Pete took his foot off the can, stood up straight, and looked Aunt Babe square in the eyes. Then it all came spilling out.

"I'm goin' to the pig wells, Aunt Babe. Roy and Lamar, they said Isaac prob'ly got hisself killed over cards or something and that somebody mighta pitched his body over in them wells with all that cholera. Don't seem like nobody else is even lookin' for him. So I *mean* to find out if he's in there. And if he is, I know Daddy Ballard will come and get him out. And Hattie can have him a funeral. Isaac never woulda left

67

Daddy down in no hole, and we oughtn' to leave Isaac in one neither."

Aunt Babe took a step back and studied Pete's face. "How old is you?"

"Thirteen."

"Mm-hmm. That's when all you boys gets the crazies. Come up here on this porch and let me see what do I think about all this."

Pete followed her and took a seat in the rocking chair next to hers.

"Now, let's us back up a little. You say Roy and Lamar done give you this idea?"

"Yes, ma'am."

"They ain't the sharpest tools in the shed. What exactly they say got you all worked up?"

"They said the Callahan boys —"

"*Callahan?* Now there's a no-account bunch o' white folks if ever I seen one. What that trash know 'bout anything?"

"Well, the Callahan boys told Roy and Lamar that they heard the sheriff found a bloody hammer in the grass by Isaac's truck, but he ain't told it 'cause he's hopin' the killer'll trip up somehow and give hisself away."

Aunt Babe rolled her eyes. "What that sheriff plan to do? Park his big self at the mercantile and lock up ever'body what shows up lookin' to buy a new hammer?"

"Roy and Lamar say the sheriff's a piece o' work," Pete went on. "They say he never woulda had sense enough to call the FBI if Daddy Ballard hadn'a made him."

"They got that much right. Keep on."

"Well, since the deputies found Isaac's truck in the hollow, the Callahans said somebody musta killed him and dumped him in them pig wells way back in there. And Roy and Lamar said if that's what happened, ain't nobody ever gonna find him, because ain't no sheriff's deputy 'round here gonna mess with them crazy hollow people."

"Now you stop right there," Aunt Babe said. "First off, you know good and well them *crazy* hollow people, as you done gone to callin' 'em — they got a name, same as you. It's Pickett. And they ain't crazy — well, Paul might be a little teched in the head, but all in all, they ain't crazy. They just poor. You think it make somebody crazy or bad just 'cause they ain't got as much as you?"

"No, ma'am."

"Yo' granddaddy's one o' the richest men in the state o' Alabama, and he was friends — *good* friends — with Hinkey Pickett they whole life. They growed up fishin' these creeks together. You know that?"

"No, ma'am."

"Mm-hmm. Seems to me they's a lot you don't know. That sheriff's dumb as a post 'bout ever'thing 'cept one — stealin' from colored folks. Used to come after our men with all kinda silly charges and throw 'em in the jailhouse till the families could come up with some cash money to bail 'em out. Wasn't never nobody but him in sight when we paid it. You ask me, all our money paid for that bass boat o' his."

"But he don't steal from y'all no more?" Pete asked.

"Knows he best not."

"How come?"

" 'Cause a while back, he make the mistake o' lockin' up Isaac. Hattie finally got her courage up and told yo' granddaddy what was a-goin' on. Ain't nobody paid no bail money since then." She scrutinized Pete's face. "Tell me something. What *you* think happened to Isaac?"

"Well, Roy and Lamar said —"

"I don't care 'bout Mutt and Jeff. What *you* think?"

Pete stared at her and thought it over. "I don't know what happened to him, Aunt Babe. But whatever it was, I know it wasn't his fault. Them Callahans said Isaac got in with the wrong crowd when he was playin' cards. They said whatever become of him was his own doin'. But I don't believe that. I think somebody did something bad to him, and there wasn't nothin' he coulda done to stop it."

Aunt Babe's expression didn't change. "Who you think done that?"

"I don't know," Pete said. "I was always kinda scared of Reuben."

"You best be! Reuben knife his own mama for a five-dollar bill — don't you never let me catch you nowhere 'round him."

Reuben was part of the card-playing crowd that met in an old abandoned shed on Friday and Saturday nights. Pete had been with Isaac in the field once when Reuben stopped by to tell him about a poker game. Isaac's smile had disappeared the minute he saw Reuben's truck, and he had motioned for Pete to stay behind him while they talked. Something about Reuben made you want to run home and hide under the bed.

"Now, where them white boys get the notion Isaac in the pig wells?" Aunt Babe asked.

"I guess they just figured it's the one place nobody's looked — or ever *would* look," Pete said. "Do you remember the cholera?"

" 'Course I do."

"How come only pigs got it?"

"You can't tell 'bout that cholera. Sometimes it go after people. Sometimes it go after pigs. Either way, a lotta dyin' gonna follow it. That's how come Paul made all her people pitch them dead pigs in the dried-up wells at Hinkey's old sawmill — bottle up that cholera so it can't get nothin' else dead." Aunt Babe's eyes narrowed slightly as she looked at Pete. "You know they ain't no chance you gonna find Isaac alive in them wells, don't you?"

"Yes, ma'am."

"And you know Isaac wouldn' never take off without tellin' Hattie, like some folks been a-sayin'?"

"He'd *never* dust his broom."

Aunt Babe rolled her eyes. "Listen at you. 'Dust his broom,' my hind leg. You know there ain't gonna be no happy endin' to this, don't you?"

"Yes, ma'am. But if I could just find him — find out what happened to him — Hattie could have him a funeral and put it to rest."

"Hattie the only one need to put it to rest?" Aunt Babe eyed him closely.

"No, ma'am," he admitted. "I guess not."

"You know the way to them wells?"

"Yes, ma'am."

"You got sense enough to know a well can

72

cave in — way out past them brick walls around it — and you can fall in that hole from a ways back?"

"Yes, ma'am."

"But you bound to go?"

"I'm bound to go."

Aunt Babe put two fingers in her mouth and gave a loud, shrill whistle. A beautiful hound dog came bounding out from under the porch. His legs and most of his body were snow white, but he had a patch of black fur across his back that made him look like he was wearing a fine saddle. His head and tail were a rich golden brown except for a single white stripe right down the middle of his narrow face, from his brow to his nose. He sat down at Aunt Babe's feet and looked up at her, waiting for instructions. She rubbed his head and scratched him behind the ears.

"This here's Cyrus," she said. "He gonna guide you. Cyrus know ever' inch of that hollow. He done had his breakfast, and he gonna be hungry for his supper before sundown. He never miss a meal. He come home to supper without you, I gonna send for your granddaddy. Soon as you outta sight, I gonna call yo' mama and see can I talk her outta the tree she likely done climb from worry. Give you time to get yo' doin's done. Now go on. Cyrus, you watch over this lost chile."

"But I ain't lost, Aunt Babe," Pete said.

"Yeah y'are. You just don't know it."

Cyrus trotted onto the road and waited a few feet ahead of Pete as Aunt Babe went back inside.

Pete stroked the dog's head and scratched him behind the ears just as Aunt Babe had done. "A dog will always remember you if you do that," his father once told him. Cyrus fell into step with him as they followed the western split in the road, bound for the hollow.

For now, the road was sunny and bright. All the trees on either side had been cleared for cotton fields. But about a half mile ahead, fields would give way to woods. There was another bridge there with a deep, cold creek running beneath it. Whoever named it apparently didn't have much time to think about it — it was called Deep Creek. That was the entrance to the hollow where all the Picketts lived.

They were Daddy Ballard's last remaining tenant farmers. Most of the others had found work in the cotton mills or moved away altogether. The Picketts didn't own any farmland or equipment. They farmed "on halves," working his grandfather's land with his equipment, and then giving him half the crop after the harvest. Years ago, they had chosen the most remote fields — 150 acres on the river — because it allowed them to keep to themselves. That was Miss Paul's doing.

The Picketts didn't go to church, at least not with everybody else. But Roy and Lamar said that if you drove through the hollow on a Sunday afternoon, you could sometimes hear them singing in Miss Paul's barn. Pete's cousins — like most people in town — said the Picketts were snake handlers, but nobody had ever seen them do it. Pete could imagine Miss Paul shaking a big black Bible in the air as she preached to her clan, whipping them into such a frenzy that they danced around the barn with rattlesnakes and copperheads writhing in their hands.

Pete felt Cyrus nuzzle his hand. So intently had he been conjuring Miss Paul and her vipers that he didn't realize he had made it to Deep Creek Bridge. When Cyrus trotted off the road and down the bank for a cool drink, Pete followed and fed him a leftover ham biscuit. Cyrus gave him an appreciative lick on the cheek and then took another long drink before climbing up the bank to the road.

They walked through a shady tunnel of towering oaks that overlapped high above — a welcome break from the hot sun. Hollow Road would be perfectly straight for about a hundred more yards, but then it would take a big dip, make a sharp turn to the left, and follow a serpentine path through the woods all the way to the river.

Nobody was stirring when Pete walked past Miss Paul's barn. He had never noticed how many houses were tucked along this road. Most of them were unpainted shotguns or dogtrots with tin roofs and deep front porches, and they all had big vegetable gardens off to the side. The yards had no grass but were swept clean since most of the houses were nestled under shade trees.

The very last house that he and Cyrus passed was unlike all the others. It sat on a flat, sunny patch. A morning glory vine completely covered the porch railing and was climbing up the side of the house, while a rambling rose all but filled a small flower bed lined with rocks. The front porch and both sides of the house were bordered with a crazy quilt of flowers. There were milk and wine lilies, zinnias, geraniums, four-o'clocks, cannas — Pete knew them all from helping his mother work her flower beds. This was beautiful. It was like flipping through a coloring book that you thought was blank and stumbling onto one solitary picture that had been brilliantly colored. Cyrus had to bark to break Pete out of his trance and get him moving again.

Picking up their pace, they made their way around several bends in the road, past Pickett's Pond, and finally to the piece of fence that marked the entrance to the sawmill. Every inch of it was covered in honeysuckle. A weedy path began where the main gate used to be. It led through a pine thicket to a small clearing where the mill, or what was left of it, stood. By the angle of the sun, Pete guessed that it was around ten o'clock.

He and Cyrus watched for snakes as they walked down the path. Just beyond the pine thicket, they could see the mill. The whole building leaned to one side, and it looked like the only thing holding it up was kudzu. All those vines had covered it in a leafy veil that draped around the trees surrounding the clearing, forming a dense wall of green that stretched as far as Pete could see. He would have to break through it to get to the wells.

With his hunting knife in hand, he began sawing at a small section of kudzu, but those vines were as tough as cowhide. Finally he managed to cut an opening big enough to push through. With his eyes closed and arms outstretched like a diver, he went in head-first, twisting and thrashing in the small opening till half his body was through. With one more push, the vines gave way, and he landed on all fours inside the sawmill clearing. When he opened his eyes, he found himself staring down at a pair of pink plaid tennis shoes.

His eyes followed the shoes up bare legs to faded denim overall shorts, and finally to the stunned stare of a girl who looked about his age, maybe a little younger. He raised himself up on his knees. She had shiny black hair that was pinned back at the sides and fell into big curls around her shoulders. Her eyes were a strange and beautiful shade of bluish green, and her skin looked like — how would his mother describe it? — peaches and cream. She was wearing a pink T-shirt under her overalls. Slowly standing up to face her, Pete was relieved to see that he was a head taller than her. That seemed important right now, though he couldn't say why.

"Your arms are bleedin'," she said. He looked down to see scratches and small cuts up and down both arms, and he wished to goodness he could get some words to come out of his mouth. It had been hanging open from the minute he first saw her. "Is that there your dog?" she asked.

He hadn't even noticed Cyrus at his side. "N-no," he managed to get out. "I just — sorta — borrowed him. What are you doin' here?"

"What are *you* doin' here?" She hadn't budged since Pete stood up, and she stood stock-still in front of him, while he nervously dusted himself off and blotted at his cuts with the hem of his T-shirt.

"I'm sorta lookin' for somebody," he said.

"Oh," she said, as if that were a perfectly normal thing to be doing at a deserted sawmill.

"How 'bout you?" he tried again.

"I like it here 'cause it's not as lonesome as a empty house."

"How come your house is empty?"

She stared at him without answering. "I'm Dovey," she finally said.

"I'm Pete."

"Who you lookin' for, Pete?"

"It's sorta complicated."

She sat down on a tree stump a few feet away and waited for him. Pete followed and sat cross-legged on the ground beside her as Cyrus stretched out in a shady spot and closed his eyes.

"I think my friend Isaac might be in one

of them wells," Pete began. Then he told her everything, all the way back to his father's accident.

For a moment after he had finished, she just looked at him. He imagined she was making up her mind exactly how crazy he was and whether she should take off running or hit him over the head with something. "You need any help?" she asked.

"Sure," he said. "You reckon Isaac could really be down there?"

"No," she said. "But it sounds like you need to look." She led Pete around to the back of the mill. The remains of several sheds and storage buildings circled out from it. Right in the center of that circle were three wells about ten feet apart. Their stone walls had crumbled down to low rims a couple of feet off the ground. All around them, the ground looked sunken and damp. Pete took a couple of steps toward the wells, but Cyrus leaped in front of him, blocking his path. He looked back at Dovey.

"You'd be stupid if you wasn't scared," she said.

Pete tried to step around Cyrus, who was circling his legs like a house cat.

Dovey reached out and grabbed his arm. "You'd be even stupider if you went near them wells without something to catch you

80

if they cave in. C'mon. I know where there's some rope." She led him through one of the sheds and onto a path through the woods. He wished he had known about the path before he fought his way through all that kudzu. "Watch for snakes," she said.

"But I thought —" Pete stopped himself.

"You thought what?"

"Well, ever'body says — I mean — don't y'all handle snakes?"

"What do you mean, handle 'em?"

"You know — *handle* 'em."

"When they get in the garden, we chop their heads off with a hoe — is that what you're talkin' about?"

"No, I mean when y'all are havin' church in Miss Paul's barn, do y'all pick up live rattlesnakes and copperheads and dance around with 'em while she preaches from the Bible?"

Dovey stopped in her tracks and glared at him. "Why would anybody do that?"

"I don't know. I just thought —"

"Ain't you ever seen nobody that's been snakebit?"

"Well, no, I —"

"Whatever gets bit turns black, and you get chills and fever, and if you don't die right then and there, sometimes they gotta cut off your foot or your leg or your arm or whatever has them fang marks in it. It turns my stomach just thinkin' about it. What in the Sam Hill would make you think we're crazy enough to pick up something that means to kill us and hold it in our bare hands?"

She walked quickly ahead of him, as if she were too disgusted by what he had said to share the path with him. He and Cyrus broke into a trot to try and catch up with her, but she wouldn't slow down.

"Wait!" Pete called out. "Dovey, wait a minute!" She stopped and let him catch up. "I'm sorry," he said. "I didn't have a bit o' business askin' you that. I'm real sorry."

She seemed to be thinking it over as she twirled her hair around her finger. Then she gave him an unceremonious nod of forgiveness, and they fell into step with Cyrus a few feet ahead. Pete had so many questions he wanted to ask, but he was afraid of making her angry again.

"Go on," she said.

"Go on and what?" he asked.

"Go on and ask me. If you thought we dance around with copperheads durin' the Holy Scriptures, there's no tellin' what other crazy mess you're wonderin' about. Go on and ask. I promise not to get mad."

"Well . . . how come y'all don't go to

school or to church with the rest of us?"

"What do you think people would do if we was to come walkin' into your church or that school?" she countered.

"I think it'd be fine."

She smiled at him like his mother did when she was trying to make him feel better about some idiotic thing he had done. "No it wouldn't. We don't belong there."

"Well . . . how'd you get to be smart if you don't go to school?"

"Smart don't have nothin' to do with school. Smart's in your head. You just need somebody to teach you how to use it, and my Aunt Delphine teaches all of us. She teaches us how to read and do numbers. Our mothers teach us how to cook and keep house and grow a garden, and our daddies teach us how to get around in the woods. Granny Paul teaches us all about healin' and the Bible and signs of bad weather. What else we gonna need?"

"But what if you have to leave here?" Pete persisted. "You know, like to go to college or join the army or something."

She gave that smile again. "We ain't about to join no army — and I don't even know what college is."

They had circled around behind Pickett's Pond to a small shed behind one of the shotgun houses. Dovey led the way as they gathered up two long ropes, a big lantern, and a box of matches. Then they returned to the wells, where she lit the lantern, tied one end of the longest rope around the handle, and looped the rest into a bundle. She handed Pete the second rope. "Here, tie this around you good and tight," she said. When he had secured one end of it around his waist, she tied the other end around the trunk of a stout pine tree a safe distance from the wells. Then she handed him the lantern and looped the extra rope over his shoulder.

"What's this for?" Pete asked.

"So you can see inside the wells," she said.

"But I brought a flashlight."

"Ain't no flashlight gonna shine down that far."

He took a few steps toward the wells. About halfway there he turned to ask, "What about the cholera?"

"What?" Dovey asked.

"You know, from way back yonder — all them sick pigs."

"Great day in the mornin', that was a million years ago. Anyway, the cholera lives in water, and the wells are dry. Besides, when Granny Paul made everybody throw their pigs in, she told the men to pour gasoline down in there and burn off the disease. They tell about that cholera every time we smoke a hog over the pit out back of the barn. There ain't no cholera left in them wells."

"I reckon you're right." He slipped his hand in his pocket and gave the rabbit's foot a squeeze before walking as fast as he could to the closest well. Getting down on his knees, he lowered the lantern over the side. Down, down, down it went into the dark pit. He couldn't help gasping when the lantern illuminated a skull at the bottom. It wasn't human, but it was creepy just the same.

"See anything?" Dovey called from her post by the tree Pete was tied to.

"Just pig bones — at least, I guess they're pig bones. They ain't Isaac, that's for sure." He hauled up the lantern and tried the center well, but it had caved in on itself. It was full of dirt almost all the way up to the stone wall and had been that way a while, because a thick carpet of moss covered the dirt, and there were little pine saplings growing out of it.

"Anything?" she called.

"Caved in." He sidestepped his way over to the third well and lowered the lantern, but this time he leaned way out over the well to get a better look. The rope around his waist was stretched as far as it would go. Nothing. Not even pig bones. Just a deep, dark, barren hole. As he slowly pulled the lantern up and shut out the light, he could feel his eyes begin to sting. It would truly be the end of him if this girl saw him cry like a baby.

Keeping his head down, he took a few reluctant steps in her direction. But when he stepped on a mossy crack a couple of feet from the well, the ground opened up. "Pete!" he heard Dovey yell as the damp earth swallowed him down and the lantern went sailing out of sight, somewhere far below. His stomach jumped up in his throat, just like the time he had ridden a big roller coaster at the state fair. After that, he was just flailing through nothingness.

His head was two or three feet below ground level when the rope caught him. He could see the sun above but couldn't see his hand in front of him and felt only cold air beneath his feet. Struggling to get his bearings in this dark, dank hole, all he could do was cling to Dovey's rope and pray that it held.

"Pete, I'm comin'!" she called.

"No!" he yelled. "Dovey, can you hear me?"

"Yes, and I'm comin'!"

"No! Don't come near this hole or you'll fall through and you ain't tied to no rope! I'm gonna try to climb out. You can run for help if I fall. Dovey? You hear me?"

"I hear you!"

Cyrus was barking his head off. Pete hoped he could get out of the hole and calm the dog down before his barking summoned everybody in the hollow to the sawmill. He had never been especially interested in sports, but he now wished he'd tried a whole lot harder when Coach made the boys climb that rope in the gym. What was it — right hand, left foot, then left hand, right foot? Or was it right-right? There was a wall of dirt in front of him, so he had something to brace his feet against as he climbed. The hole that had swallowed him reached all the way back to the wells. His hands burned from squeezing and pulling on the rough rope, and he slipped and fell all the way back down the first time he made it to the rim of the hole. It took forever, but he pulled and climbed and sweated and cried till at last his head was in daylight.

A few more heaves brought him facedown on the damp ground, where Dovey started to run to his aid, but he knew it could cave in again. "No! Stay back!" he yelled. She obeyed, but Cyrus didn't. He sprinted to Pete, licking his neck and sniffing around his head. Mercifully, the sight of his companion made the hound stop barking. Pete didn't even try to walk for fear of punching another hole in the ground. Cyrus stayed right beside him as he dragged his body along the rope line, all the way to the tree, and finally let go at Dovey's feet. For a while he just lay there breathing hard and trying to recover from the fright and the disappointment and the whole awfulness of everything. He could feel Dovey sit down beside him as Cyrus kept sniffing all around his head and neck, trying to see his face.

"All that for nothing," he said, finally sitting up and untying the rope around his waist.

"All what?"

"Me gettin' this stupid idea and plannin' this stupid trip and thinkin' I could do something stupid like rescue somebody that's already dead."

"But you wasn't tryin' to rescue him," Dovey said. "You was lookin' for a way to tell him goodbye. And now you know this ain't the way. So you'll just have to keep on lookin'."

Man, she was something! And she had

been right here in this hollow his whole life.

"What time you reckon it is?" he asked.

She looked up at the sun. "Around two. C'mon to the house. I'll doctor your hands before you go home." They gathered up their supplies and retraced their path through the woods with Cyrus.

"I'll bring you a new lantern," Pete promised as they returned the other supplies to the shed. He and Dovey followed the path back to Hollow Road, where it came out right in front of the house with the flowers. Dovey led Pete to a rocking chair on the porch.

"This is *your* house?" he asked.

"Yes," she said with a frown. "Why? What's wrong with it?"

"Nothing's wrong with it, Dovey. It's just that I noticed it when me and Cyrus came by on our way to the mill. All the flowers, I mean. They're real pretty. Like my mother's."

She gave him a big smile that made him forget all about his throbbing hands. "Thank you. Granny Paul says flowers are my gift."

She disappeared into the little house. A few minutes later, she came out with a bowl of water for Cyrus and a boxful of small jars and strips of cloth. Then she brought out a wash pan filled with water and set it on a little table in front of him. Pulling up a chair for herself, she sat down and began carefully washing all the blood and dirt from his hands and arms.

"Holler if I hurt you," she said.

"No, you're doin' fine."

She dried his wounds with a clean dish towel and then dabbed them with salve from the jars.

"What's that?" he asked.

"It's Granny Paul's healin' balm," she said. "It'll make your cuts quit hurtin' and close up faster."

His hands were a real mess, so she took her time getting lots of salve on all the rope burns and then wrapped them in soft strips of cloth from the box.

"There," she said, examining her work. "All done. Leave the bandages on till morning. Then your mama can doctor you again."

"Thanks — for everything," Pete said. "I'd be down in that hole right now if it wasn't for you."

"I reckon you would." Cyrus came and put his head in Dovey's lap. She scratched him behind the ears. "A dog'll never forget you if you do that."

Pete grinned. "Yeah, I know."

"Well, I guess you better be goin'," she said.

Pete and Cyrus started down the porch steps. "Hey, Dovey, can I come back sometime — you know, just to visit?"

"You don't belong here."

"I know. But can I come anyway?"

"I reckon so — till my daddy runs you off with his shotgun." She was already in the house, and he couldn't tell if she was teasing about that last part. He sure hoped so.

Pete looked up at the afternoon sky, which seemed a little bluer now that he had met Dovey. Maybe he hadn't done what he came to do, but he had done something. He felt different. With a smile and a wave just in case Dovey was watching from inside, he set out for Aunt Babe's. He and Cyrus would make it home before dark.

SEVEN

May 23, 1964

Paul Pickett stopped dusting the rough-hewn mantel over her fireplace and picked up the only picture she owned of her whole family. She needed help, but which of the women to call on? They were all there, staring back at her from a tarnished frame.

Years ago, a traveling picture man had posed the family together in front of her house. At the center of the clan, seated on two ladder-back chairs, were Paul and her Hinkey. How she missed him! Gathered around them were their four sons — Adam, Noah, John, and Joseph — and daughters Lydia and Selah, along with their spouses and all the grandchildren. Most of the older children in the picture had since grown up and left the hollow for paying jobs in the cotton mills.

Mammon, cursed mammon. Family should come before possessions.

She studied the women. Her two oldest, Lydia and Selah, stood with their husbands on either side of Paul and Hinkey. They didn't look anything like her. Paul had a small frame, but she was strong and wiry from years of hard work. Her eyes were a very pale blue. As a girl, she was known for her long golden hair, which hung to her waist. Age had turned gold to silver, but she still kept it long. She wore it plaited and pinned into a bun at the nape of her neck. Because she did not believe in women wearing britches, she did all her work, even milking two cows, in a simple shirtdress — cotton in the summertime and wool in the winter.

Both of her daughters were tall and lean like their father, and they had his dark eyes and hair, just like their brothers. All of her children were the spitting image of Hinkey, which was such a comfort now that he was gone.

Just behind Paul and Hinkey in the photograph stood Adam, her oldest boy, and his wife, Delphine — the smartest of her daughters-in-law. Delphine had more schooling than most. Better still, she had plenty of walking-around sense.

Off to the side stood Noah and his sweet wife, Aleene, a trusting soul who always saw the best in people, even when they didn't deserve it. If anybody should ever try to hurt Aleene, Paul would take up her shotgun and lay them out herself. She was keeping it even handier now — loaded and laid across her bureau at night — what with all the talk about Babe's grandboy gone missing and his truck found in this very hollow. Trouble to come from it — intruders and meddlers. She would deal with that in due time.

Gently she ran her hand over John and Lottie, looking at each other with such love. They had just married when the picture man came around. Of her four boys, John was the one who melted her heart. He had married an angel. But now Lottie was in heaven with all the other angels. There had been no way to shield Dovey from what that sickness did to her mother. None of Paul's healing could touch it, and even when John insisted on trying a doctor, the man proved useless. First sign of trouble came in late summer, and Lottie crossed over two days before Christmas.

Since she died, all the women in the family (except for Ruby, who was useless) had tried to mother Dovey and do for her. But Dovey never asked for much. Since Lottie passed, it was as if she felt she didn't have the right to, and that's a heartbreaking thing to see in a child.

Paul traced Lottie's face with her finger before turning her attention to the couple on the far right of the image, standing at a noticeable distance from the rest of the family. That was Ruby's doing. Ruby was a loudmouth without a lick of sense who had talked the youngest of the Pickett boys, Joseph, into running off and getting married before anybody could put a stop to it. Paul had made a secret promise to herself that if Ruby should ever drop dead from unforeseen circumstances, she would slip over to the burying ground and dance on her grave.

Sometimes Paul felt a sorrowful longing for the days when her children were first married and the grandchildren were just beginning to come along. The hollow was running over with family back then. But things were different now. Most of the remaining grandchildren were old enough to work and soon would fly. That would leave only Dovey.

Dovey. Paul was reminded of the task at hand. She had a choice to make, and she had chosen Delphine.

Delphine would be her eyes.

EIGHT

Dovey stood before her mother's dresser and looked into the tall mirror hanging above it. Her father had made both pieces from a hickory tree he cut down himself, planing the boards till they were smooth as glass and dovetailing all the joints. The mirror tipped out from the wall a little at the top, so you could almost see your whole self. Her mother used to say that every time she looked into that mirror, she remembered how blessed she was.

Her hairbrush was still there on the dresser. Dovey knew the reason why. Her father couldn't bear to put it away. For him it must've brought comfort, a way to feel her mother's presence in some small way. But for Dovey, the brush was a sorrowful reminder that she would never again feel those gentle hands in her hair.

Before she got sick, Dovey's mother used

96

to stand her on a footstool in front of the mirror and brush her hair till all the tangles were gone and it fell into smooth, shiny ringlets. So patient and gentle she was that it never hurt, even when Dovey had been on the creek bank with her cousins all day, leaving her hair a tangled mess. After her mother died, Dovey had made the mistake of letting Aunt Ruby try to brush it. She had yanked and pulled so hard that Dovey ran out of the house and hid in the barn to cry.

From then on she kept the tangles out all by herself. She did just about everything by herself except when Pete was with her. The few cousins who were still in the hollow could all drive, and they took off together whenever they could scavenge a pickup from one of the uncles, rarely thinking to include her. It wasn't that they meant to leave her out. They were just older and tended to forget she was there.

Running her mother's brush through her hair, she began gathering it into a ponytail. She glanced at the radio on the corner of the dresser. Dovey's father had bought it for her mother, who loved music, but now he never turned it on except to hear the weather. Dovey kept it on all the time when she was home by herself. She especially liked a lady singer named Patsy Cline whom she had once seen on the *Grand Ole Opry* on Aunt Ruby's television. When Dovey heard that Patsy had died in a plane crash, it hit her just as hard as losing a family member.

She loved to hear Patsy sing "Crazy" and "Sweet Dreams" and that song about falling to pieces. But her absolute favorite was "Walkin' After Midnight" because it was a happy-sounding song about being lonesome, which never failed to lift her spirits. Whenever they played that one on the radio, she would dance through the house, singing at the top of her lungs.

Today, thank goodness, Dovey wouldn't need the radio to pass the time because it was Saturday, and that meant Pete was out of school and could spend the day with her. Not only that, but they were on a special mission. She straightened her ponytail and set out for Deep Creek Bridge, where Pete would be waiting for her.

Ever since they had found each other back in the spring, Pete and Dovey had spent lots of time together, fishing or wading in the creeks or climbing trees and exploring the woods. Now and then Pete would slip a saddle out of his granddaddy's barn and ride one of his horses to the hollow so that he and Dovey could explore the creek bank on horseback. Neither of their families knew anything about it.

Dovey looked up at the warm September sun. Everything had been so much easier in the summertime. Without school, Pete was free to do as he pleased once he finished his morning chores, and he usually made it to the hollow by lunchtime. The first time he came back to see her, he had walked right up to her front door and knocked. She nearly had a fit. If the aunts saw — especially Aunt Ruby — they'd tell her daddy, and heaven only knew what he might do. She and Pete couldn't call each other because nobody in the hollow had a telephone except Aunt Ruby, who couldn't be trusted with a secret. So whenever they got together, they would settle on a time to meet again. The meeting place was always the same — Deep Creek Bridge.

But then when school started back, everything got harder. It still made her insides hurt to think about that Saturday a couple of weeks ago when she had carried their lunch to the bridge and waited and waited and waited. Pete never showed up. Then Sunday, neither one of them could go anywhere. Sundays were for the Good Lord and family. By Tuesday afternoon, when she still hadn't heard a word from him, Dovey decided Pete had forgotten all about her. She sat down at her mother's kitchen table and sobbed till her head hurt. She was still crying when she heard him at the back door.

"Dovey? Are you alright? Can I come in?"

She walked over to the screen door but didn't open it. "I don't think you oughta come here no more," she said.

"Dovey, wait a minute —"

"I told you from the start you didn't belong here, and you don't. You make promises you don't keep, so just go away."

"Now, you let me in so I can tell you what happened, or I swear I'm gonna sit down on your front porch and explain everything to your daddy when he gets home."

The door flew open. She sat down with Pete at the kitchen table but kept sniffling and blotting her eyes with a dish towel.

"Are you cryin' because of me?" he asked.

"Yes," she said. No point in lying about it.

"Well, that ain't never gonna happen again. Listen, Dovey, I couldn't help it. Saturday morning Mama got up and said we were goin' to Birmingham to buy school clothes, and nothin' I said or did could talk her out of it. And then she wanted to stop and visit my Aunt Geneva on the way home. Then Sunday was Sunday, and Monday they took us on a stupid field trip to the Wheeler Dam and Helen Keller's house in Tuscumbia, and we didn't get home till dark, so I couldn't —"

"Who's Helen Keller?" Dovey asked, sniffling into her dish towel.

"Huh? Oh, she's this famous writer from up in north Alabama. Can't see nor hear, but some teacher figured out how to spell words in her hand so she could understand what people were sayin'."

"That sure would be lonesome, not bein' able to hear nor see nobody," Dovey said.

"I guess. Listen, I think we're gettin' off the subject."

"I reckon I'd rather talk about Helen Keller than remember bein' forgot. How'd you get here so quick after school let out?"

"One of my cousins was on his way to Childersburg, so I asked him to drop me off at the creek to fish. I bet he's wonderin' how come my cane pole's still in the back of his pickup. Look, we can figure this out, Dovey. For starters, you've got to believe that I would never ever just not show up. If I'm not here, there's a reason for it."

She looked up at him. "That's hard to remember when I'm all by myself."

"I know. We just need some way to signal each other when something comes up."

"Nothing's gonna come up for me."

"Well then, let's figure something out for me," he said. "I got this idea. See, Daddy Ballard had a phone installed at Aunt Babe's. He pays the bill and everything so she can talk to her kids or call somebody if there's some sort of emergency. And then she's got Cyrus, who can track like nobody's business. Bet we could teach him to track you. If I could call Aunt Babe and she could send Cyrus to you, then you'd know I had a good reason for not comin'. What do you think?"

Dovey shrugged and said, "Worth a try, I guess."

They had waited to visit Aunt Babe until Dovey's family was especially busy and distracted with the cotton harvest. Today was the day.

When she reached the bridge, she spotted Pete waiting on the creek bank below. She had heard her older cousins talk about their girlfriends and boyfriends. It wasn't like that with Pete. Still, it made her happy just to sit beside him. She liked the dimples in his cheeks when he smiled and the way he looked at her as if there wasn't anything else in the world he would rather be looking at.

Waving to her, he climbed up the bank to meet her. "You ready for Aunt Babe?"

"I guess we're fixin' to find out," she said.

They fell into step on the dirt road. "You still lookin' for Isaac?" Dovey asked.

"Hattie told me not to," he said, "but it don't seem right to quit."

"What did she say?"

"She said Aunt Babe told her what I did — about me goin' to the sawmill. And she said I shouldn't do anything like that again because I might get hurt. She says she's not disappointed in me — but I'm kinda disappointed in myself."

"I think you had to be really brave to even try," Dovey said. "You must love Hattie and Isaac and Aunt Babe a whole lot."

Pete smiled. "Hattie said something else. She said you can love somebody so much and mourn 'em so much that it'll run you crazy if you let it. She says I gotta find a way to put it away and carry on, because good people can end up in the wrong place at the wrong time, and terrible things happen to them, things they can't help and can't never make right. Hattie says that's what happened to Isaac, and she's worried it'll happen to me too, if I don't quit lookin' for him."

"So what are you gonna do?" Dovey asked.

"I don't know. I really don't."

When Pete and Dovey made it to the crossroads, Aunt Babe was sitting on her front porch. Cyrus came running out to meet them, taking the biscuit Pete offered him and ushering his young friends to the house. Aunt Babe left her rocking chair and stood on the porch, staring down at the boy and girl who had stopped at the bottom of her concrete-block steps.

"Aunt Babe," Pete said, "could we talk to you for just a minute?"

"Who this girl, Pete McLean?"

"This here is Miss Dovey Pickett."

"Paul's grandbaby?" Aunt Babe asked.

"Yes, ma'am," Pete said.

Looking at Dovey, Aunt Babe suddenly clasped her hands to her face and shook her head as if she had just solved a mystery. "Sweet Lord," she said. "You Lottie's chile."

Dovey's eyes flew open almost as wide as her mouth. "You knew my mama?"

"I wept in sorrow when I heard the Lord done called her home, but I can understand why he need her up in heaven," Aunt Babe said. "Sweet Lottie prob'ly teachin' them angels a thing or two 'bout kindness. She used to stop by here reg'lar to see do I need anything. She don't know me from the milk-man — just knowed I was a old woman by myself, and that was enough for her to do for me. I wonder what become of that cuttin' I give her from my ramblin' rose?"

"I take real good care of it," Dovey said. "It fills up a whole flower bed."

Aunt Babe smiled. "You a angel like your mama?"

"I hope so."

Aunt Babe looked down at Pete and Dovey standing side by side on the step below. "Dearly beloved," she said, shaking her head. "Come on in."

They sat down at the little table in Aunt Babe's red kitchen, and she gave them each a tea cake from a jar on the counter before taking a seat herself.

"Aunt Babe," Pete began after he had thanked her for their tea cakes, "it's like this. Me and Dovey, we like doin' things together."

"What things?" the old woman asked, frowning and leaning in toward Pete as if to read what was really on his mind.

"Well, all kinda stuff. Sometimes we fish. Sometimes we go wadin'. Sometimes we slip one of Daddy Ballard's horses out for a ride — 'preciate it if you didn't tell him that, though. But Dovey's got this idea that my folks and her folks wouldn't go along with it, and she don't want none of them to know. She ain't got a telephone, so I can't call her and let her know if Mama decides to drag me off to Birmingham to buy school clothes when me and Dovey had already made plans."

"Mm-hmm. Keep talkin'."

"So I got to thinkin' about *your* telephone and Cyrus," Pete said. "He's the smartest dog in the whole county, and I bet we could teach him how to track Dovey. That way I could call you if I can't make it, and you could send Cyrus to let Dovey know so she won't think I forgot about her and get her feelin's all hurt. Maybe you could tie a kerchief or something around Cyrus's neck — that could be our signal that something's gone wrong and I can't come to the hollow. What do you think, Aunt Babe? Will you help us?"

She leaned back in her chair and studied the two of them. "Pete McLean, her people works for yo' people. This ain't the proper order o' things, what you tryin' to do."

"You mean we can't fish together just because her folks work for Daddy Ballard?" Pete countered. "You worked for Ma Ballard but y'all were friends."

"That was different."

"How?"

" 'Cause your grandmama was like a daughter to me! There wasn't never no danger that me and Sweet Ginia was gonna get it into our heads to run off and get married to one 'nother."

"Married?" Pete and Dovey said together.

"But I just turned thirteen!" Dovey said.

"And I ain't even outta school!" Pete said.

"You talkin' 'bout *now*," Aunt Babe said. "I'm talkin' 'bout down the line. Y'ain't gonna be thirteen forever. Time I was fourteen, I was done married with a baby on the way. What you wanna do now's fine. What you gon' wanna do later is somethin' altogether different. *That* gonna stir up a hornet's nest."

"But I don't see why we oughta let something bad that *might* happen down the line mess up something good that's happenin' right now. Besides, just because you run up on a hornet's nest, that don't mean you gotta stir it up. You can slip right by it if you're careful."

Dovey was proud of him for arguing their case so well.

Finally Aunt Babe gave in. "Done my best," she said, shaking her head. "Can't nobody say I didn't. Do what you will with Cyrus. I got a red kerchief 'round here somewhere. Just be one more aggravatin' phone call for me to fool with since yo' granddaddy pushed that durn telephone off on me."

Pete jumped up and hugged her neck. "Thanks, Aunt Babe!"

"Go on then," she said.

Pete had already run outside to start training Cyrus when Dovey stood up from her place at the table. "Would it be alright . . . if I hugged you too?" she asked.

Aunt Babe opened her arms wide and let Dovey in.

Pete and Dovey sat on a flat outcropping of limestone and dangled their feet over Copper Creek while they ate their lunch. It was an especially good one because Pete's mother had fried a chicken for supper the night before. Usually they stayed on Deep Creek because Pete didn't want Dovey to walk this far by herself. But since they were already at Aunt Babe's, they took the opportunity to enjoy a new spot. He could walk her back to the hollow before he went home.

The two of them had followed the clear little stream from the bridge till it took a wide bend, carrying them out of sight of Hollow Road. Here they wouldn't have to worry too much about being spotted. Thanks to Aunt Babe, they both felt like a load had been lifted.

Pete was eating his chicken and looking down at the clear water beneath their feet.

"You're thinkin' about Isaac," Dovey said.

"We used to walk by this spot a lot," he said with a smile, "and I'd always tell him we ought to try fishin' from this rock, and he'd always say the bream wouldn't bite here, and I'd always get a little aggravated. He was right, though. I ain't seen a sign of a fish since we got here." And then he got really quiet.

Dovey knew he didn't feel like talking, so she just hummed to herself, swinging her feet over the clear water. Pete started to hum along with her, and once they got to their favorite part, they gave each other a big grin and started singing loud enough to shake the cones off the pine trees. "Walkin' After Midnight" never failed to chase the clouds away.

NINE

September 12, 1964

The next week, Pete and Dovey were back on Deep Creek.

"You tell me when you get tired o' hearin' this, okay?" Pete was saying.

"I don't mind," Dovey answered, keeping her eyes on her cork bobbing in the water but listening intently to every word he said. Dovey had learned something about Pete that would forever be true. He couldn't stand to think he had let somebody down. That, more than any other kind of worry, would eat at him until he figured out how to make it right. So when he talked about Isaac, she could tell he just needed her to stay close by while he wandered around the situation and looked at it from every direction.

"It's just that Glory's such a small place," he went on. "Everybody knows everybody. Everybody's *kin* to everybody. So how could something awful happen to somebody we all know, and nobody has any idea what it was?"

"Somebody does know," Dovey said, pulling in her line and casting her cork in another direction.

"But they woulda told the sheriff or Daddy Ballard or Hattie — *somebody* — wouldn't they?"

"Maybe not." She sighed, setting her fishing pole down. "Pete, what's throwin' you off is that you think there's just one world we all live in, but there's not. There's a bunch of 'em. There's the world you come from and the world I come from and the world Isaac comes from — there's all kinda worlds. And the only people that don't seem to know that are the ones that come from yours."

He looked like she had hurt his feelings.

"I'm not tryin' to be mean," she went on. "But I don't want you to keep on gettin' disappointed either. You're lookin' for Isaac in *your* world. But whatever happened to him, happened in *his.*"

Pete was quiet for a long time before he said, "You're right. Always are. Aggravates the stew outta me." But he was smiling when he said it.

"I guess we better get on home," she said.

"Yeah. Wanna meet right here next Saturday at lunchtime?"

Dovey nodded.

"Before we go, I got something for you," Pete said. He pulled a small square package out of his knapsack. It was wrapped in pink paper and had a narrow white satin ribbon around it. Dovey had never seen anything like it. "I'm sorry I missed your birthday, but I just didn't know," he said. "And I couldn't get nobody to carry me shoppin' till the other day."

Dovey carefully unwrapped the little box, trying hard not to tear the paper because she wanted to keep it. Inside was an oval-shaped silver locket with pretty scrolling around the edge and a pink rose in the center.

"Hattie carried me to get it," he said. "I only had that one chance to shop, though, so I hope you like it okay."

Dovey had already fastened the delicate silver chain around her neck and was holding the locket up so she could see it. "I've never *ever* seen anything so pretty," she said.

"Happy late birthday." He smiled, standing up and holding out his hand to help her up before they said their goodbyes on the bridge.

■ ■ ■ ■

Aunt Babe wasn't on her porch when Pete got to her house, which was a relief. Most of the time he would remember to bring her a little something, like peach preserves from his mother's pantry or some cut flowers in a Mason jar, but he had forgotten today, and he hated to meet her empty-handed after she had been such a help. He was almost past her house when he heard the screen door slam and a voice — not Aunt Babe's — call to him. "Pete McLean! I would speak with you on this porch!"

Most of the porch was in deep afternoon shade, but a shaft of light filtered through one of the pecan trees and fell on the old white woman in the cotton dress standing at the top of the steps. He had seen her only a few times in his life, but there was no mistaking who she was. Slowly he made his way to the porch and climbed the concrete blocks till he stood face-to-face with Miss Paul Pickett.

"Sit down," she said, gesturing to a small straight-back chair next to Aunt Babe's rocker, where she took a seat. "You know who I am?"

"Yes, ma'am."

113

"Then you know why I am here. And before you even ask, no, Babe did not summon me. She has kept your trust. I was gathering roots in the woods when I spotted you with my granddaughter on that horse of Ned Ballard's. Dovey's Aunt Delphine has been keeping watch over you ever since. Babe revealed nothing to me but your name."

"Miss Paul, we ain't done nothin' wrong."

"I know that," she said, "else you would not be breathing. And while we are on the subject, if you ever take it into your head to dishonor Dovey in any way, I will hunt you down and kill you myself to spare her father the sin of murder and the fires of hell. Do you take me at my word?"

"Yes, ma'am."

"You mean to continue keeping company with Dovey?"

"Yes, ma'am."

"Then you must walk in the light. No good comes under cloak of darkness."

"Yes, ma'am."

"I would speak with Ned Ballard — alone — at my house. Tell him I would have a moment of his time Monday morning."

Pete swallowed hard. "You wanna talk to Daddy Ballard — about me and Dovey?"

"Are you ashamed of her?"

"No, ma'am! I'd take her to church if she'd let me. But she's always been so sure that something terrible would happen if any grown folks found out — 'specially her daddy — and she's always right about pretty much everything —"

"Well, she is wrong about this. Out in the light. That is how it will be, if it is to be at all."

"Does Dovey know about all this?" Pete asked.

"She does not. First you and Dovey, then Ned Ballard, then — God be with us — her father. That is how it must go."

Miss Paul had said her piece. She left the porch and walked toward a pickup now idling in the road. Pete was sure it hadn't been there before. Aunt Babe came out and put her arm around him as the truck slowly drove Miss Paul back into her hollow.

"Baby chile, you done come through the fire," Aunt Babe said, giving his shoulders a squeeze. "If you was old enough, I'd offer you a shot o' whiskey."

"If I was old enough, I'd drink it," Pete said.

Aunt Babe looked at him and burst out laughing. She laughed till she couldn't catch her breath, and her laughter had always been contagious. The two of them were still giggling when Pete hugged her goodbye and started home.

TEN

September 14, 1964

Miss Paul and Ned Ballard sat across from each other at her kitchen table. They had known each other for at least fifty years but had never had a conversation that wasn't absolutely necessary. That was her doing, not his. He and Hinkey had grown up together. Hinkey had been a good friend to him when he had next to nothing, and Ned saw no reason for their friendship to change just because he married into money. Neither did Hinkey. Paul, however, didn't believe in mixing. You stick with your own kind — that was her way. And she had just dealt her landlord a shock. Pete, she said, had spent the better part of the summer in the hollow with her granddaughter.

"Well, Ned Ballard, what say you?" Paul asked.

Ned was reminded of Paul's longtime dilemma, which Hinkey had once explained to him. She could not bring herself to call him Ned, as Hinkey always had, because she thought it unseemly to be so familiar with one who held her family's livelihood in his hands, nor would she stoop to "Mister." That left her no choice but to address him by his full name.

"I don't quite know what to say," he replied. "Has Pete behaved himself?"

"Delphine reports that he is both kind and protective toward our Dovey."

"And Dovey? Where does she stand?" he asked.

"God have mercy, I divine she loves him dearly — or will — though she's too young to know it."

"Well, Paul, it's been my experience that there's not much use in tryin' to tell young folks who they can love and who they can't. If they're not doin' any harm and they help each other get through some sadness, which they've both had, I don't see any need to get all worked up about it."

"But what comes later, Ned Ballard? They are children now, but not for long. What say you when they are fifteen or sixteen? What say you when Pete wants to marry her, as I divine he will? What say you if the devil has his way and that boy *needs* to marry her?"

"Pete's been raised right, Paul. He knows

the difference between right and wrong, and he's a good boy. As for me, I think you've known me long enough to predict what I'd do in most any situation. I don't believe in duckin' and dodgin'. I believe in ownin' up to my choices. That's how Pete's been raised."

She nodded. "Best to have no muddy water," she said. "Best to be clear from the start. You know well as I do that if these children wed, all those Baptists of yours will say your grandson's marrying down."

Ned shook his head. "Look, Paul, everybody around here with any age on 'em knows I got most of my land from Virginia's family. Plenty of folks back then said she married down when she put my ring on her finger, but I've tried to be a good steward, and Virginia and me, we did alright. I don't care about that marryin' down business. But I do care about Pete. And if he's spendin' all his time with your granddaughter, I'd like to meet her."

"Agreed," Paul said.

"And one more thing," he said. "Let's us promise that whatever happens between these children is up to them. They're mighty young. They may well get married one day and stay married for sixty years. On the other hand, either of them could wake up tomorrow and decide they've outgrown the other one. That'll be real hard on whoever gets left behind. But they'll just have to take their knocks like the rest of us and go on. I don't fault you one bit for keepin' an eye on 'em, but whatever comes of it has to be their choice. If Dovey leaves Pete, it won't affect your farmland one bit. And if Pete leaves Dovey, I trust you not to set my cotton on fire. Agreed?"

"Agreed."

ELEVEN

September 19, 1964

Pete and Dovey couldn't stop fidgeting. Miss Paul had told them to sit and wait at her table, but there was no way they could be still, so they paced around the kitchen like a couple of caged bobcats.

First Miss Paul had cornered Pete at Aunt Babe's house. Then she had summoned his grandfather to her house. That meeting, Pete gathered, had gone surprisingly well. But now Dovey's father had been called in from the fields by Miss Paul, and who knew what might happen next? She was waiting for him on the front porch.

After what seemed like an eternity, Pete heard footsteps coming onto the porch, followed by a deep, smooth-sounding voice. Wonder if he could sing like Dovey?

"Something wrong, Mama?" the voice said.

"Come inside, John," Miss Paul said.

Pete and Dovey were standing side by side in front of the sink when John Pickett followed Miss Paul into the kitchen. Pete had never laid eyes on him before. He was tall, lean, and muscular, with angular features. His hair was as shiny black as a crow's feather, and it sort of feathered back like a bird's. He wore it longer than the men in town — all the way over his collar — and definitely no Brylcreem. His skin was dark from working long days in the sun, and he had dark eyes too — nothing like Dovey's. Her daddy's eyes were like onyx, and they had a way of looking through you so that you couldn't be sure whether he was listening real close or deciding how he meant to murder you.

"Who's this?" he asked when he saw Pete.

"Sit down, son," Miss Paul said, pulling out a chair for him.

He sat down next to his mother. "Who's this?" he asked again.

"He is Ned Ballard's grandson," she said.

Pete felt he should offer his hand and a "pleased to meet you," but since the only adults in the room were talking *about* him, not *to* him, he was at a loss for protocol.

"This is Pete," she went on. "Pete *McLean.*"

"Mc—" He frowned a little and studied

Pete like he was trying to decipher something on his face. "What's he doin' with Dovey?"

"They have been keeping company this summer," Miss Paul said.

Dovey's father was still staring at Pete, and though he said nothing, his expression had changed. Something about it, Pete thought, was kind of dangerous. John Pickett slowly stood up, but Miss Paul put a hand on his arm. He resisted for a moment but slowly sat back down, never taking his eyes off Pete.

"John, there has been no wrongdoing. I have seen to that. Delphine has kept watch over them. Dovey was lonesome. And now Pete is her friend. He is a good boy, for a Ballard. They have been keeping this a secret because Dovey knew you would do what you just did. But I believe you are in the wrong. Pete, come here and pay your respects to Dovey's father."

Pete walked over and extended his hand. His voice cracked a little as he said, "Pleased to meet you, sir."

John Pickett shook his trembling, sweaty hand. "Mama, I would never disrespect you, but I don't know what you're thinkin'. Dovey ain't got no business keepin' company with a boy. Besides that, we got no

123

idea how that Reynolds man's pickup ended up over here — a boy ain't enough protection, roamin' around these woods, till we find out what's been goin' on."

"And who would you have protect your daughter and keep her company?" Miss Paul asked.

"Well . . . her family, her cousins —"

"Her cousins are full grown and don't give her the time of day. Her father and her uncles are busy in the fields. Her aunts are busy in the home. Do you mean for her to spend every waking minute alone in that house of yours without a single companion? She might be safe there, surrounded by family keeping watch, but she is not happy. You know good and well Lottie would never have wanted such a life for Dovey."

"It's not fair bringin' Lottie into this." Pete could barely hear him, he said it so quietly.

"Who ever told you life would be fair, John? Certainly not me."

"But she's just a baby!" he cried.

"No, John, she just turned thirteen," Miss Paul said. "Did you remember to get her a present? Because this boy did."

Dovey's father looked stunned, as if Miss Paul had thrown cold water in his face. And as he shifted his gaze to his daughter, he didn't seem scary anymore — just terribly sad.

Miss Paul put her hand on her son's shoulder. "You haven't really looked at your child in a very long time," she said as gently as Pete had ever heard her speak to anybody.

"That's not true," he said, closing his eyes as if to shut them all out.

"Yes it is, Daddy," Dovey said from across the room, and her father opened his eyes to look at her. She had begun to cry, not the wails of a child, but the silent tears of a weary soul worn out from fighting the hurt and ready at last to surrender to it. "It's alright, though," she continued in a steady voice as she walked toward him. "I know you can't help it. I know I look like Mama, and that's why it makes you sad to be with me, and you're already feelin' more sadness than you can stand. It's alright if you need to look away. Don't feel bad."

She put her arms around her father's neck, and for the longest time he clung to her as if she were his only hope of staying afloat. When he finally let go, he had tears in his eyes just like Dovey.

"But I don't even know this boy," he said when he could finally speak.

"Then get to know him," Miss Paul said. "Pete McLean, do you know your Bible?"

"Not all of it, but —"

"Do you know the story of Jacob and his wives?"

Pete thought for a minute and was mighty relieved when the answer came to him. "Yes, ma'am! Jacob saw Rachel tendin' to her lambs and thought she was real pretty. So he asked her daddy if he could marry her. But her daddy said Jacob would have to work seven years for her hand, which is what Jacob did. But then at the wedding, Rachel's family tricked him and sent her older sister down the aisle underneath a veil. I can't remember her name . . ."

"Leah," Miss Paul said.

"Yes, ma'am, Leah. So Jacob got real mad because he wanted Rachel, and her daddy said he could marry her too, but only if he promised to work seven more years. And that's what he did. He ended up workin' fourteen years for Rachel's daddy because he wanted to marry her so bad."

"And how long would you work for my granddaughter?" Miss Paul asked.

Pete looked over at Dovey, who was wiping her blue-green eyes with the back of her hand. He thought about Miss Paul's question long and hard, but when he spoke, he was sure of his answer. "As long as it takes," he said.

TWELVE

Pete was so excited he could barely breathe. Back in the fall, he would not have been surprised if Miss Paul had told him he had to work the Picketts' cotton for fourteen years before he could take Dovey to an all-day singing at his church, but he only had to work one summer. He had been farming with her family three days a week since he got out of school — that was all his mother would allow — and somewhere along the way, Dovey's father had apparently decided that he might not kill Pete after all.

Daddy Ballard had paved the way with Pete's mother, who said she still wasn't sure how she felt about all this. While she reminded Pete almost every day that he was far too young to get serious about any girl, she was clearly fond of Dovey. She would allow Pete to work with the Picketts as long as they swore on a stack of Bibles that they

127

would not put him on any tractor that might end up in a sinkhole.

Daddy Ballard would be driving Pete and Dovey to the church today because Pete's mother was going to the singing with Mr. Garland Harris. Pete remembered how anxious she had looked when she first told him that the nice man who bought the cotton gin had taken her to the Boat Dock restaurant on the Coosa River and wondered if they might see each other again. But by then, Pete knew a thing or two about loneliness. So he had told his mother that if Mr. Harris made her happy, he was all for it.

Mr. Harris looked older than Pete's mother — and nothing like Pete's father. He was medium height with blond hair, which was always neatly trimmed and smoothed back with hair tonic. He had a kind smile and a quiet manner. Pete had never seen him wear anything but a suit and wondered if he even owned a fishing rod. Even so, he did his best to like Mr. Harris.

Pete ran a comb through his hair, which seemed to grow a shade darker and, mercifully, a little smoother every year. He couldn't believe he was actually getting ready to take Dovey to First Baptist with him. It wasn't just the concerns of their families that had to be overcome. Dovey herself was the real obstacle. She had rarely been out of the hollow and was scared to death of being surrounded by strangers. Somehow he had managed to lure her with the promise of music — and not just the usual fare, but traveling quartet singers with guitars and fiddles and everything.

He had convinced her that if she would just work up enough courage to visit his church once, she would never be scared to go again. And in his experience, it was always good when you could cross something off the list of stuff you're scared of. For example, he wasn't scared of Miss Paul anymore. He didn't even get a knot in his stomach when she quizzed him about the Bible to make sure he was still a Christian.

Sometimes Pete had the urge to hide Dovey away so nobody could steal her from him. But that wouldn't be right. Dovey deserved to be seen. And she deserved to see his world, even if she decided in the end that she didn't want to be part of it.

At the blare of Daddy Ballard's Cadillac horn, Pete checked himself over in the mirror. He had grown nearly a foot in the past year and was almost as tall as Dovey's father. Working the fields had tanned his skin, and he was thrilled to have the beginnings of real muscles. Even so, he still had that lanky look of young teenage boys whose arms seemed to grow faster than everything else. He was wearing his navy blue Sunday suit, a white dress shirt, and a tie his mother had picked out.

Daddy Ballard blew the Cadillac horn again. Time to go.

Dovey had no idea what to expect from church people, but she was willing to take a risk to hear the music Pete had told her about — and to make him happy. Her Aunt Lydia had made her a sundress of pale pink eyelet. It was simple, with a square neck ("nothing too low," Aunt Lydia had assured Granny Paul), wide straps, an A-line skirt, and a white sash at the waist. Dovey had grown taller, and she was "starting to fill out," according to Aunt Ruby, who embarrassed the daylights out of her when she talked like that. Her father had bought her a pair of white patent-leather shoes. She wore Pete's locket, like always, and barrettes with tiny silk flowers on them — a present from Aunt Aleene. From her open bedroom window, Dovey heard a car out front, then footsteps on the porch.

"Morning, John."

"Mr. Ballard."

Dovey imagined the two men were shaking hands. The screen door made its familiar *whap* as they came inside. It was strange to think of Pete's grandfather right here in her house, just a few feet away from her bedroom. He was probably used to much bigger houses.

She heard her father calling, "Dovey, honey, don't keep Mr. Ballard waiting."

As she came into the small front room, she was thrilled to see the look on Pete's face. He had never seen her in a dress before.

"Hey," he said with a smile.

"Hey," Dovey answered. On the creek bank together, they talked about anything and everything, but here in Dovey's house, with adults scrutinizing them, they didn't know what to say.

"John, these Baptist singings can go on for a while, especially if they decide to throw in a long-winded preacher, which they generally do," Pete's grandfather was saying. "Prob'ly won't be over till about three o'clock, but if you need Dovey home before then, we'll leave as early as you want us to."

" 'Preciate that. It's alright if she stays, long as she's happy, if you get my meaning?"

"I do. We'll let Dovey decide then. The

minute she wants to come home, why, we'll get her here. But it shouldn't be any later than three thirty."

"That'll be fine."

"Alright, you two, your chauffeur's not gettin' any younger," Pete's grandfather said. "Let's get ourselves to the meetin' house."

"Bye, Daddy," Dovey said, hugging her father.

"Bye, baby," he said and kissed her on the forehead. "You have a good time. I'll be right here if you need me."

John watched from the porch as a rich man's Cadillac carried his daughter out of the hollow. When he came back inside, he paused for a moment in the doorway of Dovey's room. It was changing so fast. No more paper dolls and coloring books. His baby girl's childhood was almost over. He went into the bedroom he had shared with Lottie, switched on the small lamp on the dresser, and ran a finger over her hairbrush, still in the same spot where she'd always kept it.

Gazing at his own desolate reflection in the mirror, he had to wonder — was that how he looked to Dovey? Had he looked that way since Lottie died? John knew he had become a stranger to his daughter — in some ways, a stranger to himself. He turned the brush over in his hands one last time before slipping it into a dresser drawer and turning off the lamp.

By the time Daddy Ballard parked his Cadillac at First Baptist, the churchyard was a beehive of women scurrying back and forth between their cars and the fellowship hall, their arms laden with Tupperware, casserole dishes, cake plates, and gallon jugs filled with sweet tea.

Dovey's eyes were as wide as saucers. Pete guessed she had never seen such a sight — or heard such a commotion as the women called out to each other:

"Vonelle, is that a cobbler, I hope? I waked up in the middle of the night just worried to death we was gonna run low on desserts."

"Did anybody remember to slice us some lemons for the tea?"

"Where's Inez with that electric knife? If she's come off without it, I'm gonna throw myself in the Coosa River."

"Now, honey, don't you give that pie crust another thought. Ever'body has one go a little gummy now and then. Just rip off that masking tape with your name on it and nobody'll ever know that plate's yours."

Dovey stopped in front of the church and looked up at the steeple. "It's so beautiful, like it's pointing the way to heaven."

Pete smiled. "In a way, I guess it kinda is." He opened the church door for her and watched her take it all in.

"It's just so . . . *beautiful,*" she said again. "What's up there?" She pointed to a tall, rectangular opening behind the choir loft.

"That's the baptistery — you know, where we baptize people."

"You mean there's water back there?"

"Not right now, but there's a pool back there that we can fill up when we're baptizing."

"Granny Paul baptizes all of us in the river," she said.

"Ever'body used to do it that way," Pete said. "Daddy Ballard was baptized in the river. I think that'd be pretty neat."

"Were you baptized in that pool?"

"When I was nine."

"And what's that over there?"

"Tell you what," Pete said. "Let's get out of the middle of this aisle so we don't block traffic, and I'll explain anything you want me to."

From their pew about midway down, he pointed out the piano and the organ, the choir loft, the communion table and the offering plates, the American flag and the Christian flag.

Something else had caught Dovey's attention. "Up there on that sky-blue wall behind the baptistery — that pretty bird — is that . . . ?"

"Yeah," he said. "It's a dove."

She smiled and settled back into their pew like she suddenly felt right at home. He had taken the seat on the aisle, with Dovey sitting next to him so he could show her what to do if anybody came up and wanted to share their pew. "Now, Dovey, the church'll likely fill up, and some folks might come up and want to sit on the other side of you. The way it works is, I stand up and step out into the aisle, and you stay sittin' down but tuck your feet way up under the pew so they can get by."

"Like this?" she asked, doing a practice tuck.

"That's perfect," Pete said.

Sure enough, not five minutes later some visitors from another church came up and wanted a seat. Pete stepped into the aisle, Dovey tucked her feet, and a lady sat down on the other side of her and said, "Why, what nice manners you have." Dovey looked like she had died and gone to heaven.

Miss Beulah came in and took her seat at

the organ. "Brace yourself," Pete whispered. As usual, Miss Beulah had the volume pedal all the way to the floor when she opened up with her prelude, "Brethren, We Have Met to Worship." A couple of visitors sitting in front of Pete and Dovey visibly jumped.

Pete's Aunt Geneva came into the sanctuary and got herself situated at the piano on the opposite side of the choir loft from Miss Beulah, and then Brother Jip came in and took his seat behind the pulpit. Next came Brother Alvin Lackey, the song leader, followed by the choir. They were wearing their burgundy robes, which they had never been able to do at the August singing because it was too hot, but the church was air-conditioned now, so the robes were sort of a salute to progress.

With the choir in place, Brother Alvin opened his hymnal on a music stand facing them and gave Aunt Geneva a nod for the intro. The choir began to sing.

When we all get to heaven,
What a day of rejoicing that will be.
When we all see Jesus,
We'll sing and shout the vic-tor-y!

As Brother Alvin motioned for the choir to sit down, Brother Jip walked briskly to

136

the pulpit. The preacher was about five feet ten and built like a tree stump, with pudgy cheeks and a toothy smile. He was clean-shaven and wore his brown hair combed straight back into a pompadour smoothed down with Brylcreem. Everybody liked him, though Pete's mother thought he went too heavy on the Old Spice and "could be a little much sometimes." Even so, this was her church and he was her pastor, so she did her best to overlook his shortcomings.

"Aw, that was some *fine* singing, choir!" Brother Jip exclaimed, gripping the podium on both sides. "And all the people said?"

"Amen!" the congregation responded.

"Aw, you can do better than that!" Brother Jip said. "And *all* the people *said*?"

"Amen!" the congregation roared.

"Aw, praise God. Thank you, Brother Alvin and choir, for that wonderful call to worship. What a glorious message in song. 'When we *all* get to heaven, what a *day* of rejoicing that will *be*!' Amen?"

"Amen!" the congregation answered.

"We are so blessed to have a houseful of visitors today, and all of us here at First Baptist Church of Glory just want you to feel welcome and right at home. I am Brother Jip Beaugard, the pastor. My *good-ness*! I see folks out in the congregation from Mt. Zion, Mt. Pisgah, Mt. Olive, Highway 9 Full Gospel . . . Why, somebody even let Brother Leon Sparks and his Methodist flock in!"

With the whole church laughing, Dovey whispered to Pete, "Y'all *laugh* in church?"

He nodded.

"Now, I hope you know, Brother Leon, that the *only* reason you Methodist brothers got to come is on accounta your ladies being such fine cooks," Brother Jip was saying as the congregation kept laughing. "And of course we like to pay tribute to our Methodist friends since they *named* our town. Did you all know that? Sure enough, it was the wife of the very first Methodist minister here, way back in 1811, who said this little valley was the closest thing to heaven on earth and recommended that the settlers call it Glory. Brother Leon, you can put a little extra in the offering plate since I'm paying such fine tribute to the Methodists this morning."

"Mighta known a Baptist would get around to that offering plate!" Brother Leon called from his pew, which made the congregation laugh again.

"Before we bring Brother Alvin back up here for some singing, if you're visiting with us today, would you stand up right where you are and be recognized?" Brother Jip said.

Dovey shot Pete a look. He shook his head — *don't do it.* All over the church, the visitors stood up, and the ushers went around handing them little cards to complete and drop into the offering plate.

"The deacons will show up at your house if you fill out that card," Pete whispered, "and your daddy will strangle me."

"Aw, what a blessing. Praise him with our hands!" Brother Jip cried. And everybody clapped till the visitors sat down.

"Now, I know y'all didn't come to hear me preach today —"

"Amen!" came a man's voice from the back, which brought more laughter.

"That musta been the chairman of my deacons," Brother Jip joked. "And just so you'll know for sure that you have received a blessing this Lord's day, I ain't *gonna* preach — can I get an amen?"

"Amen!" the congregation yelled, playing along.

"I just have a couple of quick announcements," Brother Jip said. "First of all, Willadean needs all the church hostesses in the kitchen as soon as y'all can get over there after the service. Now, ladies, if the Spirit's working with you and you need to come down here and pray with me at the altar, why, don't you worry about that fellowship table. It'll take care of itself. But if you're right with the Lord and there's not a doubt in your mind where you'll spend eternity when that trumpet sounds, why, it won't hurt my feelings one bit if you scoot on over and warm up them dinner rolls during the invitation. I'll leave that decision up to you. Second, our offering today will be going toward this wonderful air-conditioning that's keeping us all so nice and cool, so whatever you can spare, we appreciate it, and if you can't spare a dime, we'll be happy just to have your fellowship."

After that, Brother Jip said a word of prayer and then turned the podium over to Brother Alvin.

Pete took *The Broadman Hymnal* from the rack in front of them, found the hymn Brother Alvin called out, and held the music so that Dovey could see. He could tell she was scared to sing at first, but by the time they got to the chorus, she appeared to be so caught up in the music that she couldn't help herself.

Leaning, leaning, safe and secure from all
    alarms;

140

> Leaning, leaning, leaning on the everlasting
>   arms.

Pete noticed with great pride when several people on the pew in front of them glanced back to see where that voice was coming from. Dovey could sing like Anita Carter.

Next, Brother Alvin introduced a quartet from Childersburg. There were three men and a woman singer, plus two guitar pickers and a bass fiddle. When they began to sing and play, the whole congregation came alive, clapping along in time.

> Oh, they tell me of a home far beyond the
>   skies,
>   Oh, they tell me of a home far away;
> Oh, they tell me of a home where no storm
>   clouds rise,
>   Oh, they tell me of an uncloudy day.

They sang two more songs after that, including one of Pete's favorites, "I Feel Like Traveling On." Several more groups and a few soloists got up, and before everybody knew it, Brother Jip was offering the invitation and then blessing the food.

After the blessing, the whole congregation herded into the fellowship hall, where the church hostesses had arranged six or seven folding tables into a big U-shape and covered them with so much food that they were beginning to bow.

Pete and Dovey filled their paper plates with fried chicken, potato salad, baked beans, sweet potato casserole, deviled eggs, dinner rolls, and chocolate cake (best to go on and get your dessert, Pete knew, or anything chocolate would be gone when you came back for it). He found two empty folding chairs in some shade, where they sat and ate with their plates in their laps.

Just as they were about to finish, Judd Highland walked over. Pete despised him. He was a year older, a head taller, and thought that because his daddy was a big shot in Birmingham, he was better than everybody else. The Highlands had moved here several years ago — into what they called "the country house" — and Judd's daddy commuted back and forth to the city. Pete had once overheard Aunt Geneva tell his mother that there was something fishy about the whole thing and that Judd's mama was a real piece of work.

Judd played football and liked to lecture anybody who was dumb enough to listen about the importance of athletics. Worst of all, he was too arrogant to realize that he wasn't very good at sports, but even so, some of the girls liked him — probably because they wanted to be seen in his red Thunderbird. He didn't even have his license yet, but he had a car, and there was never any shortage of older boys who would tag along with him just to get a turn at the wheel.

The Highlands didn't go to First Baptist. They were Presbyterians who had to step down a notch and join the Methodist church when they moved out here since the nearest Presbyterian congregation was twenty miles away. But they always came to the August singing, probably because everybody else did and they thought they needed to be seen.

"McLean, my man!" Judd said, sauntering up with his hands in his pockets.

"Hey, Judd," Pete said.

"Who's this?" he asked, pulling up a chair right in front of them. He was leaning back with his legs stretched out in front of him, his arms crossed over his chest, and a big know-it-all grin on his face.

"This is Dovey," Pete said. "Dovey, this is Judd."

"Hello," she said.

"*Dovey.* Well, well, well. I don't know where McLean's been keeping you, but I'm about to take you off his hands."

"Hey —" Pete started to object, but Judd

ignored him.

"You see that *smokin'* red T-bird parked right over there?" He leaned toward Dovey like he was telling her a secret.

"What's a T-bird?" she said.

"What's a — that *car* over there, sugar!"

"I see it," she said.

"Well, it's got a fine leather seat with your name on it," he said, as if he had just done her the biggest favor of her life.

"What are you talking about?" she asked, looking him square in the eyes. Pete knew that look. But Judd didn't.

"I *mean,* you and me and maybe one of my linebackers in that T-bird, cruising down the highway to the Dairy Queen the minute this shindig's over," he said.

"Why would I do that?" Dovey calmly stared him down.

"Sweetheart, my daddy is an executive — in *Birmingham.*"

"But who are you?" she asked with that unflinching stare.

Judd suddenly spotted some people in the churchyard he needed to speak to.

Pete had never been happier in his life.

Thelma Bunch sat in front of a pretty little plum tree, enjoying her third piece of cake before her afternoon solo. She wore a bright blue dress with a pink silk flower as big as a salad plate on the right shoulder. Her wide-brimmed, white straw hat was crowned with silk flowers in every color of the rainbow. Everything her girdle couldn't contain was spilling over the sides of an overburdened folding chair, which gave her the appearance of a big blue hen trying to hatch an egg.

No one was looking when a little green snake dipped down from a low-hanging branch in the plum tree and settled into the flowers on Thelma's hat.

Back in the church, the singing resumed with quartets and duets and a choir special or two. Pete knew Dovey could handle *The Broadman Hymnal* just fine by now, but it made him feel good to find the songs and hold the book for her. Everything was going so well till around two thirty, when the inevitable could be avoided no more. Like the children of Israel who had to wander in the wilderness before they reached the Promised Land, the congregation of First Baptist would have to endure Miss Thelma's solo before they could go home. She had the shrillest soprano in ten states and didn't bother herself with staying on key, but a handful of old folks in the church kept requesting her solos — most likely because they couldn't hear it thunder and had no idea what she sounded like. It fell on poor Brother Alvin to introduce her.

"I apologize in advance," Pete whispered to Dovey with a grin as Miss Thelma came to the podium.

"Thank you, Brother Alvin, for that kind introduction," Miss Thelma said. "As you all know, I do not sing for the praise of man but for the glory of the Almighty. And because this is a time of worship, I'll ask that you hold your applause till the very end."

She gave a dramatic nod to Pete's Aunt Geneva, who rolled her eyes and began playing the intro to "He Lives," which, Pete was painfully aware, had a very high note near the end. Their ears might actually bleed.

Miss Thelma hadn't even made it through the first verse when an odd murmur rolled through the congregation like ripples on a pond. She closed her eyes and sang louder. Knowing Miss Thelma, she probably thought everybody was so overcome by her music that they were struggling to contain themselves.

The murmuring was quiet at first because the congregation wasn't exactly sure what they were looking at — or maybe they just couldn't believe it. But by the time Miss Thelma got to the chorus, there was no denying that something was moving on her hat — that something on her hat was, in fact, *alive.*

Pete and Dovey looked at each other, then back at Miss Thelma, then back at each other.

A little green snake was having a look around. He had slithered his way to the front of Miss Thelma's spacious hat brim and raised himself up, flicking his tongue and moving his head from side to side. The whole church — the *whole church* — sat in stunned silence, mouths hanging open, unable to move or speak. Just as Miss Thelma hit the long-dreaded high note and opened her eyes to take in the admiration of her audience, the snake dipped over the brim of her hat and looked her in the eyes with his flicking forked tongue.

Miss Thelma's high note turned into a bloodcurdling scream. She screamed till she ran out of breath, and then she sucked in some air and screamed again — screamed but did not move. A simple tip of her hat would've sent the snake to the floor, but apparently Miss Thelma couldn't gather her wits enough to do it. She just kept screaming, and the snake kept flicking his tongue and swaying from side to side, right in her face.

Daddy Ballard was the first to come to his senses. "Hold still, Thelma!" he called as he ran up the three steps to the podium. With a wave of his hand, he tapped the underside of her hat and it went sailing to the floor, snake and all. But Miss Thelma kept right on screaming.

"Thelma!" Daddy Ballard said. "Thelma!" Finally he grabbed a glass of water that Brother Jip kept inside the podium and threw it in her face. She looked at him as if she had just come out of a trance and then fainted dead away with a loud thud.

Ladies swarmed the pulpit with the cardboard fans First Baptist had held on to just in case the power went out. "Willadean, grab the revival salts by the organ!" one of the women yelled. (You never knew when somebody would get overcome with the high emotion of the spring revival, so the church hostesses thought it best to keep smelling salts conveniently tucked away in a cubbyhole by the organ.)

The little green snake was slithering up the aisle toward the front door, as if he needed to hurry into position to greet the congregation after the benediction. One of the ushers opened the door and shooed him into the sunshine.

In all the ruckus, Pete hadn't noticed until now that Dovey had her head in her hands, and her whole body was shaking. "Dovey?" he said. "You okay? Are you cryin'?"

When she looked up, he saw that she was not crying but laughing — so hard that tears were rolling down her cheeks, and she was trying desperately to stop before the church got quiet again.

Pete grinned. "I know we just witnessed a circus, but I've never seen you laugh so hard. What are you so tickled about?"

"Well, I guess . . ."

"You guess what?"

"I guess now y'all know . . . what snake handlin' looks like!"

He laughed and handed her the starched white handkerchief his mother had put in his coat pocket. Along with everybody else in the congregation, they did their best to collect themselves while the church ladies helped Miss Thelma to her feet and ushered her toward a side door.

Brother Jip, who probably wasn't quite sure what else to do, stood up like a football coach saluting an injured player exiting the field and said, "You all, let's give Miss Thelma a round of applause for a fine effort under very difficult circumstances."

And they did.

"This has been a glorious day in the house of the Lord," he went on. "Have you received a blessing?"

"Amen," the church answered.

"Once again, we want to thank all of our visitors for being with us, and if any of you don't have a church home, why, we'd love to have you here at First Baptist of Glory. Ladies, that was some fine cooking y'all did for us — amen, husbands?"

"Amen," all the men in the church said.

"We like to close every singing with that great old song of the faith, 'Amazing Grace,' so if you all will join hands across the aisle, I'll ask Brother Alvin, Miss Beulah, and Miss Geneva to come on up and lead us. This will be our benediction. God bless."

Pete had forgotten about this part. Had he remembered, he would have made plans with Dovey to slip out before it began. "Amazing Grace" had been his father's favorite hymn. He and Isaac used to sing it together in the fields, and every time Pete heard it, he felt the loss of them both in a way that was hard to bear.

Everybody was joining hands. Judd Highland's mother came over to meet Pete in the aisle and took his right hand without looking at him. He held Dovey's in his left and took a deep breath as the music began.

Amazing grace, how sweet the sound
That saved a wretch like me;
I once was lost but now am found,
Was blind but now I see.

Halfway through the last verse, Mrs. Highland dropped his hand and returned to her pew to gather her belongings, as if she didn't have any more time for this sort of thing. Dovey stayed with him. Pete didn't realize it at first, but he had actually begun to squeeze her hand, holding on for dear life. He wasn't hearing the choir or the congregation, but instead a rich baritone and a crystalline tenor — the voices of two men who, for Pete, always stood for harmony and friendship. But they were both taken — in different ways, maybe, but both taken — before anybody had a chance to do anything about it or even realize it was happening.

Once the song ended and everybody began filing out of the church, Pete and Dovey stood together in the aisle. He had told her how his father and Isaac used to sing together, and how Isaac had made him promise never to forget his father's favorite hymn.

"Well," he finally said, "I guess you've got quite a story to tell your daddy when you get home." He kept her hand in his as they made their way to the car.

Outside, Pete caught a glimpse of his mother and Mr. Harris standing at the far edge of the churchyard. Mr. Harris was handing her a handkerchief from his coat pocket, and Pete could tell that she was crying. He knew why too. "Amazing Grace" had brought his father back to her for a moment, and now she had to let him go again.

■ ■ ■ ■

PART II

■ ■ ■ ■

THIRTEEN

March 15, 1966

Ned Ballard drove his Cadillac to the crossroads faster than he should have. He knew the rocks and clods of red clay in the road could do untold damage to the automobile he had petted and pampered ever since his Virginia died.

He had taken such pleasure in buying it for her. Virginia wasn't like a lot of women. She didn't want everything in sight, and she didn't want anything just because it cost a lot of money. She would wear a sale-rack dress for thirty years if she knew it looked good on her, and she would pass up the most expensive frock at Loveman's if she thought it made her look matronly — or worse, "like one of those silly women trying to dress like a teenager." Virginia was discerning, but from the minute she saw that Cadillac on the showroom floor, she was smitten.

Since she died, he had done his best to keep it the way she would've wanted. He never drove it over fifty miles an hour, kept it away from loose gravel and fresh tar, and wouldn't dream of parking in the shade for fear of what the birds might do. But Aunt Babe had just called him. She had called him on the very telephone she professed to despise, though he knew good and well she loved talking to her children and her grandchildren on it. Two of them lived long-distance, and he paid the bill. Aunt Babe didn't have the foggiest notion about long-distance charges, and he meant to keep it that way. Virginia would have wished it so.

The one number Aunt Babe had never dialed was his own — until now. Something was wrong with Hattie. And so he flew down Hollow Road, rocks and clods flying, to the little shotgun house at the crossroads.

Aunt Babe met him at the door. " 'Preciate you gettin' here so quick, Mister Ned," she said, motioning him to her kitchen.

It was one of the oddities of their relationship that Aunt Babe had always called Ned's wife "Sweet Ginia" but addressed him as "Mister Ned." He figured that made sense to Aunt Babe because Virginia had been like a daughter to her, and his wife adored her as much as any member of the Jackson family. It was Aunt Babe, Virginia always said, who listened to her troubles, advised her about the ways of men, and wasn't afraid to tell her when she was in the wrong. The bond between the two women had been fierce, but Ned knew Aunt Babe felt no such bond with him. To her, he was just a white man and a big landowner, which would always make him a "mister" in her book.

He followed her to her crimson kitchen and the sound of a woman sobbing. "Hattie?" he said.

She looked up with red and swollen eyes. The handkerchief she clutched was no match for the weeping she was doing.

"Hattie," he said again, taking a seat next to her, "what's this all about?"

"It's a foolish thing, really," she said. "All this over a old chair."

"A chair?"

"See, I've got this green wingback chair with a real thick seat cushion that Iris found on the curb — just put out on the street for throwaway — when she was at Spelman. Her and a girlfriend carried it all the way back to her do'mitory. She cleaned it up real nice and talked some boy with a truck into drivin' her home for the Thanksgiving break so she could bring it to me. Don't ever let on to Iris, Mister Ned, but I always preferred my rocker, and I never set in that chair but maybe one time when I first got it. Isaac, though, he loved it. Said it made him feel like he was settin' in his very own liberry when he read his books there.

"Well, this mornin' as I was straightenin' up, I thought to myself I hadn't vacuumed underneath that cushion since . . . well, since it was used a lot. And when I picked it up to clean under it, I seen my boy's bookmark layin' there. I guess it had slipped down under the cushion while he was readin'. Right away I know what I'm lookin' at because I give it to him — a little gold cross with a purple velvet ribbon attached to it."

"Hattie —"

"I found my Isaac's bookmark, Mister Ned. I found his bookmark, but I'll never find him. Why they got to kill the good ones, Mister Ned? He was just tryin' to do right — and find a little happiness besides. They quarrel with him, fine, but why they got to kill him? He was a *good* boy."

"Hattie," Ned said, "do you know who killed Isaac?"

"No, sir," she said. "Most folks think Reuben, that thug from down around Four Mile. I wish to goodness Isaac never took up them cards. I always told him they was trouble. Then again, there's that awful Klan . . .'"

"You want me to find out?"

"You done tried your best, Mister Ned."

"Yes, but I tried my best workin' with the law. This time I mean to use money. Money can find things county sheriffs can't. 'Specially the one we're stuck with — for now. But I won't do anything you don't want me to. So you just tell me — do you want me to?"

In the comfort of her mother's kitchen, Hattie thought it over. "Yes, sir, I do," she finally said. "I think I got to know — not so much who done it, but what happened to my boy. I don't want you gettin' yo'self hurt, though."

"Don't you worry about me. I got sense enough to know when to handle something myself and when to hire it done. Galls me no end to think about some no-account sleepin' like a baby, thinkin' they got away with this. Whether they turn out to be white or colored, I hope they spend the rest of their sorry life in the pen. Did one of your girls give you a ride over here?"

"Junie brung me."

"Aunt Babe, you want to go over and stay with Hattie tonight? I can drive you both so Junie won't have to make another trip."

"What we gonna do 'bout Cyrus?" Aunt Babe asked.

"I'll have Pete and Dovey look after him. They can fix him a bed on John's porch till you get back."

Aunt Babe disappeared into her bedroom. When she came back to the kitchen, Ned could see that she had packed a sack big enough to hold more than she needed for one night.

"Mama, what you doin' with so many clothes?" Hattie asked.

"Ain't no good to be all by yo'self with a mournful heart in the springtime," Aunt Babe said. "All the happy flowers in bloom just make the darkness inside you that much meaner. I'm gonna come be with you for a while."

Ned followed them out to his car and held the door for them. Cyrus watched from the porch as he drove them out of the hollow. The sun was sinking down as the Cadillac turned onto the highway, bound for the shotgun houses and dogtrots clustered up and down the road to Morning Star Baptist Church.

FOURTEEN

May 14, 1966

Lila stood before her son, tying his black bow tie. She couldn't believe she had to reach up to do it. Just a year ago, Pete had shot up so fast that he had been lanky and rail-thin, and he was still growing. But now his muscles were beginning to catch up with his frame, his voice had changed, and he was losing that awkwardness that plagues all teenage boys early on. He was broad-shouldered like the Ballard men, and he had inherited Lila's dark blue eyes. Still, he reminded her so much of his father. They shared the same dimpled smile and the same thick, wavy hair, though Pete's was getting darker and softer than his daddy's as he matured.

Really, where Pete favored Jack most was on the inside. They both genuinely cared about other people, maybe a little too much, and they both had a sixth sense when it

161

came to the ones they loved — how they were feeling or when they were hurting. They would put themselves out in front to shield you even when they were the ones who needed shielding the most, and that made you pray for them a little harder than you prayed for anybody else.

"Mama, do you mean to turn me into a soprano?" Pete asked with a grin, tugging at his collar. She straightened his tie and helped him slip on the white dinner jacket she had bought for him at Loveman's.

"You're not too big for me to whip." She smiled, smoothing the jacket over his shoulders and stepping back to make sure it hung perfectly. "You're lucky we're still having some cool nights. Your daddy and I got married in July, and bless his heart, he was sweltering in that tuxedo I made him wear. That reminds me — what do you do if Dovey gets chilly?"

"I offer her my jacket."

"That's right. And at the dance?"

"I walk her to a seat and ask her if she'd like some punch."

"You *escort* her to a seat. She's a girl, not a horse."

"Yes, ma'am."

"You've been good about opening doors for ladies since you were little, so I'm not worried about that. But don't forget, now, to offer Dovey your hand and help her out of the car like I showed you. And then you offer her your arm —"

"Mama, how we gonna get home if I ain't got no arms and hands left, what with me offerin' her this one and that one all night?"

" 'Ain't got no'? Really? Is that how they teach you to talk at that school?"

"Okay then, if I *don't have any* arms and hands left . . ."

"Oh, hush up," she said, fussing with his lapels. "Good manners are important. They tell other people, especially girls, what you think of them — and whether you've got any sense. One of these days you'll be glad I taught you not to act like a hooligan."

"I know."

"Now, you've got a full tank of gas?"

"Yes, ma'am."

"And the extra money I gave you is in your wallet?"

"Yes, ma'am."

"And you won't forget Dovey's wrist corsage in the refrigerator?"

"No, ma'am."

"And you remember she has to be home by nine and you need to be home not long after that?"

"Yes, ma'am."

"And you know you're only allowed to pick up Dovey — and I mean you slow that car down to a *crawl* going over those bridges in the hollow — drive to the dance, and come straight home, no place afterward? I don't want to hear about my car being seen in Childersburg tonight."

"Mama, if I even looked toward Childersburg with Dovey in the car or got her home five minutes late, her daddy would murder me."

"That's true," Lila said. "I guess he's pretty scary, huh?"

"Yes and no," Pete said as he thought it over. "He's not mean or anything. And he teaches me a lotta stuff in his shop. I sorta like him. It's just hard to know what he's thinking."

Lila smiled. "So I've heard. Long as he's got the bluff on you, I guess all I need to do is tell you to act like a gentleman and have a good time."

He started for the kitchen.

"Oh, son?" she said.

"Yes, ma'am?"

"Your daddy would be real proud."

Lila hugged Pete and kissed him on the cheek before he went into the kitchen to get Dovey's corsage out of the refrigerator. She watched from her screen door as he pulled out of the driveway in her Buick.

When Pete was out of sight, Lila went into her kitchen and readied the coffeepot for a long night. Part of her was so happy for Pete and Dovey, setting off on their first real date, and part of her wouldn't stop worrying till they were safe at home again. This house felt so empty the minute Pete walked out the door. It took everything she had to make sure he never knew that. She would not allow her own loneliness to deny him even a minute's happiness. He had been through enough.

She glanced at the three messages by the telephone. They were all in Pete's handwriting and all said the same thing: "Mr. Harris called." Sooner or later she would have to face the music. A kind and decent man, Garland Harris made no secret of being smitten with her. Shouldn't she be grateful for that? Shouldn't it be enough? She poured a cup of coffee and picked up the phone.

At least half the boys driving to the spring dance tonight didn't have a driver's license yet, but since most of them had been plowing cotton and hauling it to the gin since they were twelve or thirteen, the town policeman, Chief Thurgood, looked the other way this one night of the year. As long as you were at least fifteen and didn't speed or do something really stupid, you could take your date to the dance without the humiliation of being delivered to the school by your parents. And almost none of the boys ever got out of line because they knew the chief could match every car in town to the parents who owned it and wouldn't have any trouble figuring out whose daddy to call.

Pete didn't really care about the dance, but he was beside himself to have a real date with Dovey. His mother had given the two of them a couple of dance lessons in the front parlor. As with everything else, Dovey caught on right away. Pete was a real klutz at first, but once he stopped trying so hard and just followed the music, he did alright.

Lately his mother and Dovey had been spending a lot of time together. Awhile back, Dovey had mentioned that his mother seemed to talk a little differently from her. Later, when she heard Pete's mother correct his grammar, Dovey had asked if she could be corrected too.

One day Dovey was helping rearrange the china cabinet at Pete's house and asked his mother what those smaller plates were for. In a flash, his mother had taken down a whole place setting and gathered some of

Ma Ballard's silver out of a wooden chest on the buffet. One piece at a time, she showed Dovey how to set a formal table. Pete left the two of them alone, but he could hear them from the front parlor.

"How did you learn to do all of this?" Dovey asked with that slightly forlorn tone that crept into her voice anytime she came upon some bit of information that she thought everybody else had known all along.

"Someone taught me, just as I'm teaching you," his mother said. "No woman's born knowing all of this, Dovey. We all have to learn, and we all make mistakes. Don't ever let anybody tell you otherwise. Just always remember, the whole point of setting a pretty table or cooking a special meal is not to prove anything to your company but to make them feel comfortable and welcome. As long as you manage to do that, you can serve the salad in a soup bowl and the pot roast with a shrimp fork — it won't make one bit of difference."

For the past couple of weeks, it was the dance, not the china cabinet, that had Dovey's full attention. Every time she saw Pete, she peppered him with questions. What did the girls wear? How did they fix their hair? How many people would be there? What did a gym look like? Who decorated it for the dance? What did every-body talk about? He knew she was scared to death of the school, so he kept reminding her of how terrified she had been the first time she went to church with him. Now she went every Sunday and was thinking about joining the choir, mostly because everybody begged her to the minute they heard her sing.

When word first got out at First Baptist that Dovey was a Pickett, the church ladies had seized the opportunity to gather infor-mation — always with a polite smile, but it wasn't hard to guess what they were up to.

"And how is your grandmother faring, honey? Now, does she still preach in your family barn on Sundays? Well, what a bless-ing that must be, worshiping together and all. Anything . . . unusual happen . . . in your lovely family services, dear?"

Dovey took it all in stride — all except for Miss Thelma, who had made the fateful mistake of coming at her with "I believe in speaking my mind, and if you ask me, Pau-line Pickett has absolutely *no* business keep-ing children out of a proper Sunday school."

"But I didn't ask you," Dovey had said, giving Miss Thelma the stare. And Miss Thelma, just like Judd Highland before her, had suddenly found someone in the churchyard who needed her immediate attention.

Pete pulled the Buick slowly into Dovey's yard, hoping her father would notice what a careful driver he was, and carried the white corsage box to the front door.

John Pickett greeted him with a shotgun in his hand. "C'mon in, Pete," he said. "I was just cleanin' my gun — thought I might go after some rabbits next week."

"Yes, sir," Pete said, eyeing the Remington.

"What you got there?" Dovey's father asked.

"A wrist corsage for Dovey. Mama helped me pick it out. Hope she likes it."

"Dovey, honey," her father called, "Pete's here."

Dovey came into the front room. She and Pete had grown up right in sync. Now that he was fifteen and she was close to it, he was still about a head taller than she was, just as he had been the day they first stumbled onto each other at the sawmill. But Pete wasn't thinking about that. He wasn't really thinking about anything at all because the first sight of Dovey on any given day tended to shut his brain down, and that was especially true tonight.

She told him that her Aunt Lydia had worked on her dress for a solid week. Dovey chose the pattern, and Pete's mother some-how managed to buy the fabric without of-fending the Pickett women. His mother said they had decided on silk and lace for the bodice, whatever that was, and silk and chif-fon for the floor-length skirt. All Pete knew was that the dress was a pale shade of Dovey's eyes — a beautiful bluish green — and it made her look like a princess.

She wore her hair down, with a pretty pearl barrette on one side. A few weeks earlier, she had shown Pete a picture in a magazine of a girl with her hair teased high and piled on top of her head. "Is this what I should do for the dance?" she asked.

"Why would you want to gunk up all those pretty curls in your hair?" he replied. He truly needed help understanding such a baf-fling thing, and that had made Dovey smile. The only jewelry she wore to the dance was Pete's locket. He had given her other pres-ents, but he could tell the locket was still her favorite. She had told him that she kept it on a little table by her bed so it would be the first thing she saw every morning and the last thing she touched each night.

"I need to remind you of anything?" her father asked Pete.

"No, sir," Pete said. "To the school and back and no place after, home by nine or

I'm a dead man."

"That's exactly right. Now, y'all have a good time." Dovey's father kissed her on the forehead as he told her goodbye.

Pete had pulled into the school parking lot and shut off the engine before he realized he had never given Dovey her corsage. He had carried it into her house and back out again, set it in the car, and driven it all the way to the dance.

"Oh, man!" he exclaimed. "You must think I'm the biggest lunkhead, Dovey. This is for you." He took the delicate flower out of its white box and slipped it over her wrist.

"I've never seen a flower like that," she said with a little gasp. "What's it called?"

"It's an orchid. Mama said it would look pretty with your dress. Now, why didn't you thump me on the head and tell me to take this durn flower out of the box and give it to you?"

"Because I didn't know there was a durn flower *in* the box. For all I knew, you coulda packed us some leftover chicken in there."

They both laughed, like they had so many times as kids teasing each other on the creek bank. But Pete saw Dovey's expression change when she looked up to see all the couples start filing toward the gym. Some of the girls had that big hair she had shown him in the magazine. Little clusters of them were scattered here and there, admiring each other's dresses and giggling about whatever it is that makes girls like that giggle. The stag boys were huddled at the back corner of the gym, smoking Lucky Strikes.

Dovey looked at Pete with terror in her eyes. "I don't belong here," she said.

"You belong anywhere you wanna be," Pete said, turning to face her. "You're the prettiest girl here tonight, Dovey — and the smartest, school or no school. Do you wanna be here — with me, I mean?" A little afraid of her answer, he stared down at the corsage on her wrist, lightly running a fingertip over the delicate orchid.

"I want to dance with you in this dress and wear your pretty flowers," she said. "But I don't think I can go in there with all them — all *those* — girls."

"How many kids you reckon we've seen go into that gym while we were sittin' here?" Pete asked.

"I don't know . . . thirty or forty? Why?"

"Well, I'd say I'm friends — real friends — with maybe six or seven of 'em. And the same is true for everybody else in that gym if they're honest about it. Don't nobody feel like they belong in high school, Dovey, except maybe the cheerleaders and the football team, and they might be fakin' it for all I know."

He could see her hands trembling, so he wrapped his own around them. "Look, if you just flat out don't want to go inside, that's fine by me. I don't give a rip about that dance. I just wanted to take you some-place besides church — and someplace where your whole family wasn't standin' over me with firearms."

That brought her smile back. "So what are we gonna do?"

He thought for a minute. "Well, we're gonna go dancin' someplace else." He gave her hands a little squeeze, then turned and cranked the Buick.

"But Daddy said —"

"He said we couldn't go anyplace *after*. He didn't say nothin' about before. All we gotta do is stop back by here and run inside that gym for two seconds on the way home, and we can truthfully say that we went to the dance and no place after. And I hope you'll do me the honor of singin' at my funeral if your daddy ever finds out, because I've always thought you had a real pretty voice."

Pete eased the Buick out of the parking

lot and drove a few miles up the highway. He turned onto a side road next to the billboard that read "McAdoo's" and followed it to a café on the bank of a crescent-shaped lake, which glowed in the soft rosy light of early sunset. He opened Dovey's door for her and helped her out of the car, just as his mother had shown him, then offered her his arm as they walked across the gravel parking lot to the café.

"Evening, Mr. McAdoo," Pete called to the man wiping tables with a dish towel on the far side of the café.

"Hey, Pete!" he called back, checking out his dinner jacket and tie. "Whoo-ee, son, look at you all gussied up! You must be preachin' somewhere tonight."

Pete laughed. "No, sir — just out on a date. This is Dovey."

Mr. McAdoo came over and shook her hand. "Pleased to meet you, Miss Dovey. You know, even a pretty girl like you could do a lot worse than ole Pete here. That scalawag's been swimmin' in my lake since he was yea high, and I can tell you right now, he's good people."

Dovey smiled. Pete could see that she already liked Mr. McAdoo.

"Pete, I don't start openin' the café for supper till next week — I'm just gettin' things ready — but I'll fix y'all a bite if you want me to. I'm guessin' you're on your way to the spring dance?"

"Yes, sir. We didn't come to eat, but thank you for offerin'."

"Well, what can I do for you?"

Pete cleared his throat so his voice wouldn't crack and make him sound like a big baby. "Has your swimmin' pier still got those speakers hooked up to the jukebox?" he asked, fidgeting with his bow tie.

"Sure does." Mr. McAdoo frowned slightly as if he were trying to figure out where Pete was heading. "The kids love my jukebox," he explained to Dovey, "but my wife hates it. Says the racket gets on her last nerve. So I had to run me some speakers out to the pier, where Mertis can't hear the music from the kitchen, or else she throws a fit and won't fry my hamburgers for me."

"Well, we were on our way to the dance," Pete told him, "but neither one of us has ever been to one before, so we chickened out a little when we got there. I thought maybe we could practice with a few songs out on the pier till we get our nerve up — if you don't mind changin' a dollar and lettin' us play your jukebox for a little while?" He fished a dollar out of his wallet.

"Don't mind it a bit," Mr. McAdoo said,

getting their change from the register. "I've got to run Mertis up to her mother's in a few minutes. Won't be gone long, but if y'all have to leave before I get back, there's a spare key in a Mason jar underneath that flat-bottom boat that's flipped over right out yonder. So lock up for me if you don't mind. And be careful if it gets dark on you. The corner lights work on the pier, but all the others blowed down in a storm last summer and I haven't got around to puttin' 'em back up yet. If you want a Co-Cola or anything, just get you one out of the cooler."

"We sure thank you," Pete said. "And Mr. McAdoo, if we could . . . you know . . . keep this between us? See, we're not supposed to go anywhere but the dance, and Dovey's daddy's a real good shot."

"Haven't seen hide nor hair of you in weeks." Mr. McAdoo winked.

"I'll leave our Coke money by the register," Pete said.

"No need. I think I can spot y'all a couple of Co-Colas in honor of the occasion." Mr. McAdoo shook Pete's hand. "And Miss Dovey, I hope to see you again when we can visit longer." He gave them a little wave as he went out the front door.

The café had a wall of floor-to-ceiling windows facing the lake. A door in the center led out to a deep porch, which ran the length of the café and connected to a pier that angled down slightly for a few yards then leveled off over the water. At the end of the pier, about ten yards from the bank of the lake, was a big square platform with a plank floor and a ladder attached to one side so swimmers could climb up and dry off in the sun. The platform rested on stilts, but right now the water was high enough to cover them, so it looked like it was just floating on the lake. As Dovey stepped onto it, Pete loaded the jukebox with nickels and selected as many of her favorite songs as he could find. If anybody could chase away her jitters, it was Patsy Cline.

He started outside to join her, then stopped for a minute on the porch just to look at her standing there with her back to him, silhouetted against the lake in her flowy blue-green dress. A slight breeze lifted her hair away from her face as she watched a mother duck swim by with her babies and nudge them into the shelter of the tall grass on the bank. Pete suddenly got a terrible feeling that Dovey was about to cry. Switching on the pier lights, he hurried out to her just as Patsy began to sing "Crazy."

Pete took Dovey's hand but didn't say

anything. She was still watching the ducks. "Do you ever feel just . . . lost?" she finally asked, looking up at him.

"About ninety percent of always," he said.

She smiled. "Sometimes I think there's just so much I don't know, things you're supposed to learn from your mother, maybe . . ."

"Or your daddy," he said.

"I don't know what to do at a dance, and I don't know if Mama was still scared of things like that when she was as old as I am. I don't know how she met Daddy. I don't know if they ever got in trouble for stayin' out late or what songs they liked to dance to. I don't know how it was with them. Why don't I know that?"

"Because you were still little when they were together," Pete said. "And when you're little, your parents aren't real people — they're just your mama and daddy. All that stuff you don't know about 'em — that's not your fault, Dovey. And it's not theirs either. They didn't have no way of knowin' what was comin'. They just had a rug pulled out from under 'em."

"Them — *those* girls at that gym — they all looked so . . . so sure," she said.

"Sure of what?"

"I don't know! That's the problem."

"Well then, what are *you* sure of?" Pete asked.

"What do you mean?"

"Well, are you sure you'd rather be out with me in Mama's big ole Buick than sportin' around with some hotshot like Judd Highland?"

Dovey rolled her eyes. "I'd rather be on a three-legged mule with you than sportin' around with that silly Judd Highland."

"Okay, then that's something you're sure of." He smiled at her and took her other hand so they faced each other. "Are you sure . . . that I'd rather be out with you . . . than with Miss Thelma?"

She laughed. "Are you makin' fun of me?"

"Just seein' where I stand." He grinned. "You know, when Miss Thelma's wearin' her good girdle, can't you nor anybody else hold a candle to her."

"Hush!" Dovey laughed again.

"All I'm sayin' is that if you're sure about me and I'm sure about you, then maybe the rest of it we can just . . . kinda figure out together?"

She nodded.

"Think you might ever dance with me," he asked, "or do I need to call Miss Thelma and see if she's free?"

"Maybe if you get real lucky, she'll wear

her snake hat for you."

The sun had slipped into the water like a scoop of vanilla ice cream sinking into a Co-Cola float, and a dark, misty twilight had fallen over the lake. Pete put his arm around Dovey's waist and took her hand in his. Their dance began just as his mother had shown them, with Dovey's "keep him at arm's length" hand on Pete's shoulder. But then Patsy began to work her magic. "Sweet Dreams" came on the jukebox, and the longer Patsy crooned, the closer Pete and Dovey drifted. Her hand inched across his shoulder and around his neck, and he lifted her other one up to join it so he could put both arms around her. She rested her head on his shoulder as he leaned his face against her hair and wished like everything that Patsy would keep on singing forever.

When the music stopped, they both stood very still, holding each other and gazing into each other's eyes. Pete didn't even hear the next song begin as he slowly bent down to kiss Dovey for the very first time. And the miracle of it was — she kissed him back.

Thank you, thank you, thank you, Patsy Cline.

Ned Ballard sat at his usual booth at the Tomahawk Café, having a cup of black coffee with his strawberry pie. The waitress had put some of that canned whipped cream on his pie, which he didn't care for, but she was so jittery that he didn't complain. Instead, he just raked it onto the saucer with his fork. He had seen some of the young people come in for a hamburger on their way to the dance and wondered if Pete and Dovey were having a good time.

On the table in front of him was a thin binder that contained the latest report from the private detective he had hired out of Atlanta. Even though two years had passed since Isaac disappeared, the detective, who was a former FBI man, had already discovered a lot more than the county sheriff did back when all the evidence was fresh. And it was a good thing too, because that detective didn't come cheap. He would be worth every penny, though, if Hattie and Pete could finally put Isaac to rest. He knew Hattie had made Pete promise to stop looking for Isaac — and that she and Aunt Babe kept a sharp eye out for any signs that he might go back on that promise. But Ned also knew how much it still ate at the boy, even after all this time. He promised Pete he would share all the detective's reports with him, and he meant to do exactly that. Might give him a little peace to know that somebody was at least trying.

He thumbed through the report. They still didn't know who had killed Isaac, but they knew who didn't do it — everybody's prime suspect, Reuben. The detective had paid Lucius Hays, one of Isaac's card-playing buddies, enough money to get the names of everybody around that poker table the night Isaac vanished.

According to Lucius, Reuben was there, but he was in no shape to kill anybody. He couldn't even stand up. A few hours before the card game started, he had met up with some of his Talladega cousins, who were even meaner than he was. They had spiked his cheap whiskey with some drug. Nobody knew what it was exactly, but it was bad news, Lucius said, because when they dumped Reuben out at the poker shed, he had stumbled into a corner and curled up like a baby, humming to himself and occasionally hollering for his mama.

Isaac wasn't having a good night either and had folded early, almost broke except for whatever cut of his pay he had already given to his mother. That meant nobody could accuse him of cheating — the usual cause of bad blood at the shed.

Still, the detective had retraced the footsteps of every last one of the card players till he was sure they hadn't followed Isaac up the road that night. And they all confirmed what Lucius had said about Reuben, which they had no reason to do, since clearing him might hang the blame on one of them.

"Can I get you anything else, sir?" the waitress asked just before she knocked over his water glass with her ticket pad. "Oh! I'm so sorry, Mr. Ballard! It *is* Mr. Ballard, ain't it? Lemme get that right up!"

He grabbed the report before it could get wet. "No harm done," he said. She wiped all the ice cubes back into the glass and blotted up a small puddle of water before backing into a customer and knocking over a dishpan full of silverware on her way back to the kitchen.

Ned opened the report again and swore under his breath at what he read. A Chevrolet dealer from Huntsville had stopped to use the pay phone at the Sinclair station in town the night Isaac disappeared. He had been in Phenix City for a sales meeting, which was followed by an awards dinner that hadn't wrapped up till almost eight. On his way back to Huntsville, he had stopped in Glory to call his wife and let her know he was tired and had decided to look for a motel.

For miles before he found the Sinclair, he had kept his eyes peeled for a phone. Just outside of town, he spotted bright lights on a side road and turned onto it to see if there might be a filling station with a pay phone there. It turned out to be floodlights at the lot where the county road crew left their equipment on weekends, so he had pulled into the short driveway at the gate to turn around. That was when he saw a pickup and a car pulled over to the side of the road.

They were parked facing each other, with both hoods up, and a colored man was fiddling with jumper cables running between the two. That was around nine thirty or ten o'clock. He hadn't paid it much attention until he read a newspaper story about the FBI's investigation of a disappearance in Glory and saw the picture of Isaac's truck. It was the same one he had seen that night.

As soon as he read the article, he called the county sheriff's office and gave a detailed description of the other car — he had gotten only a glimpse of it, but that was all he needed. Both the car and the pickup were Chevys, which he had been selling for almost twenty years. And the floodlights on the nearby lot were bright enough so that he could even tell what color they were.

The sheriff didn't include the salesman in

his report because he said he had lost the notes his secretary made when she took the call, and he apparently didn't think Isaac was worth the trouble it would take to gather that information again. Or maybe he was just plain lazy. But the secretary remembered it, and now that she had found a better job and didn't have to put up with that worthless sheriff anymore, she didn't hesitate to tell the private detective all about it.

She remembered every last detail of the call — the salesman's name, where he worked, why he was passing through Glory, even what awards he had won at that dinner down in Phenix City. She remembered absolutely everything except his description of the car, which she said "just had a bunch of numbers and car talk in it." The salesman's name, she was certain, was Frank Wheeler. But there was no Frank Wheeler in the Huntsville phone book, and the detective was still calling Chevrolet dealerships in Alabama, Georgia, and Mississippi, trying to find him.

Ned checked his watch. It was already eight thirty. He left a generous tip for the nervous waitress, tucked the report under his arm, and paid his ticket at the register. Outside he heard the distant rumble of thunder, and a cool wind was beginning to blow. Pete and Dovey might get rained on before the night was over with, but he hoped not.

Pete drove the Buick into Dovey's yard just as the rain began to fall. A quarter to nine — they had made it home with time to spare. Every light in the house was on.

"Gee, I wonder if he's still up," Pete said with a weak smile. "Ready to make a run for it?"

"Guess so," Dovey said. "Are you sure you wanna do this?"

"I'm sure I *don't* want to," he said. "But I think I have to. Maybe he won't get too mad. Go on and pick out my funeral music, though, just in case."

He took off his jacket as he went around the car to open Dovey's door. Holding it over her with one arm, he helped her out of the Buick, and they ran for the front porch, where Dovey's father held the screen door open. He brought them both a towel as they sat down on the edge of the couch. Her father took a seat in the armchair across from them, his shotgun propped in the corner.

"Mr. Pickett," Pete began with a glance at the Remington, "I think I need to tell you something."

"I'm listenin'," Dovey's father said.

"We didn't go anywhere after the dance, but we went somewhere before."

John Pickett said nothing, and his expression gave Pete no clue what he was thinking.

"When we got to the gym, we got a little nervous about going inside —"

"Daddy, that's not true," Dovey interrupted. "Pete wasn't scared at all. I was. When we got to that gym and I saw all those girls with their teased-up hair and the boys smokin' their cigarettes, and they all knew each other and I didn't know any of them, it just — I felt like I didn't — well, I just couldn't see myself in there. And all I could think about was how hard Aunt Lydia worked on this dress and how much time Pete's mother spent teachin' us to dance, and you bought me these shoes and this pretty hair clasp, and it was all gonna be wasted because of me bein' so silly and scared."

Dovey's father was looking down, running his hand over a small tear in the arm of his chair.

"Mr. Pickett, I never cared anything about that dance," Pete continued. "I just wanted to take Dovey out. And she really wanted to go dancin' in her new dress, but that gym was just makin' her so unhappy. So we drove up to Mr. McAdoo's café and played the jukebox and danced for a little while." He decided not to mention that he and Dovey had been alone at McAdoo's. There was such a thing as honesty, and there was such a thing as suicide.

"After we left the café," Pete went on, "we stopped back by the gym and stayed for one song just so we could truthfully tell you we had been to the dance and no place after. But then on the way home, I got to thinkin' about how that was kinda lyin'. And Dovey would hate lyin' to you. So would I. I mean, you trusted me with her and I didn't do what I said I'd do. Anyway, I just felt like I owed you the truth, and please don't blame Dovey or Mr. McAdoo because this was all my doin'."

Dovey's father looked at her and then at Pete before getting up from his chair and picking up the Remington.

"Daddy —" Dovey began as her father came toward them and propped the gun on the floor next to him, holding it upright by the barrel. He didn't let her finish.

"Pete, you know there's always consequences," he said calmly.

"Yes, sir." Pete's throat was completely dry.

"I'll expect to see you in the field four days a week instead of three for the whole month of June. If I need to speak with your mother about it, I can stop by next week."

"Yes, sir. I don't think that'll be —"

He held the shotgun out to Pete. "Do me a favor and put this back in my gun cabinet when you leave. 'Night, you two."

Pete's hand trembled a little as he took the gun from Dovey's father, who left them alone but called from the back of the house, "I wanna hear that Buick crankin' directly."

"Yes, sir," Pete called back. He and Dovey leaned back on the couch and exhaled the breath they had been holding. Pete rested the shotgun on his lap.

"For what it's worth," Dovey said with a smile, "I was gonna sing 'I Feel Like Traveling On' and 'Far Side Banks of Jordan' at your funeral."

The two of them burst out laughing.

"I've got more than one gun," her father called out.

"We better quit while we're ahead," Pete said, returning the shotgun to a cabinet in the hallway. Dovey followed him out to the porch, where he had left his jacket to dry on the back of a rocking chair. He put his arms around her and held her close, listening to the rain drip off the tin roof.

"Dovey," he finally said almost in a whisper, "do you think you might — I mean, would you maybe — could we, do you think, get married when I get out of school?"

She smiled up at him. "I was sorta countin' on it," she said.

FIFTEEN

"Pete, you mind comin' out to the barn for a minute and helpin' me load a few tools into my truck?"

"Sure, Daddy Ballard," Pete said as his mother began making a pot of coffee. Pete's grandfather had taken them out to Sunday dinner after church, and they were spending the afternoon with him. He followed Daddy Ballard out to the barn. "What you need me to load?" he asked as his grandfather shut the barn door behind them.

"Nothin', son," he said, taking a seat on a hay bale and motioning for Pete to do the same. "I need to talk to you. Got something I feel like you've got a right to know before anybody else."

Pete felt a familiar knot in his stomach. No good news ever began like this, at least not in his experience. He took a deep breath and tried to steady his nerves. "Did you —

191

did you find Isaac?" He felt a little dizzy as he said it.

"No, son, but we did find something," Daddy Ballard answered. "We found out that a salesman passin' through town the night Isaac disappeared saw him — saw him *after* he left that card game."

Pete struggled to take it in. "But if he was just passin' through, how did he know it was Isaac?"

"He didn't — not at first, anyway. But when he saw a newspaper story about a colored man disappearin' in Glory, he recognized the truck — remember they ran that picture of the truck in the newspaper?"

Pete nodded but couldn't quite find his voice for a minute. Then the questions came tumbling out. "Well, who was this salesman? Where'd he come from, and what did he see, and how come he ain't said nothin' all this time? And how'd you finally find him? Where's he at?"

"Hang on, Pete, and I'll tell you everything," his grandfather said. "That sorry excuse for a sheriff made one royal mess outta this. And I still don't know if we'll ever untangle it. But I'm gonna do my best — for you and Hattie."

"I know," Pete said. "And I didn't mean you any disrespect. It's just —"

"No need to apologize, son. We're all sick and tired o' chasin' our tails, but I really think we're on to something."

Pete's grandfather recounted everything he had learned about Isaac's disappearance, down to the last detail. When he finally finished, Pete struggled to put it all together.

"So . . . the Chevy man saw another car but didn't see anybody with Isaac?" he asked.

"That's right," his grandfather said. "And I can't explain why just yet. But if we can find that car, we can find the owner. Think about it — Isaac wouldn't have any reason to jump off a car with no driver. Somebody *had* to have been there. And if we can find 'em, we'll finally know what happened to Isaac because whoever he was helpin' either killed him or knows who did."

Killed him. Even though Pete knew those words to be true, they still hit him like a kick in the gut. Something about saying them out loud made them too real to stand.

Daddy Ballard reached over and put a hand on his shoulder. "I'm sorry to be so blunt, son," he said. "But the way I see it, you've done been through enough to deserve the truth. And I think way too much of you to sugarcoat the situation or try to hide anything from you."

193

Pete felt his lower lip tremble slightly — imperceptibly, he hoped — as he tried to smile and thank his grandfather.

"I'm going in to tell your mother," Daddy Ballard said. "It'll give you a little time to yourself. You come and get me if you've got any questions after you've had some time to think about it."

"Yes, sir," Pete said. "And thank you, Daddy Ballard — thank you for tellin' me."

Alone in the barn, Pete slowly climbed the wooden ladder into the hayloft and wandered over to the opening where he had first overheard his cousins speculating about Isaac. He sat down and dangled his legs over the ledge, looking out at the pastures and fields.

If Isaac hadn't stopped to help somebody in trouble, he might still be here. If he weren't so kind, he wouldn't have gotten killed.

The world made no sense — except when Dovey was in it. Pete lay back in the hay and tried with all his might to remember every detail of the night before. If he could see Dovey clearly in his mind, if he could conjure her voice and her laugh and her touch, then maybe he could endure the hours that would have to pass before he could hold her again.

SIXTEEN

May 16, 1966

On a rainy Monday morning, John Pickett took his old seat at Lila's kitchen table while she poured them both some coffee.

"Still take it with just a little cream?" she asked.

He smiled. "Good memory."

She handed him a cup and sat down across from him. It had been raining almost steadily since Saturday night, and right now John was looking out Lila's rickety screen door, watching water splash off a concrete table underneath the pecan trees.

"Cleaned a lot of catfish on that old table, you and Jack," she said. "It's a wonder I didn't wear out my percolator keeping you in coffee back then. How do you ever fall asleep at night?"

He shrugged. "Lotta nights I don't, but I doubt it's the coffee."

"Our kids got anything to do with it?"

"I take it we're still not telling Pete that his daddy was a friend of mine?" he asked.

"No. And I made Daddy and Geneva promise not to — Aunt Babe and Hattie too — for now anyway. I think the fear of God and your shotgun are good for Pete. Makes him think twice."

"My family's keeping it quiet too."

"I'm surprised he hasn't put it together, though," Lila said. "I won't even let him ride around with Geneva's boys because I spotted a beer can in their truck, and yet he thinks I'd let him work for a man who might actually murder him."

She smiled and sipped her coffee. Even that smile — Jack had always thought it was so pretty — looked sad to John now. He had to wonder if the same was true of his.

"Your sister still keeping everybody straight?" he asked.

Lila shook her head. "I'll put it this way — don't ask her what she thinks unless you really want to know."

John hadn't thought of Geneva in forever — or of this kitchen table, where he had once felt so at home. That seemed like a hundred years ago.

"As long as we're talking family, there's something I've always wondered," Lila said. "I know you and Jack sort of stumbled onto each other on the creek bank when you were kids, but how'd you square that with Miss Paul?"

"Daddy."

Lila nodded, and he knew she understood. Hinkey Pickett and Ned Ballard had been boyhood friends. Over the years, Mr. Ballard had helped the Pickett family so many times that John's father didn't share his mother's distrust of outsiders.

"Prob'ly the only time I ever saw him put his foot down with Mama," John said. "None of my brothers and sisters could understand why me and Jack were friends or why I liked going over there. But you know how his family was — his mama 'specially. About every other week, I had to remind that sweet lady I wasn't her kid."

"Well, when you've already got six . . ." Lila said. "I don't know how on earth they fed everybody on that small farm, but they managed."

It's a lot harder when you don't even own your land. He would never say that out loud because it wasn't Lila's fault. Or her daddy's, really. And it would hurt her feelings.

"I just remember a lot of laughin' around the table and in the fields," John said. "That was the happiest bunch of folks I ever saw. So different from our family."

Lila nodded. "It took me awhile to get used to all their teasing and carrying on, but once I did — oh my goodness, we had some good times over there."

John remembered when Jack had first worked up the nerve to ask Lila out. They were all still teenagers back then. He had fallen hard for her and started saving for an engagement ring after their first date.

To John, Lila had always been a puzzle. Her daddy was one of the richest men in the state, yet she didn't have an uppity bone in her body — or a selfish one. Never had. Now that he thought about it, she was probably one of the kindest people he had ever met. The two of them had rarely spoken without Jack in the room, and John had been anxious about coming here. Talking to Lila was easier than he had imagined it would be, but the two of them were still circling each other, not quite sure how to face the questions they needed to answer together.

"How's the front porch holdin' up?" he asked.

"You do good work." She smiled. "I take care of all my serious thinking in that swing."

When Jack and Lila first married, John had helped them restore their old farmhouse, adding a deep wraparound porch and building them a swing as a wedding present. As the men hammered and nailed, Lila worked on her cooking skills. Every afternoon she would put down her paintbrushes, take out a thick cookbook that the church hostesses had given to her as a wedding present, and attempt something new. Up until then, John had never even seen a shrimp, but when Lila got to the seafood section of her cookbook, he and Jack had to eat shrimp five different ways in one week.

Lila pushed a plate filled with tea cakes in his direction.

"These got shrimp in 'em?" he asked.

"I'm never gonna live down shrimp week, am I?" She laughed as he took a tea cake from the plate.

He looked out at the rain still pouring down. "Hard rain always makes me think of Jack. I used to go to worryin' whenever the fields stayed wet too long, but he would tell me that a wet field is just an invitation to fish. I miss the way he could turn things around like that. Seen Pete do it a couple of times . . . Sure wish things coulda been different — for all of us."

"I know. Me too." After a long silence, she looked at him with a straight face and said, "You know, not many women could beat me at frying catfish, but your Lottie came close."

John had to laugh. "Man, Lila, your catfish was awful."

Lila laughed with him. "My secret was cold grease. I can just see Lottie spreading newspaper over y'all's kitchen table and dumping out a mountain of the lightest catfish in the whole world. Now, that girl could cook."

"Prob'ly the only reason her sorry daddy didn't put her out of the house before I came along."

John had never thought about it before, but it was a remarkable thing that Lila, with her mahogany china cabinets filled with fine dishes and linens, had come to Lottie's table with Jack and eaten fried catfish off newspaper like it was the most natural thing in the world. Lila had an easy grace about her, and to her credit, she had done everything she could to make his wife feel comfortable. But Lottie would always come away from their visits feeling — what was it she used to say — "a little lost." And John loved her too much to watch her go through that again and again.

"You're making the only choice you can, my friend." That was what Jack had said when John struggled to apologize for letting go of their friendship. He had felt some relief to know that Isaac Reynolds had become a friend and a help to Jack — took away some of the guilt he felt. But now nobody had any idea what had become of that man. If Jack were here, he'd be out looking for him. That's just how he was.

It was Jack who had found a doctor for Lottie when she got so bad. And then a year later, he was gone too. No one noticed when John slipped into the back of the church the day of the funeral. And no one saw him slip out midway through, when the weight of his loss overcame him and he had to flee First Baptist for the seclusion of the woods.

"I guess we both know what's coming for these kids of ours," Lila said, finally broaching the subject they had been talking all around. "Pete hasn't been able to focus a thought or complete a sentence since Saturday night, so I think it's safe to say he's got it bad. If things keep moving in this direction, they're bound for the altar as surely as any pair I've ever seen."

John looked up from his coffee and asked her straight on, "How you feel about that, Lila?"

"Sometimes I wish they'd give themselves time to date around a little, just to make sure. Then again, Pete could go out with every girl at that high school and never find anybody better to walk through life with. And I honestly think the sight of Dovey with another boy would do him in. He might have to be hospitalized."

John smiled as she went on.

"I seem to remember making up my mind about Jack the first time I danced with him, and we weren't that much older than they are now. Sometimes two people just know. What do *you* think?"

"Jack would be proud of how you've raised Pete. And I know the boy really cares for Dovey or he never coulda faced me like he did after that dance."

"They're just so young," Lila said. "There'll be the draft to contend with when he turns eighteen. I've been trying to talk him into at least thinking about college so they'd have some options down the road, but he swears he wants to farm."

"You don't believe him?"

"Who knows? You of all people remember how Jack was, and Pete's just like him. He might truly want to grow cotton, but then again, he might just be saying that because he's worried about leaving me alone or taking Dovey too far away from you or disappointing his granddaddy. He'll do whatever he thinks he has to, just to make everybody else happy. About the only thing besides farming that he's shown any interest in is the woodwork you've been teaching him. I've heard about every power tool in that shop of yours, by the way. You still selling pieces to a dealer in Birmingham?"

He nodded.

"And Miss Paul still has no idea you're chasing mammon in Sodom and Gomorrah?"

John smiled. "You're a meddlesome woman, Lila." He sat there quietly for a minute before raising the next question that had troubled him. "If Pete does decide on college, would you want him to finish before . . . before he and Dovey . . ."

"Before they get married? Are you kidding me? We'll be lucky to hold them off till he gets home from school this afternoon."

"Maybe me and my Remington can be of some help in that area."

"Keep it prominently displayed at all times."

"I wanna thank you for spendin' time with Dovey — teachin' her things," he said. "She's at that age where I don't know what she — I mean, I just don't want her to be afraid — Lottie never could get past it, and it was so hard for her."

"She did the best she could, John — we

all did. We were kids ourselves back then." Lila took a long sip of her coffee. "Listen, there's one other thing, and I want you to just hear me out before you say no. I talked this over with Daddy, and we think he should deed that land on the river to your family."

"Now, Lila, we ain't takin' —"

"Wait, now, before you decide. First of all, you're not taking anything. You've earned it. And second, I mean, think about it — anything else would be awkward for Pete and Dovey. Business needs to be business and family needs to be family, but the two will be all crossed up for our kids if we keep things the way they are with that land. Y'all have worked it for years, and you ought to have it. Daddy's already had the papers drawn up. He just needs to know whose name to put on the deed. And as for the equipment, you can trade Daddy some cotton and keep using his or keep all the cotton and buy tractors and a picker some-place else. That's up to you. Miss Paul, I imagine, won't go along with this. So should it be your name on the deed?"

He ran his fingertips around the rim of his coffee cup while he thought about what Lila was saying. She was right and he knew it. If things stayed the way they were, then one day — maybe not tomorrow, but one day — he and his brothers would be working for his son-in-law. That would be more than their pride could stand. And seeing their pride hurt would be more than Dovey could stand. Still, his mother would declare it charity and throw an unholy fit. But he would just have to take that as it came, for Dovey's sake.

"All four of us," he finally said. "That's the best way to keep things right between me and my brothers."

"Then it's settled," Lila said. "We'll do as you say. And as far as we're concerned, it's nobody's business whether any money changed hands. Word will get out, though, that the land is yours, which is why we wanted to do it now. Let them do their talking and speculating and forget all about it before anything happens with Pete and Dovey. That way the two of them can start fresh without any nonsense in their way."

For a while, John and Lila sat there with no sound but the ticking of her kitchen clock between them until he said, "So while you're easin' the way for everybody else, how are you makin' it?"

"I'm fine," she said, her eyes fixed on her coffee cup. But when she looked up at John her smile faded. "I'm fine except when I'm miserable — when I'm missing Jack so much that I just want to run screaming across a cotton field. Or when I'm lying awake wondering if I'm doing what's best for Pete and trying to figure out how on earth I can help him through yet another heartache if Daddy can't find out what happened to Isaac. And when I'm done worrying about all that, I move on to my *own* life — what in the daylights is that supposed to look like? You know I was seeing Garland Harris for a while."

"Seems decent enough."

"Oh, he is. Only he's not Jack, and there's no helping that. Almost four years have gone by, and I swear some evenings I still expect to see him come walking in that door right there, tracking up my kitchen floor with those muddy work boots and grabbing supper off the stove before I could get it on the table."

"Got a pretty good idea how you feel."

"I know you do," she said. "And I just think — feeling that way — it's not fair to somebody like Garland. He wants a wife, and he deserves one who isn't wishing he were somebody else. So I told him I thought it would be best if we — well, you know . . ."

"I'm sorry, Lila. I didn't have no right —"

"You didn't say anything wrong. It's good

to talk about Jack with somebody who knew him so well — and cared about him so much."

After another silence, he had a question for her, one he had turned over and over in his mind ever since Lottie passed. "Do you ever wish you didn't know?"

"Know what?"

"What you had — what you lost."

"I never thought about it before . . . Might be easier . . . But no. I'd live my life with Jack again even if I had to lose him again. Living through all of that gave us Pete and Dovey, and neither one of us could ever give them up."

"No — you're right." He closed his eyes and let out a long, tired sigh. This was getting to be too much, all the churned-up memories and the grief. But then Lila did something that John would see her do again and again — walk into a pitch-black room and turn a light on.

"You know what I could use?" she said, as if she'd had a sudden revelation. "I could really use a good friend. Somebody who doesn't ambush me with dinner parties where there just happens to be an unattached insurance salesman or a widowed tax accountant prattling on about nothing. Somebody who'll tell me straight up that

208

my Shrimp Panama is disgusting. You up for it?"

He frowned as he thought it over. "Never had a woman friend before."

"Well, there's a first time for everything."

"Always figured you can't trust 'em." He was finally smiling again.

"Oh, you can't. You absolutely can't."

"You ever learn to fish?"

She shook her head. "Still despise it."

"Being your friend ain't gonna be much fun."

"No, but there could be an occasional supper in it for you."

"Hold up, now — I've had your cooking."

Lila laughed. "I am *much* better than I was back then!"

"Okay then."

"So now that we're friends, can I meddle some more?" she asked with a big smile. "Anybody new in *your* life?"

"Just your son, God help me," he said.

They had one more cup of coffee as the rain finally began to let up.

SEVENTEEN

April 18, 1967

Pete opened his high school locker and crammed in all the books from his morning classes. After lunch, all he had left were shop and PE. Then the final bell would ring and set him free.

It wasn't that he hated school. He actually liked history and geometry. Shop was okay, but it was pretty lame compared to what he was learning from Dovey's family. Her father, he had discovered, was a master wood craftsman. Her Uncle Hollis was the best mechanic in the whole county, and her Uncle Noah could fabricate anything from metal. Unbeknownst to Miss Paul, all three of them had quietly used their skills to supplement the family income for years. And all three were willing to teach Pete what they knew as long as he did his part in the fields, which he was happy to do. So making a cutting board in shop class wasn't much of a challenge, given that he already knew how to dovetail joints and turn wood on a lathe.

As for PE, what a total waste of time. You didn't need dumbbells to "bulk up" if you were pitching hay bales around all summer and spending long autumn days tromping on cotton to pack it down in the wagons.

Now that Pete was a junior, his mother let him decide how much he could farm as long as he kept his grades up, and he found himself working more and more. He worked for free with the Picketts during the summer and for pay with Daddy Ballard the rest of the year. Whenever he was rained out, he was either with Dovey or in her father's woodworking shop. He had saved up for a used truck, but when he turned sixteen, Daddy Ballard bought the pickup for him and told him he would likely need every dime he had saved for repairs, gas, and the Dairy Queen. He actually got to take Dovey there now, all the way to Childersburg, because the longer he worked with the Picketts, the more Dovey's father seemed to trust him. Work, for Pete, had translated into time alone with Dovey, and there was no such thing as too much of that.

Still, every afternoon he had to waste a whole hour doing push-ups and sit-ups and running laps and tossing free throws. He didn't mind the rope climb because he had learned long ago that such a skill could come in mighty handy, but there wasn't much chance he would ever free-throw his way out of a deep hole in the ground.

His family probably thought he didn't participate at school because he didn't want Dovey to feel left out. But that wasn't true. All of Pete's life, he had felt a little alienated from kids his own age, even though he got along with them well enough. He could sense things they were missing, like an undercurrent in the river. The world looked so different to him than it did to them. But Dovey could feel the currents. She saw everything Pete saw and some things he missed.

As he closed his locker, he heard giggles behind him and turned to see a cluster of freshman girls gawking at him. He smiled to himself. "You can call me Lucky," Isaac would've said to them. But that image conjured another, much darker one. It was the way Daddy Ballard's private detective had described what the car dealer saw the night Isaac disappeared. Isaac had been helping somebody, like he always did. And somehow his very kindness had gotten him killed. The whole thing made Pete feel a little sick. He doubted the lunchroom menu would do much to help that.

Pete eyed his cafeteria tray and sorely regretted turning down the sack lunch his mother had offered to pack. Tomato soup and peanut butter sandwiches — that was today's menu, only the peanut butter had an oozy, grainy consistency that made even hungry teenagers suspicious of its origins. He looked around for an empty chair and saw plenty of them at the table where the only six colored students in the whole school were sitting. They had come in January, one of Alabama's federally mandated baby steps toward integration.

They were like a solitary island of color floating in a sea of white. Seeing them there reminded Pete of the day he first met Dovey at the old sawmill, when she had told him why she didn't go to school: "We don't belong there."

Pete thought most everybody seemed polite enough to the new students in the hallways and in class, but for three months they had sat together at the same cafeteria table with no one coming near them. That, Pete decided, was crazy. What was the difference between sharing a lunch table with them and sharing a kitchen table with Aunt

Babe or a creek bank with Isaac? He found himself walking steadily toward them, every eye in the cafeteria fastened on him.

"Mind if I sit with y'all?" he asked.

"We're not looking for trouble," said the tall, thin boy at the head of the table.

"Me neither." Pete shrugged, and the tall boy motioned for him to sit down.

"You some kinda crusader?" one of the girls asked.

"No. I just figure y'all put your shoes on one at a time, same as the rest of us. It's not like you're from Mars." They stared at him without saying a word. "Then again, maybe I'm wrong," Pete went on, tasting the awful soup and making a face. "Maybe y'all *did* beam down here from outer space to vaporize all us white folks. If that's the case, I'd sure 'preciate it if you started with the football team, 'cause some of them are real jerks."

One of the girls was still staring at him like he was crazy, but the others were smiling. "Who *are* you?" the tall boy asked.

"Pete McLean." He grinned, reaching across to shake hands. "And you might as well know that I'm pretty much a nobody at this school, so the fact that I'm gracing you with my presence won't exactly get you elected to the student council."

"That's a shame," the tall boy said. "And here we thought we'd finally found us a white boy to pin all our hopes and dreams on."

Pete didn't know what to say at first, but then the boy broke into a grin and the two of them laughed.

"I'm Lenny," he said. "And that's Theo, Wanda, Reesie, Sharon, and Florence."

"Hey," Pete said. "Where y'all from?"

Coach Gilbert "Buster" Thrash loved football. He especially loved it when the crowd, after every victory, sent the opposing team off the field with a humiliating chant: "You've been Thrashed! You've been Thrashed!"

Coach had made himself something of a legend in Alabama. He had carried five teams in as many counties all the way to the state championship, which continued, maddeningly, to elude him here in Glory. In three years, he had yet to put together that winning combination of raw talent, Spartan discipline, and evangelical devotion to football that would bring home the trophy.

For the past few months, though, he had kept his eye on one boy who just might be able to tip the scales in his favor — a strapping junior who had yet to see the light and follow it straight to the goal line. McLean was a sad case, really. Something about a dead daddy and a backwoods girlfriend — he couldn't remember the details. But that sad case was a strong six feet two with speed *and* brains. Let him work out his childhood trauma on the playing field, that's what Coach thought about it.

McLean had breezed through the rope climb and agility test. Now came the final bench press. Coach was eager to see what this boy could lift once Judd Highland did his predictable eight reps at 210, mediocre as always.

"Never seen you in the weight room, McLean — what you press?" Coach asked as Judd finished and took his place with the team.

"I really don't know, sir," Pete said.

"Well, let's start you off at —"

"Hey, Coach!" Judd called with a smug grin on his face. "Why don't we let McLean pick up where I left off — *if* he can?"

"McLean?" Coach said.

"If you want me to, sir — I really don't know what I can lift."

Coach motioned for Pete to take his position on the weight bench. Pete gripped the crossbar, looked up at the weights on either end, and pushed high. He lifted the barbell up . . . five, six, seven, eight, nine, ten, eleven . . .

"Whoa!" Coach said. "Looks like you need a little more weight, boy." He added ten pounds and Pete lifted. Ten more and Pete lifted again. Coach stopped him at 230, guiding the barbell back into the rack, and Pete returned to the civilians.

"Highland, you want another go?" Coach asked.

"Uh . . . can't today, Coach — Doc says I strained my bicep when I went for 240 last week."

Coach could see that even the freshmen weren't buying it. His quarterback looked like he might actually punch Judd in the face.

"In that case, hit the showers, everybody," Coach said. "Say, McLean, hold up a minute." He motioned for Pete to sit down with him on the bleachers. "Pretty impressive, what you did on that bench."

"Thank you," Pete said.

"What's it gonna take for me to get you on the team?"

"I 'preciate it, sir, but I'm working after school and in the summers — hoping to schedule all my classes in the morning next year so I can go to the fields in the afternoon. That doesn't leave any time for practice."

"Mm-hmm, mm-hmm." Coach was nodding earnestly as if he completely understood and sympathized, but he wasn't really listening. He was too busy plotting his next move. If he could hook this boy before the end of spring training, they might have a shot at the state championship come fall.

"Tell you what," Coach said, "I can let you stay a while and use the weight room if you like."

"Thanks, Coach, but I've got to get home," Pete said. "I'm helping my granddaddy with his crop."

"Well, that's admirable — helping the poor old fellow scratch out a living. You go on home, son. We'll talk another time."

Pete thanked him again and headed for the locker room.

EIGHTEEN

April 19, 1967

Ned Ballard glanced at his watch — a quarter to nine. That should work out about right. Tate Harwell, an old friend and the principal at Pete's school, had asked him to come down a little early for their nine o'clock appointment. Tate's secretary greeted him just outside the principal's office.

"Would you care for some coffee before you go in, Mr. Ballard?" she asked.

"No thank you, Jewel. But I 'preciate the offer. Tate's forever braggin' on your coffee."

"He's telling the truth too." She smiled as she ushered him in.

Tate Harwell stood up when Ned came into his office. With his wire-rimmed glasses and silver hair combed back, he was a dead ringer for Lyndon Johnson. He had been running the school for twenty-two years.

"Morning, Ned," he said as they shook hands.

"Tate, 'preciate you callin' me," Ned replied, taking a seat in one of five chairs arranged in a semicircle in front of Tate's desk. "Looks like you're expectin' a crowd."

"Well, it's like I told you on the phone, I believe in having all parties represented," Tate said. "Never cared much for a stacked deck."

"What's the situation?"

"Last night around suppertime, Whit Highland called the house spouting off about some fight Pete and Judd got into yesterday afternoon."

"A *fight*? Pete's never been one to fight."

"I know. I also know what Judd's made of, which isn't much. Highland apparently thought I didn't have sense enough to know what's goin' on at my own school."

"Well, that's his mistake." Ned smiled. As long as the two men had been friends, Tate had always known what parents wanted to say to him long before they walked into his office. He likely already knew everything about the fight — who started it, who finished it, who saw it, and what he meant to do about it.

"I'll not make any bones about it, Ned — I despise the Highlands, and Pete was

220

absolutely not at fault yesterday. Fact is, you ought to be mighty proud of him. Still, when a fight happens on my school grounds, I have to make a formal investigation, just to show the students and their parents that I mean to be fair."

"You'll get no objections from me," Ned said.

Jewel knocked. "I've got the boys."

"Send 'em on in," Tate said.

Pete came in and sat down next to his grandfather, with Judd taking a seat as far away from both of them as he could get. Four other boys filed in behind them and stood along the wall. There was a tall colored boy Ned had never seen before; Burl and Ted, two roustabouts who rode around town with Judd all the time; and a much younger boy — likely a freshman, given the terrified look on his face.

Judd's jaw was bruised and puffy, and he looked confused. "Mr. Harwell, there's been some mistake. I'm not supposed to be here — my parents are handling this."

Tate didn't look up from the folder he was pretending to study on his desk. "Were your parents in that parking lot yesterday afternoon?"

"Well — no, sir, but —"

"Then they can't tell me what I need to

know, can they?"

Judd slumped down in his chair as Jewel ushered in Whit and Celeste Highland. They stopped just inside the door when they saw the crowded office.

"What's this?" Whit Highland demanded. He pointed at Pete. "That boy is the only one with anything to answer for. You had no business taking Judd away from his studies — and no right bringing anybody into this meeting without my say-so."

Ned had a sudden vision of himself opening the window behind Tate's desk and pitching Highland out on his head. But that would set a bad example. Sure would feel good, though. And he was pretty sure it would qualify as righteous anger.

Tate did not get up to shake hands. "I have every right to conduct business in my office as I see fit," he said calmly. "It's been my experience that most fights involve two boys, not one. And if Judd's entitled to have his family with him while he explains himself, so is Pete. Fair's fair. Take a seat, won't you?"

The Highlands sat down next to Judd.

"Now, it's my understanding that some sort of skirmish occurred in the parking lot yesterday around three p.m. and that these two were involved. Am I right so far, boys?"

"Yes, sir," Pete answered. Judd said nothing.

"Judd, why don't you describe the events as you remember them," Tate said.

"Well — uh —" Judd stammered.

"Judd has nothing to explain!" Whit Highland thundered. "As I told you on the phone, he was on his way to his car when he encountered that boy and made an innocent joke about some silly girl, and *that* one turned on him like a common thug."

Ned clenched his jaw but somehow managed to say nothing. He would let Tate handle school affairs as he saw fit.

"Pete turned on Judd for no reason?" Tate asked.

"That is a *fact*," Highland said.

"Mm-hmm. Pete, why don't you tell me your side of the story?"

"For the last time, he doesn't *have* a side," Celeste Highland interrupted.

"Mr. and Mrs. Highland, I mean to hear both of these boys out," Tate said. "If you don't want to stay for it, that's fine with me. You can wait outside. But I mean to hear what Pete has to say. Are you staying or going?"

Ned took one look at Whit Highland and saw exactly where Judd got his sulking, selfish ways. They were both slumped in their chairs like a couple of pouty kids. Celeste, though — she was something else altogether. Right now she was glaring at Tate like she might take a gun out of her purse and shoot him at his desk. She bullied most of the women in town — but not his Geneva. Nobody bullied her.

Ned wished Geneva were here with him right now. It would be the next best thing to having Virginia at his side again. His oldest daughter had inherited her mother's fire. That wouldn't have been fair to Lila, though. She might hate ugly confrontations like this, but she would still be very hurt if she found out he had asked Geneva to accompany him instead of her. And somehow, he knew, Lila would find out. By coming alone to the school, where he often had business to attend to, he might be able to spare her this episode altogether.

"Pete?" Tate prompted.

"Well, sir, I was on my way to my truck when Judd came up behind me," Pete began. "We'd just taken our fitness test and he was raggin' on me about how I just got lucky on the bench press and how I didn't know anything about sports and wouldn't ever make the football team."

"And what did you do?" Tate asked.

Pete shrugged. "Just kept walkin'. But

then he started in on Dovey. He said I must like my women dumb since I went to the backwoods to find one. That's when I stopped and turned around. I told him to take it back, but it just got worse. He said maybe she could bring some moonshine and squirrel brains to the next August singing. I told him to shut up. And then he said I didn't really need to lift weights because he'd heard backwoods girls were easy and I'd likely get my workout pushing a baby stroller pretty soon. And that's when I hit him. I hit him as hard as I could, and he didn't get up. And if he ever says anything like that about Dovey again, I'll hit him again."

"There, you see," Highland said. "He admits it."

"Yes, he does," Tate said. "He admits defending the honor of a young girl whom your boy attacked just to salve his own pride."

The Highlands looked shocked.

"Boys," Tate said to the witnesses lined against the wall, "I understand that at least twelve students saw what happened yesterday, either from the parking lot with you all or out the school windows, and I've already spoken with six of them. Now I want you to tell me which version of this incident sounds the most like what you saw." He looked straight at Burl and Ted. "Keep in mind that if the majority says one thing and one or two of you says another, why, I might be inclined to think you're lying to me."

The tall colored boy and the freshman vouched for Pete. Burl and Ted said there had been so much noise in the parking lot that they couldn't rightly hear what Judd said.

Tate dismissed the four back to class. Whit Highland was livid, not because he actually believed his boy had been abused, Ned suspected, but because Judd had put him in this awful position and now he had no alternative but to keep fighting a lost cause.

"I don't care what those two think they heard," he said, his voice rising by the minute. "That thug hit my boy, and if you don't expel him right now, I'll sue!"

Ned would be silent no more. He spoke calmly and evenly, looking straight at Judd's father. "Highland, you call my grandson a thug one more time, and you and me are stepping outside."

Highland turned pale. He was a loud man. He was a rich man. But he was a small man. And Ned was a very big man.

With the Highlands at last stunned into silence, Tate continued. "You can sue alright. But you can't sue Mr. Ballard here because he wasn't involved. I guess you could sue Pete if you really want his pickup, but his granddaddy would just buy him a new one. As for the school and the county, they don't have much that's worth suing for, but you can try. Might get enough to cover your court costs if you win."

Before Highland could collect himself enough to answer, Coach Thrash came barreling into the room with Jewel chasing after him. "I'm sorry, Mr. Harwell," she said.

"Not your fault, Jewel."

"Now, Principal," Coach Thrash said, as if he meant to take this situation in hand, " 'scuse me for busting in, but I heard what happened, and I can settle this. I'm sure that if Pete could see his way clear to sign on for next season, why, I could persuade my most valued boosters here —"

"Coach Thrash," Tate said, "this is a private meeting, but as long as you're here you can stay, because there's a part of this that I do need your help with. You wanna stand right over there?"

Coach Thrash looked a little crestfallen, but everybody on the faculty knew better than to push Tate. Thrash was the kind of coach who thought his football boosters should run the school, and Ned had always admired Tate for having none of that.

"Pete," Tate was saying, "you did a bad thing, but you had a good reason. Do it again, though, and I'll have to suspend you during final exams, and you'll be spending your summer here with me instead of in the cotton fields."

"Yes, sir," Pete said.

"Judd, you tried to sully the good name of an innocent girl knowingly and intentionally. Do it again and I'll suspend *you.*"

Judd said nothing.

"I would just like to remind you," Celeste spoke up, "that my husband bought and paid for football uniforms for the *entire* team, as well as a whole weight room full of *expensive* equipment."

Ned could just imagine what Virginia would've said to that: *How gracious of you, dear, to leave the price tag on your gift.*

"Yes, ma'am, I'm aware you bought the uniforms and gym equipment," Tate said. "How long have you all lived here — five or six years?"

"What does that have to do with anything?" she snapped.

"Well, seeing as how y'all are newcomers, I don't fault you for being a little in the dark."

Ned knew what was coming and shifted a

little in his chair. It made him uncomfortable to talk about his own money. It felt like bragging, a trait he despised in other people and never intended to be guilty of himself.

"The county was near about broke when we built this school," Tate said. "Mr. Ballard here, he owns all the surrounding land, which the county couldn't afford to buy. But when he heard some of the boys at his church talking about how much they wished they could have a ball team, he told the school he'd let them use his land free of charge, which he has done for the past twenty-two years. So whenever your boy runs down that football field, he's running on Mr. Ballard's property. Same situation with the baseball diamond. And if the board of trustees weren't such blabbermouths, wouldn't nobody in town know any of that because Mr. Ballard never tells a soul what all he gives to this community. So if I were you, I'd go on down to the Tomahawk and have myself a nice family breakfast and forget this ever happened. Otherwise you might find Judd and the other players looking for a cow pasture to do their spring training in.

"And Coach Thrash," Tate went on, "I want you to tell your players in no uncertain terms that I mean to see no retaliation against anybody involved here today. If even one player — *one player* — on your football team casts so much as a hostile glance at Pete or any of my student witnesses or Dovey Pickett — most especially Dovey Pickett — I'll suspend the whole team for the first three games of next season."

The coach tried to protest. "*Principal,* I think that's a little —"

"I don't care what you or anybody else thinks," Tate said. "I know how ball players can be when they gang up on somebody. They go anywhere near these students — on or off school property — and they'll be sorry. And if they're thinking they can't touch Lenny but can take it out on the other colored boys and girls, think again. They're covered too. Don't think I haven't heard about some o' your players thrill-riding down in the hollow on Saturday nights — call themselves ghost-hunting for that Reynolds man. They can chase all the ghosts they want to, but if they go anywhere near Dovey Pickett, it's all over. I mean what I say. This ends right here and right now, or I'll suspend the whole lot of 'em for three games, so help me God. Now, everybody, get on back to your business."

The Highlands slipped out of the office like three ghosts themselves, followed by

230

Coach Thrash.

Ned gave Pete a pat on the back and shook Tate's hand as he got up to leave. "So you really had twelve witnesses, Tate?"

"You know, now that I think about it, mighta been closer to four. Never been all that good with numbers." Tate stopped Pete at the door and placed a hand on his shoulder. "Son, I meant what I said. You ever hit that boy on my school grounds again, and I'll have to suspend you. I won't have any choice."

"Yes, sir, I understand," Pete said.

"You tell Dovey I said the choir sounds a hundred percent better with her up there," Tate said on his way back to his desk. "I wish to goodness she'd take over the solos and put Thelma out to pasture."

"I'll tell her," Pete said. "And Mr. Harwell?"

"Yes, son?"

"Thank you."

"We still having breakfast at the Tomahawk on Saturday, Ned?" Tate asked.

"Wouldn't miss it. See you at seven like always."

Ned asked his grandson to walk him to his car. "Pete, I'm mighty proud of the way you handled yourself in there."

"Thank you, but I didn't do much — just

told Mr. Harwell the truth."

"Son, the older you get, the more you're gonna realize there's a whole lotta people out there who don't have the courage to take responsibility for their actions. I'll never have to worry about that where you're concerned."

Pete smiled. "Sure am glad you were with me. I don't know if I coulda done it without you."

"You're gonna be fine, Pete."

"What about Mama?"

"Well, now, that's a tough one. My plan was to keep this between you and me. But the more I think about it, maybe you should tell her. No point in lettin' a secret get between you two. I'll come with you if you want me to."

Pete thought it over. "No, sir, I can do it. And I think I prob'ly need to."

Ned said his goodbyes and drove away. Never in a million years did he think that, at his age, he would be helping to raise a teenager. But Pete had gotten off to a good start. Jack was a good man. All Ned could do now was help steer the boy as best he could.

Stopping at his mailbox on the way home, he took out a black spiral binder. He was supposed to have met with his investigator this morning, but when he got the call about Pete, he had canceled and asked that the report be left in his box. He carried it to the barn to read it.

Hattie had finally admitted that it made her a nervous wreck to see him with those reports. She just couldn't stand the suspense and the wondering and the hoping that it might actually all come to an end someday soon. Sometimes, she confessed, the very sight of one of those binders upset her so much that she had to take a BC powder and go lie down on the chaise lounge in the backyard. So whenever Hattie was working in his house, Ned read the reports in the barn.

He sat down on a hay bale and opened the binder. The detective had finally found Frank Wheeler, the car salesman from Huntsville who had seen Isaac the night he disappeared. For months it was as if Wheeler had dropped off the face of the earth. But just as the detective was about to give up, he stumbled onto Myra Perkins, the office manager of a dealership where Wheeler had worked ten years ago. Wheeler and Myra had become friends and kept in touch. He had written her when his wife became ill — not just sick but dying — and said he was taking her to Florida to spend her last days by the gulf, which she had always loved. Myra went to the funeral and made Frank promise to write her from Mississippi. He had decided to go back home to Clarksdale and open up a garage. That was where the detective found him — rebuilding a transmission in the Mississippi Delta.

Frank Wheeler remembered everything about that night in Glory. Not only that, but he had written down the make and model of the vehicles. He had a feeling his phone call to the sheriff had gone nowhere because he never heard a word about the case, not after that first report. And somehow he knew that what he had seen was important. But not long after he made that call, he had gotten distracted by his wife's illness and didn't have time to chase after a lazy sheriff.

Still, Wheeler was more than willing to help the private detective. The car he had seen was a 1956 Chevy Bel Air four-door hardtop with a two-toned paint job — red and white — and the wedge-shaped trim you'd expect on a Bel Air. There was a noticeable dent in the rear quarter panel on the driver's side.

At last, something useful to give the FBI in Birmingham. If they could find the car, they could find a witness, and that witness just might know what had happened to Isaac.

Ned closed the report and left it on the hay bale where he had been sitting. He would call the FBI from Lila's house so that Hattie wouldn't get her hopes up. That was for the best. But first he would make sure Pete knew they were finally making some progress.

Nineteen

April 22, 1967

"Pipe down, you idiot!" Judd laughed. "You're gonna wake up every lunatic in this hollow!"

"Sorry, sir!" Burl giggled. "Lemme lob a grenade to flush out the enemy!" He crushed an empty beer can and hurled it into the woods.

"Hand me a cold one while you're at it," Judd said in a hushed voice. Burl pulled a can out of a small cooler he was carrying and pitched it to Judd.

"You know what else would be good right now?" Ted whispered.

"What?" Judd whispered back.

"Another beer!" Ted yelled. Burl tossed him one from the cooler.

All three of them tried to stifle their laughter as they hiked through the trees, clumsily navigating by the light of a full moon and peppering their conversation with the kind of profanity that teenage boys use when they're trying to convince themselves that they're men.

"Which way?" Judd asked as the trail forked around a big oak tree.

"Highland, how long you been livin' here and you still can't find your way around?" Ted laughed.

"Excuse me for spending my childhood in civilization," Judd shot back as Ted took the lead. "There's such a thing as paved roads and street signs, you know."

Just before they made it to the deserted sawmill, Burl and Judd stumbled into a briar patch, yelping and swearing as they struggled to free themselves from the thorns.

"Ted, where are you?"

"Get us outta this, man!"

Ted managed to untangle them, but not before all three had ripped their T-shirts and taken briar scratches from head to toe. They made their way to the mill and sat in a circle on the ground, keeping away from the old wells. They might be tipsy, but they weren't drunk enough to do something that stupid.

"Won't your old man miss these brews from his stash?" Burl asked, fishing around in the cooler.

"Nah," Judd said. "Whit won't notice. He'll just figure Celeste tossed 'em back."

"Is there some reason why we couldn't bring a flashlight?" Ted asked.

"Because some of those backwoods freaks might spot us, and we'd never be heard from again. You've gotta give 'em a *little* credit, though — if they hadn't knocked off that colored guy, we wouldn't have a ghost to chase, and we'd have to find some other excuse to get gassed in this crummy little town."

"You really think they killed him?" Burl asked.

"Aw, yeah," Judd said.

"Coulda been some of his cronies — heard he gambled," Ted offered.

"Nah. One of them woulda spilled it already," Judd insisted. "I'm telling you, that Pickett clan is *nuts.* Old man Harwell might shut me up at school, but that won't change a thing. And to think I had to defend myself against that loser McLean and his little hick girlfriend — makes me wanna puke. Wouldn't neither one of 'em last five minutes in Birmingham."

"How come y'all moved way out here anyway?" Ted asked.

Judd shrugged. "Beats me."

"Well, there musta been some reason —"

"Look!" Judd cut Ted off before he could press for answers. "If you wanna know why

Whit and Celeste do *anything,* ask them. I got no idea."

"Sheesh, cool it," Ted said. "All I said was —"

"Shhhh! Did you hear that?"

"Hear what?" Burl asked.

"Thought I heard something," Judd said.

"Did it sound like a dead man lookin' for his truck keys?" Ted asked with a straight face.

"Maybe the Picketts are on the prowl," Burl said, adding a ghostly, *"Wooooo! WOOOOO!"*

"Shut up, crazy," Judd said. "Tell you one thing. Any of those loonies get near the T-bird, and they'll be in a world o' hurt. They don't know who they're dealing with."

Just then, all three boys heard it. Through their beer-induced buzz, through the chirping of the crickets and the occasional call of a night owl, they heard the unmistakable *chook-chook* of a shotgun being cocked. It had come from the shadows somewhere behind the wells.

At first they just froze. But then, from the darkness, came a deep voice that said, "Leave here."

Judd was the first to scream and run for the woods, with Burl and Ted chasing after him. They stumbled and fell and scrambled up and hurled themselves through the pines. Once they reached the T-bird, Judd's shaking hands fumbled the keys so many times that Ted finally took them away from him, shoved him into the back seat, and sped out of the hollow.

When they had made it a safe distance down the highway, Ted grinned and said, "Anybody besides me need to change his britches?"

Burl threw his head back and laughed. "That was *crazy*! My mama might have to rock me to sleep tonight!"

"Ha! Bet you'll leave the closet light on."

"Gonna wear my footie pajamas and everything." Burl laughed again. "Man, that scared the you-know-what outta me — but now that we know we ain't gonna die, it was a *gas*."

Judd was silent.

"Hey, Highland, you back there?" Ted asked, winking at Burl.

Judd didn't answer.

"Highland! You still with us?" Ted repeated, glancing into the rearview mirror. Judd was huddled into a corner, staring out the window. "Are you —"

"Just shut up and drive," Judd said, his answer barely audible.

TWENTY

April 23, 1967

Dovey stood in the churchyard, waiting for Pete. He was helping some of the men move the pulpit furniture out of the way for a wedding coming up next weekend. She was thinking that she needed to remind him to take her by Aunt Babe's before Sunday lunch so they could drop off the basket of flowers Dovey had fixed for her.

"Sure enjoyed your music, Dovey," Miss Willadean said on the way to her car.

Dovey smiled and thanked her. For the first time, she had worked up the nerve to sing with a quartet from the choir, and everybody said they sounded good enough for the August singing.

The churchyard was almost empty when Ladonna Bunch approached her. Ladonna never talked to Dovey.

"Well, how does it feel to be a celebrity?" she asked sweetly.

"Everybody's been real nice about our singing," Dovey said.

"Oh, not *here* — I mean at school."

"I don't know what you mean."

"Didn't Pete tell you? He nearly got hisself expelled takin' up for you last week. Decked Judd Highland. Everybody's talkin' about it. 'Course, Judd should *not* have said what he did about you — but you can't really blame him for thinkin' it, no offense. You'd think Pete would be used to those kinda remarks by now, but I reckon he just snapped. Guess you got yourself a genuine knight in shinin' armor. Well, you all have a nice afternoon. Bye now."

Dovey couldn't move, but her whole body was trembling and her face felt red-hot. Pete came out of the church just as the tears welled up in her eyes and she ran for his truck. He sprinted after her, but she jumped in and locked her door before he could get to her. He hurried around to the driver's side before she could lock that too. She couldn't stop sobbing — heaving and sobbing — and she wouldn't let him touch her.

"Dovey! What's happened? What's wrong? Please, tell me!" He kept reaching for her, but she kept pushing him away.

"All this time," she kept saying over and over. "All this time."

"All this time what?" he said.

"All this time," she managed between sobs, "all those — kids have been — making fun of you for being with me, and you've been — taking it, and you — you — kept it from me."

"Dovey, I swear I don't know what you're talking about."

"Ladonna said — you hit Judd — because of me."

He sighed and put his head down on the steering wheel. "Why on earth did that hateful alley cat have to tell you?"

"Well — is it — true? Is it?"

"Yes."

"And you wasn't — *weren't* — gonna tell me?"

He sat up and looked at her. "Of course not."

"What do you mean — 'of course not'? What else aren't you tellin' — *telling* — me? What else are you — having to — take at that school — because of me?"

"Dovey, I —"

"Please take me home."

"You've got to let me —"

"*Please* take me home."

When they pulled into her front yard, she bailed out of the truck before Pete could completely stop and ran past her father, who was sitting on the front porch. Pete started after her, but her father stood up and put an arm out to stop him.

Dovey hurried to her bedroom. Through the open window, she could hear them talking and prayed her father could make Pete go away.

"What's goin' on?" Dovey's father was saying.

Pete told him what had happened in the churchyard.

"Go home, Pete," her father said.

"But I can't leave her like this! I've got to —"

"You've got to go home and let me talk to her."

"But —"

"Look, I trust you to do what's best for Dovey every time she walks out that door with you. And it ain't easy. Now I'm askin' you to trust me even if it ain't easy. Go on home and let me talk to her. When she's ready, she'll call you."

"Wait — y'all have a phone now?" Pete asked.

"I want her to be able to call home if she needs to — just like any other girl her age," her father said.

"Mister John, I don't think I can stand sittin' home and waitin' for that phone to

244

ring." As the two of them had grown closer, Pete had stopped calling him "Mr. Pickett" and made the old Southern adjustment of adding "Mister" to his first name.

"Yes you can. Everything's gonna be alright. Just trust me."

Dovey watched from her window as her father walked Pete to his truck and then hurled herself onto the bed and buried her face in a pillow.

Her father came in and sat down on the edge of the bed. "Sit up, honey. I wanna talk to you." He arranged the pillows against the headboard and brushed at her tears with his fingertips as she sat up and tried to get hold of herself.

"So Pete — told you — what happened," she said in a teary hiccup. Her father nodded. "How could he — do that, Daddy? How could he — keep — such a secret from me?"

"He loves you," he said.

"But you don't — hide things — from people you love!"

"Sometimes you have to."

Dovey frowned. "But you never hid things from Mama."

"Yes I did."

"But Daddy —"

"Dovey, honey, how did you feel yesterday? Were you happy, sad . . . ?"

She was confused. "I — I was h-happy. I was with Pete at the — f-flea market and we were h-having a good time."

"And how do you feel now?"

"Like I wanna die."

"Well, now you know why he didn't tell you. He came by the shop on Friday and told me what happened at school."

"But that doesn't make any sense! Why would he tell you and not me?"

"Because he wanted me to keep an eye out for you in case any football players took a notion to come meddlin' around here over the weekend. He wanted to protect you."

She had calmed down and stopped sobbing, but the tears kept on flowing. "Daddy, I'm so mixed up."

"Move over," he said. She slid over on the bed so they could sit next to each other. He held her hand and took a deep breath. "Did I ever tell you . . . how I met your mother?"

Dovey shook her head. She couldn't believe this was happening. For so long now she had wanted to know about her parents' life together, but she never asked because she didn't want to bring on more sadness for her father.

"I was nineteen," he began. "Your mother was seventeen. Your Uncle Adam had run a trotline across the river, and he sent me to gather up the jugs and see what he'd caught. After I got all his fish in, I decided to take the boat into a little slough and try my luck with the bream. I was fishin' pretty close to the bank when I heard somebody — a girl — callin' for help. So I rowed in and followed those cries to your mother."

"Why was she crying?"

"She had stepped in a rabbit hole and twisted her ankle. Couldn't walk."

"I'll bet she was surprised to see you."

He smiled. "Sure was. I guess she was expectin' one of her brothers or sisters to hear her." He got quiet, and Dovey was afraid he wouldn't be able to finish.

"Did she think you were handsome?"

"I'm pretty sure she thought I was crazy. I just couldn't quit starin' at her. My whole life, I'd never seen anything so beautiful. I just . . ." He stopped again.

Dovey urged him on. "So then what happened?"

"I finally managed to talk — asked her what her name was and told her mine."

"And what did *she* say?"

"She just looked up at me and said my name. Sure sounded different when she said it."

"Then what?" Dovey prompted, but he

didn't speak. "Daddy?"

"Well, I asked her if I could carry her wherever she needed to go, and she said yes."

"And did you?"

"I picked her up, and she put her arms around me, and I carried her back to the little shanty where she lived. That's where her lunatic daddy threatened to blow my head off."

"But he got to liking you later, right?"

"That old moonshiner was as crazy as the day is long — and twice as mean. He didn't love your mother. She was just another mouth to feed and another kid to work to death. And he sure didn't have any use for me."

"Well then, how did you end up together?"

"When I laid her down on a cot there in the house, she whispered to me to please come back to the slough just before sunrise some morning — likely because she knew her daddy would still be sleepin' one off that early. So I did. I went every morning before daylight for three straight days, and nothin'. But then on the fourth day, there she was, standin' on the bank just as the sun came up. Me and your mother, we met three or four times at that slough, and then I talked her into crossin' the river with me.

Your Papa Hinkey went with us to the justice of the peace and convinced him she was an orphan with nobody to sign her permission, and we got married."

"Didn't her family come looking for her?"

"No, honey. Nobody ever did. But it was for the best because she found a real family here." Then he told her about Jack and Lila and the friendship that had to end. "Dovey, your mother was a gift from heaven, and I loved her so much I just about couldn't stand it. But part of her never got free of that shanty. The only place she ever felt safe was right here in this hollow. She just couldn't believe that she could belong out there in the world. And that cost her. It cost both of us. You too. If I'd sent you to school when you were little, you wouldn't be afraid of it now, but your mother was always so scared somebody was gonna take you away from her. So between her and Mama . . . I let you down, Dovey. Your mother couldn't help it, but I knew better, and I let you down. I shoulda sent you to school.

"I can't change what happened back then. But you and me, we can decide what happens from here on out. You gotta make up your mind how it's gonna be for you, honey. Because there's all kinda Ladonnas in this world. They're gonna do whatever they're gonna do. So you got to decide. You gonna let them tell you who you are, or you gonna decide that for yourself?"

She thought about that as she wiped her eyes. Then she squeezed his hand and kissed it. "I think I'll decide," she said with a smile.

"That's my girl." He put his arms around her. "Now, what we gonna do about that boyfriend of yours?"

Lila looked out her kitchen window to see John's truck pulling into her backyard. "Pete!" she called when she saw Dovey get out. "Son, Dovey's here."

Pete raced downstairs and out the kitchen door, and didn't stop till he had Dovey in his arms.

"I'm so sorry, I'm so sorry, I'm so sorry," she kept repeating.

John walked past them to Lila, who was standing at her kitchen door. She grinned at him. "Are we just worn out with it all?"

He shook his head. She motioned for him to come into the kitchen as Pete and Dovey circled around the house for some privacy on the front porch.

"Can I get you anything?" Lila asked as John took a seat at her table.

"Not unless you got a shot of the devil's brew, and I know a good Baptist like you ain't got any."

She opened a cabinet, pulled a bottle of bourbon from behind her cooking sherry, and set it on the table. "I'm Methodist on Mama's side." She smiled. "And you know what the Methodists say — everything in moderation."

Pete and Dovey sat together in the front porch swing. They had their arms around each other, with her head on his shoulder. If they could have found a way to get any closer on his mother's front porch with both of their parents in the kitchen, they would have.

She had begun to cry again when she first saw him, and he was still trying to soothe her. He began softly singing "Walkin' After Midnight."

She looked up at him with a weepy smile. "You think Patsy Cline can fix anything."

"Never let me down yet," he said, twirling a curly strand of her hair through his fingers. "I can't stand to see you cry, Dovey. I love you too much to see you cry."

"But why?" she asked.

"Why what?"

"Why do you love me so much?"

"Don't you know?"

She shook her head. "No. And I think I

need to. Why do you want to be with me instead of Ladonna and all those girls at school?"

"For the same reason I'd rather hold a kitten than a copperhead."

"I'm not kidding."

"Neither am I. Look, Dovey, from the first time I saw you in those pink tennis shoes of yours with those ringlets in your hair, I thought . . . well, I don't quite know what I *thought.* I just know I haven't wanted to be two feet away from you since."

"But what about when I'm old and all wrinkled up and I don't have those ringlets anymore? Then why will you love me?"

"For your lovely singin' voice." He grinned. "No, wait a minute — that'll be shot too."

"I'm serious!" she said, but she was finally laughing.

"Dovey, if you don't know by now that you're special in just about every way a person can be — well, you're just not payin' attention. I love you. And I don't want to be anywhere or do anything without you." He grinned and added, "I did think about makin' out with Ladonna once, but I was scared those buck teeth of hers would cut me all to pieces."

"Hush!" She giggled and settled back onto

his shoulder with a long, happy sigh.

"Dovey?"

"Hmm?"

"Why do you love me?"

She sat up again. "It's your eyes."

"What about when I get old and they're covered up with glasses — you know, that yucky old-man kind with bifocals?"

"Won't matter. I love 'em 'cause they see me like I wanna be, and I imagine they could still do that even with bifocals." She ran her hand across his brow and down the side of his face, like she was memorizing the feel of it. "You're all I ever wanted, and a whole lot more than I ever thought I'd have."

He kissed her as they rocked in the swing, listening to the cicadas and watching the sky grow dim.

Just after midnight, a brand-new pickup sat idling at the edge of a cotton field deep in the hollow. Its headlights were shut off. Inside, Judd Highland was making up his mind to get even. And what better way to take revenge on McLean than to inflict some pain on his beloved backwoods trash?

It had been a lark, chasing a dead man's ghost, but now even that was ruined. And the grip Judd had long held over Ted and

Burl was beginning to slip. He could feel it, just like with all the others before. Well, good riddance. Like his father always said, everybody's expendable.

He gripped the steering wheel and revved the engine. With the windows rolled down, he half imagined he heard someone coming, but he was not backing down. Not this time. Switching on the headlights so he could see where he was going, he hit the gas and tore across the cotton field, laughing and whooping like a madman as he turned the wheel sharply, cutting big circles in the middle of the field, crushing more and more tender young plants with each spin of his wheels.

After stopping briefly to admire his handiwork, he was about to stomp the accelerator again when he heard a gunshot, and one of his front tires blew. He tried hitting the gas, but the flat tire only churned into the red clay, burying itself and anchoring the truck to the field.

In a panic, he bailed out, leaving the engine running, and sprinted as hard and fast as he could back to Hollow Road. He gave no thought to how he would recover the truck, what he would tell his father, or how much it would cost his parents to buy his way out of this one. He just ran and ran, his heart pounding with fear.

TWENTY-ONE

April 24, 1967

Ned Ballard stood beside the disabled pickup with the Pickett men and surveyed the damage. "Of all the stupidity," he said, clenching his jaw and doing his best to mind his language.

"We never gave nobody call to do something like this." Adam shook his head.

"No, you didn't — but I know exactly who did it. I saw Whit Highland squirin' around town in this new truck earlier this week. I don't think he'd be fool enough to destroy property himself, but that son of his would."

"There's time to replant," Adam said. "Barely enough, but I think we can do it."

"I know this ain't my field anymore, but if you'll forgive me, I still feel attached to it. I've got some seed left over, and I can have it delivered to you this afternoon. I know you don't care for outsiders on your farm, but if you need any help at all, why, you just let me know."

"We didn't call you for that, Mr. Ballard — just wanted your advice on what to do about the truck," Adam explained.

"I know. But you don't have time to order seed, and I've got plenty in my barn, so let's just not worry about the particulars."

"Much obliged."

"Paul know anything about this?"

"No, sir. We thought it best."

"I agree. Now let's talk about the hole in that tire. Unless I miss my guess, one o' you put it there, and I don't blame you one bit."

All the Picketts were unreadable except for Joseph, who kept absently adjusting his hat and looking off into the distance.

"If I know Highland," Ned went on, "he'll try to turn this around on you. So here's what we're gonna do. I'm goin' back to the house and callin' that private investigator I hired awhile back. He can lift fingerprints offa that steering wheel and driver's door — if we're sure none of 'em will be yours?"

They all shook their heads. Joseph especially looked relieved.

Ned looked up at the sky as if he were merely speculating about the possibilities. "If there's no way Highland can bribe the good sheriff into sayin' any of you had any contact with that truck — and if the shell casings and the gun that fired 'em were nowhere to be found — you all can't be blamed for anything, no matter what they try to pull."

He looked squarely at John, who nodded in agreement. His younger brother was likely too rattled to pick up on what was being decided.

Ned said his goodbyes. "Gentlemen, I'll leave you to it. Look for my fingerprint man in a couple of hours. He drives a bright yellow Ford — you can't miss him. In the meantime, I'm gonna pay the Highlands a visit."

"You want company?" John asked.

"No. I 'preciate it, but the farther away from this you all can stay, the better."

"What are you doing here?" Whit Highland's greeting was hardly warm as he stepped onto his front porch with Ned.

"I'm here about your truck," Ned answered.

"What about it?"

"I'm just wonderin' how it came to tear up a cotton field over in the hollow before it got stuck there with a flat tire," Ned said, studying Highland's face.

The man's expression didn't change, but his hands, which were hanging at his sides, balled into fists. There was a brief silence before he said, "I'm sure I have no idea."

"Well, if you have no idea, I imagine Judd does. Maybe he wasn't payin' attention when the principal told him to stay away from the Picketts. Doesn't look real good for the football team if they all get suspended for three games — doesn't look too good for Judd either, once those linebackers get through with him."

"You shut your mouth!" Highland was beet-red, yelling, and pointing his finger in Ned's face, which he had to reach up to do.

"Get your finger out of my face," Ned said.

Highland took a step back. He was shaking all over. "Why would Judd take my truck when he has his own car?"

"I imagine he didn't want to scratch it up — but he had no problem ruinin' your truck," Ned countered. "If you didn't drive that truck over there and Judd didn't do it, are you tellin' me your wife tore up that cotton field?"

"Don't be ridiculous! What I'm *trying* to tell you, if you'd stop making these far-fetched accusations, is that — that — the truck was stolen last night. I was just about to report it when you came here creating trouble for my family."

"Stolen."

"Yes."

Ned glanced at the garage door. "How you reckon that thief got into your garage?"

"Didn't have to. I forgot and left the truck in the driveway last night."

"You don't say. Well, that was mighty convenient for your thief. You go on and report it." Ned made his way off the porch but turned at the foot of the steps and said, "You know, Highland, that boy ain't never gonna amount to anything if you don't teach him to take responsibility for his actions."

"I'm sure I don't need child-rearing advice from you of all people." Highland went inside and slammed the door behind him.

TWENTY-TWO

April 25, 1967

True to form, Whit Highland did exactly as Ned had predicted. He persuaded the sheriff to focus on the Picketts — not the vandal who had tried to destroy their crop. Already Harley Flowers and a couple of deputies had searched all their houses but found no incriminating gun. The deputy sent to dust for fingerprints reported back that printing dust was already on the steering wheel, and Adam Pickett told them about the investigator who had come and gone.

But on one count, the sheriff was successful. Even he picked up on Joseph's nervous fidgeting and quizzed him more than all the others about his whereabouts the night of "the incident." Somehow the younger Pickett maintained enough composure to stick to his brothers' agreed-upon story.

"So if the only prints on that steering

wheel belong to the owners, what will you do?" John asked.

"You let me worry 'bout that," the sheriff said. "You deputies push the truck outta that field and up here by the road."

"Shouldn't we wear gloves?" one of them asked.

"Nah," the sheriff said.

John ushered Joseph toward home as the deputies removed a rich man's truck from a poor family's cotton field, knowing full well that nothing would ever be done about it.

TWENTY-THREE

August 5, 1967

Just a year ago, if anybody had told John Pickett that his best friend in the world would be a woman — and a Ballard woman to boot — he would've laughed out loud at the foolishness of such a notion. But here he was, on his way to pick up Lila for yet another Saturday morning run to Birmingham to sell some of his furniture. She went with him every time now, provided he promised to take her to a place called Carlile's afterward and buy her a hamburger. Everybody and their brother, it seemed, went to Carlile's for barbecue, but Lila preferred the burgers — medium well, no onion, with lettuce, tomato, mayonnaise (no mustard or ketchup), extra dill pickles on the side (none on the burger, which Carlile's had a tendency to forget), a side of French fries (which she would salt to death), and peach cobbler with ice cream served with two spoons (because she could only eat a little of it and hated to see it go to waste, so she would just feel better if he ate the rest).

Being with Lila was so easy, and that made no sense at all. But ever since that day in her kitchen when she had just asked him outright to be her friend, it was like a window had opened up and a whole lot of sunlight came flooding in.

They both knew, without having to talk about it, that they weren't a couple. They had two children and two ghosts standing between them. So they had relaxed into a comfortable friendship, unencumbered by complications. No one had been more surprised by it than Pete and Dovey, but they were grateful because it seemed to make their parents happy — and made it easier for the two of them to be together.

John pulled into Lila's backyard and took a cypress screen door from the back of his truck as she came outside to meet him. "Oh my goodness!" she cried when she saw it. "That's the most beautiful thing I've ever seen in my life!"

He pointed to the hopelessly tattered door at her kitchen, tilted to one side and barely hanging on to its bottom hinge. "It's time, Lila. It's past time." And he switched out the old door for the new one he had made.

They stepped back to have a look. "That is just . . . perfect!" she said, shaking her head. "I love it. I absolutely love it. Thank you so much."

"Since I made you a door, have I still gotta buy you a hamburger?" he asked.

"You better believe it. I'll get my purse."

John enjoyed her company on these trips, but she had also been a big help. The first time she went with him, she had listened as Mr. Franklin quoted him a price on a meticulously crafted cherry tilt table. Lila had given the furniture dealer her warmest church-hostess smile and said, "Mr. Franklin, would you mind double-checking your price list, because I believe I paid three times that for one of these tables down at Huffman's a couple of years ago. We could always give them a call to make sure — I'd just hate to tell you wrong."

With that, John's furniture business suddenly became a lot more lucrative. Lila somehow knew the dealer couldn't get pieces like these anywhere else, and he sure didn't want them going to his competitor down the street. John's work had been luring rich customers from the suburbs who liked the idea of having something nobody else could get. So Mr. Franklin would pay more if he had to. And Lila, with her pretty smile and genteel manners, let him know he had to.

"I don't remember ever seein' a tilt table at your house," John had said on the way to Carlile's afterward.

"That's because I don't have one," she said.

Lila also wasn't afraid to talk to Mr. Franklin's customers, which John had never done. While he and the dealer settled their business, she would wander out to the parking lot and chat with the city women in their high heels and pearls. What appealed to them about this furniture? What was so special about it? What made them like this piece more than that one? What would they like to see that wasn't here? On the way home, she would pull out a red spiral notebook that she kept under the truck seat and jot down everything she had learned.

Truly, Lila had become John's spirit guide — that's what his mother would call it. He had never seen a dressing table till Mr. Franklin gave him a picture of one from a magazine and asked if he could make it. But when he showed the picture to Lila, she had turned up her nose and said, "This isn't you."

"How come?" he asked.

266

"Well, it's just not. It's cluttered up with a bunch of foolishness — the gilding around the mirror and the marble top and the gaudy gold drawer pulls. It's like a woman wearing too much jewelry. Your work is clean and quiet. Why don't you make your version of one of these? If that old miser Franklin won't buy it, I will."

John had listened to her and made one from walnut, with curved sides, an unadorned oval mirror, and delicate carving on the center drawer, which had a narrow rounded lip across the bottom so that you could open it without pulls. Each side drawer had a curved indentation in the center — just deep enough for a woman's fingers to grip and open it. He had fit those to Lila's hands.

When the dressing table was finished, Lila pronounced it "breathtaking," but Mr. Franklin didn't like it one bit. He called it "plain Jane" and wouldn't even take it off the truck. But before John and Lila could get the tarp back over the table, a woman from Mountain Brook drove up and had a fit over it. She went on and on about the "understated elegance" and a bunch of other stuff John didn't quite get. What he did understand was that she said she would pay double what anybody else had offered.

Mr. Franklin called later in the week to say he had spoken hastily. So far he had sold six dressing tables, and John and Lila were on their way this Saturday morning to deliver two more.

He opened the truck door for her, then backed out of her driveway and headed for the Birmingham highway. Just a mile or so from Glory, he did what he always did at this particular spot in the road — glanced in the direction of an old, vacant brick store. It had two floors and a solid-looking storage shed out back. Best of all, it was right on the highway.

A "For Sale or Lease" sign had been propped in the window of the store for months. But today the sign was gone. And he couldn't help slowing down to stare at that awful empty space where the sign and his secret dream used to be.

"Something wrong?" Lila asked.

"What? No — just lookin' around."

They made their delivery and had their hamburgers, but without the usual light-hearted conversation. On the way home, they were about five miles from town when Lila asked him if he would mind making a stop on the way.

"Sure," he said. "Where?"

"I'll show you," she said. When the empty

store was in sight, she told him to slow down. "There." She pointed to the gravel parking lot just off the highway. "Could you pull over right there?"

He turned to look at her and almost ran into a ditch, recovering just in time to pull safely up to the store. "What's this all about, Lila?"

"Well . . . I have an idea, but I need a little time to explain it, so bear with me," she said. "Listen, I look forward to these Saturdays so much. Part of it's just the fun of getting out of town, but I also like feeling that I'm — I'm part of something. That hasn't happened in such a long time. Daddy doesn't need me to help run the farm the way Jack did — he's got an accountant and a lawyer to handle the paperwork. Hattie takes care of him at home, so he doesn't need me there either. Pete's gonna be out of my house in a heartbeat. There's only so much volunteering I can do at the church. What I'm trying to say is, I miss feeling . . . *necessary.* And from the first time I made one of these Birmingham runs with you . . . well, I've gotten some of that back. I feel like I've gotten some of myself back."

"I'd still be sellin' to that crook for little or nothing if it wasn't for you," John said. "But what's that got to do with this store?"

269

"See, you're such a fine craftsman — an artist, really — but you don't care for selling. As it turns out, I'm pretty good at it. And I enjoy it. So I'd like to propose a business partnership. I bought this building —"

"Lila! You can't —"

"Just let me finish. You think doling out money is a big deal because you've had to work so hard for every dollar. But I've always had more of it than I could ever use. Nothing's fair about that, but there it is, so we might as well own up to it. The money it took to buy this old store doesn't mean a thing to me, and I won't miss it one bit. But the way I feel when I'm able to get the beautiful things that you make into the hands of people who will pay you what they're truly worth — I've *never* gotten to do anything like that."

"Ain't you worried about what people will say?" he asked.

"No. Are you?"

"But what would you get out of it?"

"I just want to be part of it — to be able to say I did something good."

"You do good all the time. You do more good than anybody I know."

"But this is different. You have this amazing talent — and power tools. I have an ideal location and a good read on your customers. Those things together make good business sense. If it would make you feel better to buy the building from me over time, that's fine. I'd give it to you if you'd let me, but I know you won't. And I'm not looking for a share of your profits. I imagine you've had your fill of working on halves."

He leaned back in his seat and closed his eyes, his hands resting on the bottom of the steering wheel as if he might need to make a fast retreat. "You don't exactly drive a hard bargain," he finally said, turning to look at her. "You're pretty much tellin' me you want to work for nothing."

"But that's where you're wrong," she said. "Listen, I went from daughter to mama without much time to figure out who I was in between. I think that's what I need to do now — figure out who I am in between. And I'm not sure I can do it without your help. Don't you see? I wouldn't be working for nothing. I'd be working for a chance to prove to myself that I can do something besides organize bake sales. I am unbelievably tired of organizing bake sales, John."

"You would *have* to agree to take a share of the money."

"Well . . . okay. We'll put my share into some kind of savings account for Pete and Dovey. Heaven knows I don't need it. So what do you say? Deal?" She held out her hand.

At first the old doubts swirled in his head. He could hear them all in his mother's voice. *Shame of charity . . . Accept your lot . . . Courting disappointment . . .* But when he looked at Lila so filled with excitement, that voice of hopelessness faded away. "Deal," he said, and they shook on it.

"Well, hallelujah!" she said as she handed him the keys. "Wanna look inside?"

TWENTY-FOUR

August 10, 1967

Thursday had long been the traditional shopping day for Lila and Geneva. Once a month they would pick a Thursday, get to Birmingham right when the stores opened, and make a day of it. They would hit all their favorites — with extra time for Loveman's — then enjoy a late, leisurely lunch before going home.

They would do all those things today, but in between, Lila knew she could expect a grilling. Geneva had spotted her with John Pickett outside the empty store, and true to fashion, she had whipped her car into the parking lot to get the scoop. She "just wanted to say a quick hello," she had said that day. But Lila knew better.

She heard her sister's Cougar in the driveway and went out to meet her.

"Hey, baby sis," Geneva said as Lila got in the car.

"Ready to shop?" Lila smiled brightly, hoping to steer the conversation to retail.

"Oh, I'm ready alright," Geneva said. They had barely made it to the Birmingham highway when she set in. "So. Let's talk."

Lila rolled her eyes. She adored her big sister, even if Geneva was a handful. Both girls were blue-eyed blondes, but that's where the similarity ended. They had inherited the exact opposite traits from their parents. Lila had a petite frame like their mother, paired with their father's easygoing disposition. Geneva was tall like Ned and had a double dose of Virginia's fire.

Geneva was somewhat famous among local choir directors. A natural musician, she could play the piano with such power that any congregation would feel compelled to sing their hearts out. But she didn't take any guff from choir directors.

Once during summer revival, the guest song leader, who was a persnickety music major from the University of Alabama, had spoken sharply to her during choir practice. He had been madly flailing his arms, trying to make her speed up to a tempo that she knew was too fast for the choir. (First Baptist had two sopranos who were just this side of the nursing home and a bass with emphysema. Geneva knew their limits.) Finally, in exasperation, the college boy had snapped, *"Will you pick it up?"*

Without even looking up from her music, Geneva had hurled a *Broadman Hymnal* at him. He had to duck to avoid a concussion. "You wanna pick *that* up?" was all she said.

Never again did the college boy question Geneva's judgment.

"Are we doing this interrogation with or without the hot lights?" Lila asked her now.

"Oh, hush," Geneva said. "Now, *tell* me about that *man.* I *mean!*"

Lila sighed. "You've known him for years."

"Yeah, but I haven't seen him since he was a teenager. And believe me when I tell you he did not look like that when he was a kid. He could be an Italian movie star, for heaven's sake!"

"We're just friends, Neva. I wanted something besides volunteer work to occupy my time, so I started helping him sell the furniture he makes. It was a lot of fun, and I'm actually good at it, so now we're . . . partners, I guess. And friends. That's all."

"Friends? Have you lost your mind, Lila? You need to be making him dinner every night and picking out your trousseau."

"Geneva!" Lila laughed.

"Oh, come on!"

"Look, Neva, he was Jack's best friend. And our kids are gonna be married. It's just too weird. Think about it. If we got married, my daughter-in-law would also be my stepdaughter. That is just . . . abnormal."

"Oh, it is not. These are the 1960s, not the 1860s," Geneva insisted. "Really, though, honey, you honestly don't think . . ."

"We just don't see each other that way. There's something there — a really special something, I think. But it's not some big romance. Not yet, anyway."

"Aha! You *admit* you've thought about it."

Lila shook her head. "Okay, yes — I do catch myself thinking about him a lot. And I trust him. I feel safe with him."

"I worry about you," Geneva said with a sigh.

"You don't need to."

"Oh no? Sweetheart, you're young! Jack's been gone for a long time now. And here you've found this lovely man. Judging by the way he looked at you in that parking lot, I think ole Cupid already fired off a few arrows. If you can keep company with a man like John Pickett and not picture yourself smooching in the moonlight, honey, that worries me."

"Neva, can't we just please —"

"Sweetie, I know you. In your head,

you've probably already taken this thing to the part where you tell him you can't have any more children and he breaks it off and breaks your heart, but I imagine he already knows. Men talk just like we do — don't think they don't. And he and Jack were close — you said so yourself."

"Neva, I can truthfully say to you that I have given absolutely no thought to telling John Pickett I can't bear his children. But next time we're picking up a load of hickory wood, I'll be sure and break the news."

"I'm sorry, honey. No, really, I mean it. I shouldn't have brought it up — not like that. I'd clobber anybody else who tried it."

That much was true. Lila had seen her do it. The very idea was just so baffling. Why on earth would anyone presume to question a woman about the children she didn't have, to stand there demanding an answer while she gaped in horror at the question? Could there be anything more personal, more private, than the children you had carried — or longed to carry — inside your very own body?

The worst was that horrible Byford Crestwell at the bank. He didn't actually work there, but he was chairman of the board emeritus — whatever that meant — and insisted on keeping an office, though he never seemed to do anything in it. He was among that peculiar breed of older men who assume that their help is always needed, their advice highly valued, their attention gratefully welcomed. Pete had still been a toddler when Crestwell, who happened by as Lila waited in line for a teller, greeted her with that weird, crooked grin of his — part smile, part smirk — and said loudly enough for anybody to hear, "When you gonna give that husband o' yours some more kids so we can start 'em some savings accounts?" He actually thought he was being witty and charming, but she saw the shocked faces of several women in earshot.

For months, Lila's family knew nothing about the banker's outrageous comments — which he made repeatedly — because she was too humiliated to tell them. But then one day he made the mistake of coming at her with Geneva at her side. Unlike Lila, Geneva was never at a loss for words, and when she was angry, she threw propriety out the window. She had whirled on Crestwell like a tornado: "Just how stupid are you? My sister's childbearing is none of your business, and if you ever so much as look in her direction again, I will HURT you." Geneva saw to it that their father moved all the family banking elsewhere.

"Honey, I think maybe you're conjuring up roadblocks because you're scared," Geneva was saying as they made their way to Birmingham. "Losing Jack — it took something out of you. Anybody could understand that. But remember when we were kids and Daddy would carry us up to McAdoo's — way back when old Mr. Mc was still alive? Daddy could barely get the car parked before you'd be flying to that high-diving platform. You'd get a running start and come sailing off of that thing before I could even get up the ladder."

"Guess I'm not much of a diver anymore." Lila sighed.

"That's not true. You've just got to work up the courage to jump one more time. Even if you do a big ole belly flop, at least you'll be back in the water where you belong. Listen, I don't blame you for getting aggravated at those silly women in town who thought you should be grateful to date any man with a pulse. And if you don't care a thing in the world about John Pickett, that's all well and good too. But if you do . . . I just don't want you to miss out because you're afraid."

Lila smiled. The sisters could have their differences, but when push came to shove, Geneva was in her corner all the way. And

279

she was one mean mama bear when it came to protecting the people she loved.

"So it didn't work out with Garland," Geneva went on. "Big deal. Personally, I always thought he was too much of a suit for you. But honey, you can't give up. Jack was — well, they just didn't make but one of him. And if you keep comparing every other man to somebody like that . . ."

"Tall talk coming from you, Neva."

"What do you mean?"

"You fell stupid-silly for Glenn Masters the first time you saw him, and God forbid if anything should happen to him, you wouldn't dream of being with any man who couldn't make you feel the way he does — and you know it."

"Okay, I'll give you that," Geneva conceded.

When the girls were dating, most boys had been intimidated by Geneva. She had a show-me-what-you-got way of staring down hopeful suitors that turned them into Jell-O. But when Glenn came along, he had just stared right back and said, "I ain't scared o' you, hot potato." She had eloped to New Orleans with him the following week. Glenn was the only man alive who could turn Geneva to pure mush.

"Sweetie, I just want you to be happy,"

she said.

"I know," Lila said. "And I love you for it. I want me to be happy too. I just haven't figured out what that means right now. Whatever comes next — it doesn't have to be the same as what I had, but it has to be as good, doesn't it? Is that too much to ask?"

"Will you promise to talk to me about it — let me help if I can?"

Lila smiled. "It's so sweet of you to pretend I have a choice." Then she added, "Neva, I'm sure Daddy told you, but just to make sure . . . That land I asked him to deed to the Picketts — it's coming out of whatever I inherit. I didn't do anything that would take away from you and your boys."

"Like I need you *or* Daddy to tell me that," Geneva said, turning on the radio.

"Oh, and don't let me forget — I want to buy Dovey a bottle of Chanel No. 5. She loves my perfume, and I think it's time she had her very own bottle of the good stuff. Remember when Mama gave us ours?"

Geneva laughed. " 'Great Scots!' as she used to say. We must've smelled to high heaven the way we took turns spritzing each other. Ole Coco woulda been scandalized."

They laughed together as they drove up the highway, wondering what they'd find together in the city.

■ ■ ■ ■

"Afternoon, Mr. Ballard. Thank you for coming in."

"Glad to do it." Ned had begun to feel at home in the FBI office in Birmingham. He liked Agent Davenport. The man had some sense. The two of them had been in constant contact over the past year. A three-year-old disappearance couldn't be the FBI's priority, Agent Davenport had told him, but as long as Ned was willing to bankroll an investigator, they would do what they could to follow up on any leads that turned up. He had been true to his word.

"It's been a long time coming, but we've finally got some good news for you," the agent said as the two men sat down at a small conference table in his office. "We've found the car that Isaac was jumping off the night he disappeared." He opened a manila folder and pulled out an 8 × 10 photograph. Everything was exactly the way Frank Wheeler, the car salesman from Huntsville, had described it, with one exception — the hood was a completely different color, as if it had come from another car.

"What do y'all make of that hood?" Ned

asked. "Frank Wheeler didn't say anything about that."

"We think it might've happened after," Agent Davenport said. "But this is the car."

"How can you be sure?"

"Well, we got a call on one of those ads we asked you to place. It came from Georgia — a fellow right over the state line. Said he'd seen my ad in the Atlanta paper and had just the car I was looking for."

Once the FBI got the car salesman's description of the Chevy, they'd had agents in four or five states keeping an eye out for it, but they also suggested that Ned take out classified ads in the biggest newspapers in those states: *Wanted: 1956 Chevy Bel Air Hard Top; will pay top dollar if original red and white; call after 5 p.m.* The ad had Agent Davenport's home phone number on it so nobody would connect it to Isaac — or to the FBI.

"This man's in Georgia?" Ned said. "And y'all think he's connected to Isaac?"

"Indirectly," Agent Davenport said. "His name is Bobby Earl Bobo."

"Bobo?"

"Thought you'd find that interesting, Glory being such a small town. At first Bobby Earl pretended that he didn't know the man who sold him the car, but when our agents explained how hard the FBI would take it if he should lie to us — and how long his prison sentence would be if he impeded a federal investigation — he sang like a canary. Said the car belonged to his brother, who lives in Glory. The brother told Bobby Earl that his wife had gotten into some kind of scrape in the Chevy, but he left out the part about a possible homicide. The Bobos are on vacation down in Panama City, and I've already called the Tallahassee office to get a couple of men over there and pick them up. I've also assured Bobby Earl that if he should tip them off and they should run before we get there, why, I'll take that personally — and take it out of his hide."

"When do you expect them?" Ned asked.

"With the weekend coming up, Tallahassee offered to hold them there till Monday, but I don't want to wait that long. Soon as I find another agent to travel with me, we'll go get them and see if we can't get to the bottom of this thing once and for all."

"If you just need somebody to go with you, I'll be glad to."

"I appreciate that, Mr. Ballard, but it has to be another agent."

"I understand. Well, guess there's nothing to do but wait, and we're gettin' pretty good at that, you and me."

"Yes, we are. But I hope to have some answers for you very soon."

Ned wondered if he would pass Geneva and Lila on the highway going home. He knew his girls had been shopping in Birmingham all day. He wished they were here right now so he could tell them what Agent Davenport had said and see if they could make sense of it. For three years he had been trying to fathom what on earth had happened to Isaac. And now that he knew who the witness was, it just got stranger. *Bobo.* He did indeed know that name. He had seen it many times — on the name tag of a very nervous waitress at the Tomahawk Café.

TWENTY-FIVE

March 9, 1968

On a steamy Saturday morning, Paul Pickett stepped off her porch and looked up at the sky. A blazing summer sun shone down from the blue, but there were signs: long, narrow streaks of white — mare's tails — and blankets of rippling, coddled clouds — a buttermilk sky. Both meant rain was coming, but Paul sensed something more. She would wait and watch before summoning the men. The women, though, should make ready.

She tugged at a knotted rope and rang the iron bell hanging from a frame made of railroad cross ties. Three rings — that was the signal. Right away she heard them coming. *Whap! Whap!* One by one, screen doors slammed as the women of her clan heeded her call. The five of them gathered around her — Lydia, Selah, Delphine, Aleene, and Ruby. They were close-knit save for one.

"Come into the kitchen," Paul said. The women followed her inside and took their seats at her farm table. It stood at the center of a spotless and meticulously organized kitchen that took up the whole back third of her shotgun house.

When they were all settled in, Paul began. "Danger is coming, though I have yet to divine its nature."

"Danger?" Ruby asked as she sawed back and forth with her nail file, smacking her chewing gum and kicking her foot up and down on crossed legs. "I mean, *danger* could be anything from a stirred-up hornet's nest to a mad dog. Why, it could be a —"

"Hush, Ruby," Lydia said without raising her voice.

"Well, 'scuse me," Ruby replied, rolling her eyes. She was wearing skin-tight pink shorts with a clingy, low-cut pull-over and shiny gold sandals that looked ridiculous on the farm. Paul had a sudden urge to hit her over the head with a rolling pin — or at least throw a sheet over her so nobody had to look at her.

"Tell us what you've seen, Mama Paul," Delphine said.

"Mare's tails and a buttermilk sky," she said.

"Rain?"

"Yes. But something more. Something in the rise and fall. Something I cannot name."

"What do you advise?" Delphine asked.

"I believe we have some time, but when it comes, it will be swift. Let the men keep working while we make ready. Bring the cows out of the pasture and into the barn in case of bad lightning, but don't lock them in the stalls — something happens to the barn, they can run for shelter in the woods. Get all the laying hens into their coops. We can't afford to lose them, so we must take them with us. We should ready the cave."

"The *cave*?" Ruby was finally paying attention. "Are y'all *crazy*? Why, that cave ain't for nothin' but tornadoes, and it's bright as Sunday mornin' out there! I ain't gettin' in no cave when anybody can see ain't nothin' comin' but sunshine. Ain't gonna be no cave for me and Joey." She kicked her foot faster and smacked her gum louder.

"Do as you please," Paul said, "but Joseph will take shelter."

"Now, Mama Paul, Joey is *my* husband, and when it comes to him and me —"

Paul held a hand up to Ruby's face like a cop stopping traffic. Then she fixed her with a stare that struck fear even in the likes of Ruby. "Joseph will take shelter. If you die, so be it. But Joseph will take shelter."

Ruby looked nervously around the table in search of a defender but found none. Aleene had bowed her head, staring intently at the table. The other women were sending Ruby the same burning stare as Paul, though none could match her subdued fury. Ruby went back to her nails.

"I imagine it would be best to divide the work?" Delphine suggested. "Maybe Selah and Lydia could gather supplies for the cave while Aleene and I tend to the livestock?"

"That is wise, Delphine," Paul said.

"Well, you can count me out," Ruby said, dusting the nail filings off her lap. "I'm just swamped with work back at the house."

"I imagine so," Paul said. "Goodbye, Ruby."

"Well, I didn't mean I gotta go right this second."

"Yes, you must go."

Ruby glanced around the table and then hurried out of the house, her cheap sandals offending Paul's freshly scrubbed floor with every step.

"When should we send for the men?" Selah asked.

"I don't yet know," Paul said. "I'll keep watch and tell you when it's time. Where's Dovey?"

"I just saw Pete's truck pulling up to the house," Aleene said.

"And John?"

"He's —" Aleene began.

"He's not home, Mama Paul," Delphine interrupted. "The fields are too wet to pick, so I imagine he's . . . working on getting what he needs for his woodworking. I'll go over and leave a note on the door in case Pete and Dovey need to leave before he gets back."

"That's good," Paul said. "Be sure and tell Pete and Dovey to watch the weather. Let us make ready."

The women left the table together, then scattered to begin preparing for a dangerous storm.

Dovey met Pete on the front porch of her house and gave him a good-morning kiss.

"Reporting for duty, ma'am." He smiled, giving her a little salute. He was carrying a pickax. "I hear you've got some flower beds with my name on 'em."

"Is that what you heard?" she said. "I think maybe you went and got yourself some bad information."

He stepped back and checked her over from head to toe. "You're not exactly dressed for gardening."

Dovey had chosen an outfit that she knew was one of his favorites — white denim shorts and a bright blue spaghetti-strap top. She wore her hair down because she wanted to look pretty for him — no ponytail. And she had on his locket, which she never wore in the garden.

Dovey could see dark circles under his eyes. He had been working so hard this week that he had barely slept. The Pickett brothers had decided to move John's shop and supplies to the new store at night so they could keep the move from their mother until they figured out how to tell her. Pete had helped them every night after he did his schoolwork. Yet here he stood in tattered jeans and an old T-shirt, ready to clear flower beds with a pickax for her.

"Now that I think about it," she said, "you're the one who's dressed all wrong for what we're gonna do today. But I divined your mistake and had Miss Lila send you some clothes over by Daddy yesterday. They're in a sack on the couch. After you change, you can swing by the kitchen and grab that picnic basket I packed us. Best I recall, there's no Dairy Queen at Pine Bluff."

Pine Bluff was a wooded state park on a crystal-clear lake about an hour away. It had become their special getaway when they wanted to be completely alone.

"Just the thought of that pickax made me wanna cry," he said as he threw his arms around her.

Lila caught a glimpse of her reflection in a pedestal mirror that John had brought in that morning. The image of a smirking Geneva immediately popped into her head. Her sister had stopped by just as she was about to leave for the store and had a high old time with Lila's pretty rose-colored tank top and white capris: "Myself, I usually mop and dust in old dungarees and a ratty T-shirt, but I guess you have to look nice for your customers — oh, wait, you haven't opened yet! Whoever could you be dressing up for?"

It wasn't as if she were some giddy teenager who had never been married or raised a child, for goodness' sake. Lila assured herself that she wasn't dressing up for John. She just wanted to look nice — what was wrong with that?

She doused a soft cotton rag with Old English and began cleaning the long counter in the store. She and John didn't have any furniture to deliver this Saturday, so they could spend the whole day getting the store ready.

It was a great building, with solid pine floors, high ceilings, and tall rectangular windows all the way across the front on both levels. The upstairs had two big skylights in the roof and a few more windows along the back wall, letting even more light in.

In its fifty years, this building had been first a mercantile, then a hardware store, and finally a clothing store, which sold the ugliest clothes in ten states and quickly went out of business. Down in the basement, Lila and John had found the original brass cash register, brought it up, and cleaned it. It still worked. They had also found the original butcher block and brought that up too. They weren't sure what they were going to do with it yet, but it looked so great in the old store that they knew they could find a place for it.

Already they had scrubbed the floors and cleaned all the windows. Now Lila was ready to tackle the counter. A good six feet long, it hit her a little above the waist. It was made of solid walnut — no doubt the original owner's way of projecting "quality establishment" — and it had to weigh a ton. Every swipe of her rag made the old counter come to life a little more as the grain began to shine through. When she had finished, she stepped back for a look. Beautiful. She should show John.

She hurried upstairs where he was setting up his shop, but at the top of the stairwell, something stopped her. She stood still and silently watched. He was standing at a big worktable in the center of the room, holding the carved front piece of a new dressing table and running his hands over it to check his work. She had to admit, he had great hands — strong and a little weathered, with long, slender fingers so attuned to what he was doing that she imagined he could've felt what a piece of wood needed to be even if he had to work blindfolded. The late morning sun had so aligned itself with one of the old skylights that it looked like a spotlight shining down on him.

He glanced up to see Lila smiling at him. "What?" he asked.

"You know what I think?" she said, tilting her head to one side. "I think every now and then we get these little split seconds of perfection. I just saw you in the middle of one."

He blinked at her. "I got no idea what that means."

That made her laugh. "Doesn't matter. Come downstairs and I'll show you something pretty."

Finally, Ned got the call he had been hoping for. Despite Agent Davenport's warning, that sorry Bobby Earl Bobo had tipped off his brother and sister-in-law, who had fled Panama City before the FBI could get to them. Fortunately, they ran out of money and were also short on brains, so they had made the necessary mistakes to get themselves noticed and caught somewhere around Pensacola. They were in custody in Birmingham, and Agent Davenport felt so bad about losing them the first time that he was willing to spend his Saturday interrogating them. He thought it only fair to invite the man who had invested so much in this case to be there when the truth finally came out.

All the way to Birmingham, Ned thought he might very well explode before he could get to the FBI office. Now, at last, he stood behind a two-way mirror, watching Agent Davenport settle into his interrogation of Dolores Bobo. He had never seen her in anything but her waitress uniform, but today she was wearing her vacation clothes — gaudy Bermuda shorts and an orange "I Slept on Panama City Beach" T-shirt. If she seemed nervous at the Tomahawk on a normal day, she was just about delirious with fright in the interrogation room. Another agent was questioning her husband someplace else while Agent Davenport set about calming Dolores.

"Now, Dolores — may I call you Dolores?" he began.

"Y-yes, sir."

"Thank you. Can I get you anything? A cup of coffee or a Co-Cola maybe?"

"N-no thank you."

"Alright then. Now first off, Dolores, I want you to try and relax. I know you've been through a terrible ordeal, and a jail cell is by nature a frightening place. But I don't think you're a bad person. I think you just got caught up in something that's a little too big for you to handle. You want to do the right thing, but you're confused, and you're just not sure which way to turn. Am I right?"

"Oh, yes!" she exclaimed. "You hit the nail square on the head! I am *confused*!"

"Alright then. Let's start from the beginning, and I'll see if I can help you work this out." He turned on a big tape recorder at the end of the table where he and Dolores sat across from each other. "Today is Saturday, March 9, 1968. I am Agent Billy Davenport, and I am interviewing Dolores

Tarhill Bobo, also known as Mrs. Red Bobo, in connection with the disappearance of Isaac Reynolds on the evening of Saturday, March 21, 1964."

Dolores watched the tape spool through the machine as if it might leap out at any minute and strike her like a rattlesnake.

"Now, Dolores, let's start from the beginning. What were you doing on County Road 51 on the evening of March 21, 1964?"

She thought for a minute. "I was *drivin'* on it," she said, appearing relieved to deliver her first correct answer.

"I'm sorry, Dolores. I wasn't very clear with my question. What I meant was, *why* were you driving down County Road 51 on the evening of March 21, 1964?"

"I was goin' home from work. The Tomahawk stays open late on Saturday nights —"

"Excuse me for interrupting, Dolores — you said the Tomahawk?"

"That's the name of the café where I work, out on the Florida Short Route. It stays open till nine on Saturday nights, and I had the late shift. That's how come me to be on that road so late — County Road 51, I mean. Me and Red — that's my husband — we live in a trailer park off to the right, about a mile 'fore you get to that fork in the road that takes you way out yonder to the colored section. But I want to make it clear that me and Red, we do *not* live in the colored section."

"And why did you stop before you got home?"

"That durn batt'ry. I done told Red it wasn't no good, but he was tryin' to save a dollar and kept chargin' it back up insteada buyin' me a new one. The Chevy wouldn't crank back up after I shut it off, so there I was."

"I don't understand. You turned your engine off in the middle of County Road 51?"

"Oh! On accounta the hubcap. Did I leave that part out?"

"Yes. Would you mind going back to that, Dolores, if it's not too much trouble?"

"See, I was just a little ways down that road — not too far outta sight of the main highway — when I hit a pothole, and it jarred my hubcap a-loose. Red, he's a car nut, and I knowed he'd have a screamin' Mimi if I was to come home without that hubcap. So I pulled off to the side of the road, turnt my engine off, and got me a flashlight out of the glove box to go a-huntin' for that hubcap. The ditches alongside o' that road's real deep and weedy, though, so I couldn't see it, and I got scared bein' out there all by myself. That's how come me to decide I oughta just go on home and face the music. But when I turnt the key, my car wouldn't start on accounta that sorry batt'ry."

"I see. So you were trying to start your car when Isaac Reynolds came along?"

"I never knowed his name, but if you mean that nice colored boy in the green Chiv-a-lay pickup, yessir, that's when he come along."

"Is this the man?" Agent Davenport pushed a picture of Isaac over to Dolores.

"Yessir, that's him. Them floodlights where they park them road machines keeps that highway lit up like a Christmas tree. 'Course, all you can see from the main highway is a glow way off in the distance on accounta how the road curves around, but when you're right up on it, why, it's bright as day. I seen him plain, plus I got a eye for faces. Can't remember names worth a flip, but I remember faces. Helps in my line o' work, rememberin' who tips big and who don't."

"And what time would you say it was when you encountered Isaac Reynolds?"

"Now, wait just a minute. I never said there was no encounterin' goin' on. I'm a married woman, and he was colored, for heaven's sake!"

"Excuse me, Dolores. What I meant was, what time did you see him and talk to him?"

"Oh. I'd say around nine thirty — p.m., o' course." Dolores appeared to be enjoying telling her story now. She probably thought it was nice having a big-city detective hang on her every word.

"And how is it that he came to work on your car?"

"Well, when he passed by, I reckon on his way home to the colored section, he seen me stuck there. Like I said, them floodlights is awful bright. He woulda had to been blind to miss me."

"So Isaac Reynolds saw that you were in distress?"

"That is *exactly* what I was in. I was in me a whole mess o' distress. And that colored boy stopped to help me."

"What happened next?"

"Well, he got him some jumper cables outta that truck and went to hookin' 'em up, and I told him I didn't think it looked right, me and him out there in the dark together, if somebody was to drive by, so I was gonna go back to the ditch and look for my hubcap."

"And what did he say?"

"Well, he was real polite about it. He says

300

to me, he says, 'Ma'am, the last thing I'd ever wanna do is make somebody like *you* look bad.' Wasn't that nice o' him? Anyways, he went back to work on the jumper cables, and I got my flashlight and climbed way down in that ditch to look for my hubcap in them tall weeds. I taken my purse with me, o' course — you know how they are. Anyways, it was kinda chilly — always is that time o' year — so I wasn't worried about snakes none."

"Were there any other cars on the road?"

"Just two that I remember. I was down in that ditch, so I didn't see none, but I heard 'em. The first one sounded like it come right up on us and stopped, but then it musta turnt around and headed back towards the highway."

"And the second one?"

Dolores gazed silently across the table at Agent Davenport.

"Dolores?" he prompted. "What about the second car?"

"Do we really gotta talk about that part?" she asked in a shaky voice. "I've tried so hard to get it outta my head."

"You can do it, Dolores. I'll be right here with you."

She took a deep breath. "Well . . . I reckon I'd been rummagin' in them weeds for about five minutes or so when my flashlight hit somethin' shiny. And I was so happy because I thought I'd done fount that hubcap and Red wasn't gonna have no call to holler at me. He don't hit much, but he sure does holler. So I was bent down in all them weeds, reachin' for it . . ."

Black mascara began flowing down Dolores's cheeks as she started to cry, and then she broke into sobs. Agent Davenport handed her a box of tissues from a shelf behind him.

"Take your time, Dolores," he said. "This is always the hard part. But I'm right here. We'll just wait till you're ready."

Dolores blotted her eyes with a tissue and appeared to collect herself. "As I was reachin' for the hubcap . . . I heard another car comin' real fast — too fast for that narrow road and that big curve . . . and then I heard tires squealin' — you know, like somebody seen a deer or somethin' and stomped on their brakes — and then there was this awful thud sound . . . like maybe that car had done waited too late to hit them brakes and kilt that poor deer . . . and then nothin'."

"And what did you do?"

"I stayed hunched down in that ditch and turned off my flashlight."

302

"So you didn't see the people in the other car?"

"No, but I heard 'em talkin'."

"And what were they saying?"

"Onced they was outta the car, I could tell it was a man and a woman, and onced they went to fussin', I could tell they was up to no good."

"What do you mean?"

"Well, first I reckon they was checkin' that colored boy to see if he was breathin', but he must notta been because the man, he started hollerin' and cussin'. But the woman, she didn't sound upset even. I remember that because it kinda made the hairs stand up on the back o' my neck. She said somethin' like, 'Calm down so I can think.' But the man, he was near 'bout hysterical — kept sayin' stuff like, 'He's dead, I'm tellin' you! That boy's graveyard *dead*!' He was a-goin' on and on till I heard a crackin' noise, like a face gettin' slapped, and then he was quiet."

"Did you see them then?"

"I never poked my head outta that ditch. Somethin' about that woman's voice sent a cold chill up my spine. And to tell you the truth, I felt like I'd heard it before. But I hear so many voices down at the Tomahawk — coulda been any one of 'em, I guess."

303

"What else did they say?"

"Well, he was worried about whoever was in *my* car and whether there was a witness and all. But she says, 'Don't be a idiot . . . *Harv*' — that's what she called him. I'd forgot that till just now. She says, 'Don't be a idiot, Harv, there's not another livin' soul on this road. Can't you see that colored boy was jumpin' off that broken-down car so he could steal it?' That seemed to settle him down — settle Harv down — a little bit."

"Dolores, you're doing beautifully. Now, did he ever call her name?"

Dolores paused and scratched her head. "You know, I don't b'lieve he did. But *she* called her husband's name."

"Harv wasn't her husband?"

"Oh, *noooo,*" Dolores said, giving the detective a knowing look.

"How do you know?"

"Well, they thought they was alone on that lonesome road, so they wasn't exactly talkin' quiet. And they wasn't but a few feet away. Wasn't hard to hear ever' word. He was tryin' to talk her into takin' that boy to the hospital — you know, to have him declared dead all official. But she wouldn't have it. She says to him, she says, 'Are you outta your blankety-blank mind? If we take him to the hospital, Whit will find out and he'll divorce me.' Whit — that was her husband's name. And then she said somethin' about it bein' lucky that he was outta town so much. And then Harv says to her, he says, 'Your husband ain't my problem.' And that's when that woman got real scary.

"She told him she'd make sure he got blamed for it. Said they was in his car, not hers, and there wasn't no way he could prove she was doin' the drivin'. She says to him, she says, 'See, Harv, women with any *style* about them always wear drivin' gloves — not that *you'd* know — and gloves don't leave fingerprints.' She says she'll tell her husband she only agreed to have dinner with Harv to go over their insurance policies but that he'd got her in that car and taken advantage of her. I 'specially remember this next part. She says to him, she says, 'You won't believe how convincin' I can be, so shut up and do what I tell you if you don't want to die in jail.' Die in jail, she says. I ain't gonna die in jail, am I, Agent Davenport — on accounta what I seen but was too scared to tell?"

Behind the two-way mirror, Ned was in shock. He had to sit down, and one of the secretaries kindly brought him a glass of ice water. Harv Akers was a big, burly insurance salesman from Childersburg. Ned

305

knew of him because Lila had told him about getting stuck next to Akers at a dinner party. She had found him rude and overbearing and never accepted another dinner invitation from that hostess — and certainly not from Harv Akers. And there was only one Whit in town. Ned had never cared for the Highlands, but the idea that Celeste, who helped with the same bake sales as his daughters and served on the PTA at school . . .

In the interrogation room, Agent Davenport was getting every last detail from Dolores Bobo. "What happened after she threatened him?"

"Well, he was all for whatever she wanted to do after that. He asked her what they should do about the body, and she said hide it and hide the truck too. And then she said somethin' about helpin' her thick-skulled son with his schoolwork and how it might actually pay off tonight. What you reckon she meant by that?"

"I'm not sure, Dolores. What happened next?"

"Well, then I heard a sound like draggin' a feed sack across a barn floor and doors slammin', and then they drove off — in their car and that colored boy's truck."

"And did you happen to get a look at the car?"

"I did." Dolores beamed. She clearly liked being part of the FBI. "Onced I could hear they was headed off, I peeked up outta that ditch. They was already in the dark part of the road, but the car was a-followin' the truck, and I seen the taillights — three in a row on each side. Had to be a Impala — ain't nothin' else got taillights like that."

"You're very knowledgeable about cars, Dolores."

"You put up with a car nut like Red long enough, you pick up a few things, whether you want to or not."

"So after the Impala drove away, is that when you left?"

"I was shakin' all over when I climbed up outta that ditch. I wished I'd had the FBI lookin' after me that night, I tell you what. Anyways, I was just so scared on accounta that woman and the . . ." She stopped talking and looked down at the table in front of her.

"And the what, Dolores?"

"And the blood in the highway. Tell you the truth, I was glad to hear a hard rain later that night and know that awful blood was gettin' warshed away."

"I see. I'm so sorry you had to go through

that. What did you do after you saw the blood?"

"Well, you don't know me well enough to realize this, Agent Davenport, but I can be a little thick in the head sometimes. I jumped in my car and turnt the key, and I reckon it had charged up enough from that colored boy's jumper cables that it fired up. And I was so scared that woman would come back there — you know, to clean up the mess in the highway or something — that I just hit the gas with the hood still up and the jumper cables still on. Near 'bout blowed the hood off the car. I tell you what, it's a good thing I'd witnessed a killin', or Red woulda killed *me.* Warped that hood so bad he had to buy another one."

"Now, Dolores, is there anything else you can remember about that night?"

"No, not that I can think of."

"Alright then. I want to thank you for all your help. You've done excellent work here today. Officer Blalock will show you back to your cell." He turned off the tape recorder, then stood up and knocked on the two-way mirror to signal the officer.

Dolores looked dismayed. "You mean I can't go home? I thought I could go home after I told you what I know."

"Not just yet," Agent Davenport said.

"What you did — leaving the scene of a crime and interfering with an investigation by withholding information — that's against the law, Dolores, so I'm bound to keep you here for now. But I'll speak on your behalf and tell the DA how helpful you've been. Would you like for me to arrange for you and your husband to have some time to visit in one of our conference rooms?"

"No thank you," she said. "But will you come and see me so's I don't get scared in that cell?"

"I will. And we'll do everything we can to keep you comfortable till we can get this thing settled."

Officer Blalock came into the interrogation room. "No need for handcuffs," Agent Davenport said.

Officer Blalock put the handcuffs away and politely escorted Dolores back to her cell as Agent Davenport went to the observation room.

"Those names mean anything to you, Mr. Ballard?" Agent Davenport asked him.

"I'm afraid they do," he said, still stunned from what he had heard. "Harv Akers is an insurance salesman from Childersburg, and she — Celeste Highland — is the president of our PTA."

"You look disturbed. Are they friends of yours?"

"No. But I know them — well, I know the Highlands. I know *of* Akers. It's just the very idea that people in our own community . . ."

"I understand. I see this every day, Mr. Ballard, so I guess I'm a little jaded. But I can see how you'd be upset."

"So what happens now? Do y'all arrest Celeste and that salesman?"

"No, not yet," Agent Davenport said. "What Dolores gave us was golden, but any good defense attorney could make mincemeat out of her on the witness stand. We need to gather more evidence, which is why I'm holding the Bobos. I don't want them to have any way of tipping anybody off till we're ready. So I'm going to have to ask you, on your word, not to tell anybody — not even Isaac's mother or your own family — what you heard today. Do I have your word?"

"You do. What will happen to the Bobos, do you think?"

"Well, Dolores is in the most hot water, but I think the DA will take one look at her and see why she did what she did. Pretty sure I can help get her off with probation. Got a feeling that husband of hers has been rough on her, so I'll take this opportunity to put the fear of God into ole Red. Should make life easier for her when she goes home."

Ned smiled. "Doin' a little social work on the side?"

The FBI man shook his head. "Always tell myself I won't get roped in, but you know how it is."

"I do."

"Listen, we've been getting reports of real bad weather out around Glory. You be careful going home."

"I will — and thank you. Thank you for everything."

"If you keep doin' that, I'm gonna fall sound asleep," Pete said.

"That's the idea," Dovey said. She and Pete had spread a quilt beside a secluded little waterfall at Pine Bluff. After their picnic, dense clouds had covered the hot sun, and a cool breeze was blowing across the water. It would probably rain soon. Dovey had leaned against the tree and coaxed Pete into stretching out with his head in her lap. She was running her fingers through his hair, trying to get him to doze off and get some rest.

"If I sleep through the only time I've had

with you all week, I'm gonna hurl myself into that lake," he said.

"I'll make you a deal. If you happen to sleep through this one afternoon, I'll promise you . . . twelve more in place of it."

"Twelve, huh?"

"Yep. Twelve for one. Can't beat that with a stick."

"No deal. Can't give up one I've got for twelve I'd have to wait for." He closed his eyes and they listened to the wind in the trees.

"You're not foolin' me one bit," she said. "You're not even tryin' to go to sleep."

"I'm dreamin' while I'm awake." He smiled, still keeping his eyes closed.

"Oh yeah?" she said. "What about?"

Pete gave a dreamy sigh. "May the 18th."

"What happens May the 18th?" Dovey wanted to know.

Pete's eyes flew open.

"Pete — what happens May the 18th?" she persisted.

He sat up to face her but didn't say anything. Instead, he silently traced the lines of her face with his fingertip.

"I'll tell you after I give you your birthday present," he finally said, reaching into the sack he had insisted on picking up at his house on their way to the park. He had told her it was full of tea cakes, which she knew was a lie, but she played along. He handed her a package a little smaller than a shirt box, wrapped in white paper with a silver satin ribbon around it.

She smiled. "You know good and well my birthday's not in March."

"Dang it, you're right," he said. "Well . . . happy spring."

She carefully slipped the ribbon off the box so she could save it, just as she had saved every ribbon and bow from every present he had given her. When she opened the package, it was stuffed almost completely with tissue paper, except for a very small blue velvet box right in the center. Something about that box made it hard for Dovey to breathe.

"Open it, Dovey," Pete said.

She lifted the velvet box and opened it. Inside was a diamond ring unlike anything she had ever seen. The setting looked very old, lacy almost. The diamond was delicate too — not small, but delicate — and sparkly in the overcast light. She couldn't bring herself to touch it. Pete took it out of the box and slipped it onto her finger.

"Ma Ballard left this ring to Mama, and Mama wanted me to have it — for you. So then, Miss Dovey Pickett, I graduate from high school on Wednesday, May the 15th, and I was hopin' you might marry me on Saturday, May the 18th. Will you, Dovey? Will you marry me?"

Dovey couldn't answer. She was holding her hands over her mouth.

"Is that a yes?" Pete asked. "Because I'd hate to think it was a no after I spent a whole month workin' up my nerve to ask Mama and your daddy."

All she could do was nod and throw her arms around his neck. "Yes," she finally managed to say. "Yes, yes, yes, yes, yes!"

TWENTY-SIX

Same Day

Time had gotten away from Lila and John. It was close to two o'clock when he came down the stairs and she started to unpack the lunch she had brought, only to realize there were no chairs on the ground floor.

"Well, aren't we something?" she said, looking around. "A furniture company with nothing to sit on."

"Got plenty of chairs upstairs," he said, carrying the picnic basket and cooler for her. In his shop, they moved two chairs and an end table to a window so they could look out. Lila covered the tabletop with napkins from the picnic basket, then poured his coffee and opened a Coke from the cooler. The clouds were beginning to move faster across the sky. A storm must be coming.

"I don't think they're ever gonna play 'Wichita Lineman,' " Lila said. She had brought two radios to the store — one for downstairs and one for the shop. When it came to music, she liked a little bit of everything and always manned the truck radio when she was with John. Most of the songs she had introduced him to were pretty good. He was surprised to find that he loved what they called the blues because the music had a way of seeping through your skin and landing somewhere deep down inside. You could feel the meaning, with no need to swirl the words around in your head. That could be such a relief sometimes. Lila's favorites were Peter, Paul & Mary, Stevie Wonder, and Glen Campbell. All day long she had been hoping for "Wichita Lineman."

"Looks like that Campbell fella could find something better to sing about than voltage," John said. He pretended not to know anything about "Wichita Lineman," but he had actually heard it on the way to her house that morning. He didn't much care for the strings at the beginning, but other than that, Lila was right. It was a great song.

She laughed. "For the last time, that song is not about the power company!"

"Just goin' by the title." He took a sip of coffee.

"How on earth do you drink so much of that in this hot weather?" she asked.

He shrugged. "Always have. Long as you brought up the heat, I couldn't help noticin' that the air conditioners in this building look a lot newer than everything else. Reckon why that is?"

"Don't know." She suddenly got very busy rummaging through the picnic basket.

"It's mighty curious, don't you think? This building's been empty for years, but I'm pretty sure those air conditioners are brand-spankin' new. The two up here could cool the fairgrounds. And that's what's so peculiar — as big as they are, I don't remember seein' 'em that first day you showed me inside."

"Well, they had to have been here, John. Want some chicken? Here, have some chicken." She handed him a drumstick.

"This is really . . . not terrible," he said after he took a bite.

"It's good and you know it," she said with a smile. "I told you I had learned to cook."

"So you did. Now back to the air-conditioning . . ."

Lila gave up. "Okay, I did it. But you couldn't work up here with just a fan. You'd die of a heatstroke. Besides, Birmingham women don't like to sweat while they shop. So I called Sears and they brought them out while you were in the field, and I was hoping you wouldn't notice, which was stupid because you notice everything. I should have told you ahead of time, but I didn't because I knew you'd say you could do without them, and I didn't want you to do without them, so I just up and bought them." She paused for a minute to catch her breath and then asked him, "Are you mad at me?"

"No," he said. "I tried to be, though. You ought to know I tried."

She gave him a big smile. "Wonder what else I could get away with?"

He just shook his head, knowing he had been outdone by her again. Truthfully, though, he didn't mind.

"Seriously, you know I'm only free with *my* money, right?" she asked, and he could tell she was genuinely worried. "I'd never spend the store's money without asking you."

"I know."

You could hardly call Lila a spendthrift, especially for somebody with as much money as she had. John had been with her enough to see that. And when she did buy something, it was usually for somebody else. Every time Lila and her sister went to Birmingham, Dovey's closet got a little tighter. John had objected at first, but it was hard to argue with Lila when she said, "Do you have any idea how much fun it is to buy girl clothes for a change? Please don't take that away from me." He had given in, which was what he usually did where Lila was concerned, because he found it impossible to deny her anything that made her smile. He wasn't sure whether that made him generous or selfish, because he sure did like looking at that smile.

Lila was even thoughtful in the *way* she helped other people. She had packed Dovey's closet with "date clothes," as she called them, but she knew that John's sister took great pride in making Dovey's church dresses. So she never bought those in Birmingham. Instead, she would take Dovey to the city to pick out patterns and fabric, which they would take to Lydia. "No store-bought dress can match your beautiful work," Lila had told her. Lydia, of course, would never let on how much that pleased her. And Lila had sense enough not to try to pay her to sew for Dovey — for family — which would've been an insult.

However, once Lila told the church ladies where Dovey's finely tailored dresses came from, Lydia found herself with more sewing work than she had ever dreamed of — the kind she had no problem taking money for

— which John knew was Lila's intention all along. People underestimated her, he had decided. She was kind and easy to be with and so pretty, but she was smart as a whip too. A lot of people missed that about Lila.

"You ever buy anything for yourself?" he asked her now.

"I have my selfish moments."

"Kinda doubt that."

The two of them sat silently for a while, listening to the radio and watching the sky darken to purple as the clouds gathered up.

"Easy quiet is so nice," she said, leaning back in her chair and closing her eyes.

John thought about that for a while but eventually had to ask, "What exactly is 'easy quiet'?" She was forever coming out with some curious observation that made him think.

She smiled but kept her eyes closed. "This. This is easy quiet."

Like Lila, he leaned back in his chair and closed his eyes, listening to the thunder outside. He could hear her breathing, slow and relaxed, right next to him. "If this is easy quiet, I think I like it."

She caught him looking at her when she opened her eyes. "Easy quiet means I don't have to think of anything to say, and you don't have to think of anything to say, and if we don't have anything to say, we don't have to say anything. That's easy quiet. You're really good at it, by the way." She stared out the window for a moment. "You think he's asked her yet?"

"Have a feeling we'll hear from 'em pretty quick, once he does," John said. "Thought I'd be ready for it when the time came. But when Pete asked me if he could give her that ring . . ."

"I know. At least we don't have to actually watch them walk down the aisle till May. That gives me time to stock up on Kleenex."

"How's it gonna be for you when Pete leaves the house?"

"Lonesome as all get-out," she said. "You?"

He closed his eyes, trying to shut out the image of his lonely house, empty of Dovey. "Can't think about it." He glanced over at Lila, who looked a little forlorn, despite her best efforts to be happy for their children. And he suddenly remembered something he had made for the sole purpose of hearing her laugh. He reached into his pocket and took out a smoothly sanded wooden disk about the size of a half-dollar, slightly hollowed out in the center like a plate from a doll's house.

"This is for you," he said as he handed it

to her. "Worked real hard on it. Hope you like it."

She turned it over and over in her hand. "What is it?"

"It's a dill pickle plate. Now you've got someplace to put 'em when Carlile's forgets to serve 'em on the side. Mighty tired o' listenin' to you complain about that pickle juice in your fries." He still hadn't cracked a smile.

Lila thought it over for a minute, then frowned and said, "Well, thank you, John. How very . . . *odd* of you."

They were laughing together when lightning flashed in the distance. The trees outside were starting to dance in the breeze as the thunder came rumbling in. Since morning, the sky had turned from clear blue to vibrant purple, and the leaves on the trees looked chartreuse against the darkening sky, as if they had been plugged in and lit up.

John and Lila saw another flash of lightning and waited for the thunder.

"What's that old saying about the lightning and the thunder?" she asked. "You start counting 'one-Mississippi, two-Mississippi' when the lightning flashes, and then you stop when you hear the thunder . . ."

"You divide the seconds by five, and that's

supposed to tell you how many miles away the storm is."

"Why five?"

He thought for a minute. "Can't remember."

"Bet that wind feels great."

"You a storm girl?" he asked, surprised.

"Absolutely."

"Wouldn'a figured that. Geneva, maybe."

Lila laughed. "Neva *is* the storm — I just like to watch them. I love that cool wind on a hot day and the deep colors the sky turns and the low roll of the thunder. Don't get me wrong — got a healthy respect for lightning and hail and all, but I love a good thunderstorm."

"C'mon," he said, grabbing one of the quilts that he kept handy to protect furniture on their trips to Birmingham. Taking Lila by the hand, he led her downstairs and out the back of the store to a pasture behind the storage shed. They spread the quilt in the thick grass and sat down together. There was so much kudzu and honeysuckle draping the pasture fence that they couldn't see the cars going by on the highway or even hear much of the traffic noise — not that Glory had much traffic. The few businesses in town had been carved out of cotton fields, so there was still farmland smack in the middle of the city limits.

"There's nothing else like this," Lila said, looking up at the sky. "You can *see* the power of it — you really can. First, all the leaves on the trees start to tremble just a little — you have to be watching for it to even see it. And then the wind gets stronger, and it starts pushing the branches up and down like it's playing with them almost. But then it finally just unleashes, and there's this big . . . *hushy* noise. And then everything starts bowing to it and laying back against it. Just the power of that wind . . . I don't know. It's something . . . John? Something wrong?"

John was having trouble focusing on the weather, sitting so close to Lila with her head tilted back and that beautiful smile on her face. "What? A hushy noise?"

"That's it right there — hear it?"

A grove of pecan trees behind them was bowing to the wind as the storm crept closer and the purple sky turned smoky. The lightning was still distant, but now the thunder was following much faster. They were pushing their luck by staying outside, but neither of them wanted to leave the storm.

For the second time that afternoon, Lila turned and caught John staring at her.

"What?" she said.

"Think I mighta just seen one of those split seconds of perfection you were talkin' about this mornin'. Well, almost perfect — got a pecan leaf in your hair." His hand brushed against her face as he reached for the leaf, and for just a second he held it there. Something about the way she looked at him when he did that made his heart race.

Then there was a loud pop of lightning. The wind stopped and it got very quiet outside.

John immediately looked up at the sky. "You feel that?"

"The wind just . . . *stopped*," she said.

"No, I mean the drop — did you feel the pressure drop?"

"I don't know what you —"

"Get up!" He was already standing and pulling her to her feet. "Run!" He had her by the hand, and he knew she was running as hard as she could, trying not to slow him down, but he held back for her.

Just as they made it inside the store, the lights went out and they heard a terrifying roar churning straight for them. John knew they'd never be able to see their way safely into the basement without lights, so he grabbed Lila, flung her to the floor behind the heavy walnut counter, and lay on top of her, bracing his arms against the floor to keep most of his weight off of her. The roar of the tornado grew louder and louder. John could feel the pine floor vibrating beneath his arms and Lila's breath quickening against his neck. He heard the sound of breaking glass as the whole building shook.

In seconds it was over. The old store creaked as if it were settling back into its foundation. John shifted his weight off of Lila and propped on his elbow so he could see her face.

"Lila?" he said, but she didn't answer. She was still breathing hard and staring up at the ceiling. "Lila." He touched her cheek. "Look at me."

She finally seemed to hear him from somewhere far off.

"Did I hurt you?" he said. She just blinked at him but didn't answer. "Lila, did I hurt you?" He laid his hand over her knee. "Move your legs — can you move your legs for me?" She moved the one beneath his hand and then the other. "Can you get up?" he asked, helping her sit up and lean against the wall behind the counter. He ran his hands over her arms and shoulders, still not convinced that he hadn't broken something when he threw her to the floor.

"I'm not h-hurt," she finally said, and he

relaxed beside her. She tried to talk, but he could tell she was still too frightened to be coherent. "I've never — I mean — that was — John —"

He put his arms around her and held her tight. She was shaking all over. "Everything's alright," he said. "I've got you."

Dovey sat close to Pete on the truck seat as he drove down the highway. They were about twenty miles from home, and he had been quiet for the last five or so.

"Go on and tell me," Dovey finally said.

"Go on and tell you what?" he asked.

"Go on and tell me what you're trying to figure out. Maybe I can help."

He smiled. "You know, I might be makin' a big mistake, marryin' a girl who can read my mind."

"Well, you'll never get away with anything, that's for sure. C'mon, tell me."

Pete sighed. "It's just that I can't help feelin' like something's . . . different . . . with Mama and your daddy."

Dovey nodded.

"You see it too?" he asked.

"Yes."

"Do you think they could end up . . ."

"Together?"

"Yeah! I mean, they say they're friends,

327

but it just seems like . . . I don't know . . . maybe there's more to it than that. You think they might really care about each other — the way we do, I mean?"

"Yes," Dovey said. "But they haven't figured it out yet."

"Man! Can you believe this? Isaac told me one time that your life can take some hairpin turns, and this is a doozy."

"Would it bother you — them being together?"

"No . . . I don't think so. I think a lot of your daddy. And Mama always seems so much happier when he's there — like she's not lonesome anymore. I just didn't see it comin', is all."

"Neither did they."

He gave her a knowing grin. "You did, though, didn't you?"

She smiled. "Well, let's just say I had a feeling."

"So what do *you* think about it?"

"Daddy's so different with her — different even from how he was with Mama, what little I can remember. It's like Miss Lila chases his darkness away, even when he thinks he doesn't want her to. But that makes me worry for her."

"How come?"

"Well, you know how your mama's always

said you're just like your daddy?"

"Yeah."

"That means the last time she was in love, it was with somebody like you. But Daddy's nothing like you, Pete. It can be really hard for him to tell you what he's thinking or how he feels. When he's sad or worried, he kinda walls himself in — and walls everybody else out. I don't know how your mama would handle that."

"So what do we do?"

"I don't think it's up to us to do anything."

"Well, it's up to me to get some gas or we're gonna be walkin' home," he said. He pulled into a Texaco station and asked the attendant for five gallons. It was cloudier here than it had been at Pine Bluff, and a steady wind was blowing.

"Will that do it for you?" the attendant asked when he finished with the gas and cleaned Pete's windshield.

"Guess so," Pete said, turning to Dovey. "Unless you want something from inside?"

She didn't answer. She was staring at the diamond ring on her finger.

Pete grinned and covered the ring with his hand. "Earth to Mrs. McLean!" he said. "You want anything from the mother ship?"

Dovey laughed and shook her head.

"What do I owe you?" Pete asked the at-

329

tendant.

"That'll be two dollars," the attendant said, and Pete handed him the money. "We 'preciate your business. Where you folks headed?"

"On our way home," Pete said, "about fifteen miles from here."

"Not to Glory, I hope?" the attendant said.

"Yeah — why?"

"Ain't you heard?" the attendant said. "That little town just took a tornado. Fella come by here about ten minutes ago, said he could barely get through there. Said the Baptist church got creamed."

"What?" Dovey cried, grasping Pete's hand. And then something even worse sank in. "Pete, the store — it's not even a quarter mile from the church, and they're in it!"

"It'll be okay, Dovey. Let's just get home as quick as we can." He waved goodbye to the attendant and hurried down the highway.

Pete and Dovey started seeing signs of damage just a mile or two beyond the river bridge. It was terrifyingly random. There would've been no way to plan for it or protect yourself from it. They passed County Road 51, which led to Isaac's neighborhood, and couldn't even see the asphalt for all the downed trees.

"Hattie," Pete said under his breath.

"Don't even think it," Dovey said. "Just pray she's safe."

Lila felt John relax his arms, but he kept them around her as she slowly stopped shaking and started breathing normally again. She sat up a little so they could talk. "Pete and Dovey — should we —"

"Pine Bluff's at least thirty miles away," he said. "And they wouldn'a come home early enough to get caught in it. We'll check at our houses to be sure — if we can get the truck down the highway. Roads might not be clear."

"Daddy's in Birmingham. I'm not sure about Neva. What about your family?"

"Mama woulda predicted something this big."

"But it came up so quick. She couldn't have —"

"She woulda seen signs. Always does."

"How did *you* know?"

"Pressure in the air. And the color of the sky when the wind stopped."

"I'll bet you're thinking I'm not much of a storm girl," Lila said, disappointed in herself.

He smiled. "Matter of fact, I was thinkin' I had no idea you could run that fast."

"Yeah, well, it's a holdover from my child-hood," she said with a weak laugh. "Neva was taller, so I had to be quicker if I wanted to keep up."

"You're still a storm girl, Lila. You're just not lookin' to die. No shame in that."

A torrential rain had followed the tornado, and right now it was unusually loud, as if it were in the store with them. Some part of the building had to be open to the outside.

"Guess we gotta face the damage sooner or later," John said.

"Guess so," Lila said as he stood up, took her hands, and pulled her to her feet.

They stepped out from behind the counter to find a shattered window on the far end of the store. The tree limb that had sailed through it was lying on the floor, but that looked like the extent of the damage. Right now the wind was in their favor, blowing the rain away from the empty space where the window used to be.

"Got some plywood upstairs," he said. "I'll cover it with that for now." He started up the stairs but stopped short on the second step. Lila had closed the door to the shop behind them when they went outside, so the stairwell was dark.

"What is it?" she asked.

"What if I open that door upstairs and see

sky?" he said.

"That's not gonna happen. We just won't let it." She passed him on the stairs and went ahead of him. "C'mon. I'll go first."

At the top of the stairs, Lila opened the big door leading into the shop. She gasped as they stepped inside. "John, look!" The top floor was unscathed — not so much as a broken windowpane. Everything was just as they had left it except for the electricity, which would likely be off for a while.

They split up and walked all around the shop. It was dim, with no electric lights working and the afternoon sky still dark from the storm.

Once John made sure that everything in the shop was safe and sound, he sat down on a bench against the rear wall, leaned back, and closed his eyes. "That was mighty close."

"Made it through, though, didn't we?" Lila stood in front of the window next to him, looking out at the little pasture where they had sat together just a half hour ago. The tornado had reduced the pecan grove to matchsticks. "Think I'll let some air in now that the rain's letting up." Struggling with the latch, she tried not to think about what would've happened to them if John hadn't read the signs in the sky.

"Won't open?" He got up to help her.

"I can't tell if it's rusted shut or what."

He stood behind her and reached around her shoulders, freeing the latch and raising the window. His arms fell to his sides, but he didn't move from where he stood, so close to her that they were almost touching. He smelled like the woods after a hard rain — clean and warm. Against the purple sky, she could see his reflection in the window. He wasn't looking out at the shattered pecan grove. He was looking down at her. And it felt like those few seconds right before the storm, when the wind had stopped blowing and everything got dangerously still.

Then his hands began softly gliding up her arms to her shoulders. She leaned back against him as those hands slipped around her waist. For a moment they stood in the quiet, with nothing but the peaceful sound of rainfall on the old tin roof overhead, until he whispered into her hair, "Turn around, Lila."

Ned Ballard would've given all he had to go home this rainy afternoon and find Virginia waiting to hear about his day. He longed to tell her so many things. God only knew why, but Virginia had always taken an interest in everything he said or did. She never offered him advice unless he asked for it, but he asked for it daily, and her counsel was always sound. She would have known how to break this FBI news to Pete when the time came. In a way, he would be harder to manage than Hattie, who, sadly, wouldn't be shocked to learn that a white PTA president had killed her son. But Pete would be. Ned's one hope for Hattie was that they could prove to her beyond doubt that Isaac died instantly and didn't suffer. Anything else and she wouldn't be able to stand it.

What on earth?

It had started raining on him about ten miles out of Birmingham, but as he approached Glory, he began to see signs of a tornado's horrific handiwork. Trees were down everywhere, entangled with power lines, and the highway was littered with limbs and debris. He passed John's store and was relieved to see that it was still standing. He knew Lila was planning to work there today, and if the store was okay, so was his daughter. Even John's truck, which was parked out front, looked fine except for a few small limbs on the hood. Still, he was about to turn around and go back there, just to make sure, when he reached the only traffic light in town, which wasn't working. Looking toward the church, he saw where the tornado had actually touched down. It had played a cruel game of hopscotch, skipping up and down, back and forth across the highway, leaving this house standing, that one demolished, the cotton gin intact, First Baptist Church . . .

Merciful heaven.

He had great hands — strong and a little weathered, with long, slender fingers so attuned to what he was doing . . .

Just a few hours ago, Lila had been watching John work, thinking about his hands, which were now drawing her to him — one at the curve of her back, pulling her closer, the other caressing her face.

"Please don't let go. I don't think I can stand it if you let go." Lila almost didn't recognize her own voice.

In front of the big window, with a cool wind blowing and the storm thundering off, John didn't let go. He whispered "Lila" as he bent down and kissed her till they both couldn't breathe. Now he was holding her, waiting for her, just as he had when they were running from the storm and he'd held back to make sure he didn't get too far ahead of her.

Over static from the storm, "Wichita Lineman" was finally drifting out of the radio. But Lila wasn't listening.

Ned stood in the churchyard with a gathering crowd, relieved to see Geneva running toward him. He put his arms around his daughter and held her like he had when she was a little girl. Even this soon after the storm, word of the damage was spreading all over Glory, and members of the church were gathering to see what was left of First Baptist. Still intact, the steeple rested on its side in the parking lot of the cotton gin across the highway, but so far they hadn't been able to find the iron bell that used to hang beneath it.

The church building itself was gone. There wasn't even much debris — just a bare slab where it once had been. The piano keyboard lay in the middle of the highway, and Miss Beulah's beloved organ was nowhere to be seen. A hundred-year-old oak tree out front had withstood the storm, but it was littered with pages from hymnals and pew Bibles, which made bat-wing noises as they flapped in the breeze like tiny white flags of surrender. Miraculously, the dove that had hung on the back wall of the baptistery was unharmed. It had landed in an azalea bush — just perched there as if it had foreseen the danger and flown to safety.

As they came, one by one, the congregation instinctively formed a semicircle facing what used to be their church. Absent the heartbreaking evidence of loss, anyone driving by would've thought they were getting ready to join hands for the benediction.

"Mama!"

"Daddy!"

John and Lila hadn't heard Pete and Dovey come into the store.

"They're not —" he began.

"Ready for this," she finished for him as they reluctantly parted just before their children came running up the stairs.

"Are y'all okay?" Dovey started to cry as she ran into her father's arms.

"Don't cry, baby," he said. "We're fine."

"You look a little rattled, Mama," Pete said, putting his arms around his mother. "Did you have a close call?"

"Well, son, you could say that," she said. "You could definitely say that."

"What's it look like out there?" John asked.

"Not good," Pete said. "We heard . . . well . . ."

"What is it, honey?" Lila asked.

"We heard it hit the church."

"What?" Lila cried.

"I hate to be the one to tell you, but that's what we heard. We're on our way there — y'all wanna go?" Pete said.

Lila and Dovey both looked up at John.

He hesitated but finally nodded and said, "Pete, help me cover the broken window downstairs, and we'll all go."

John and Lila followed Pete and Dovey to the churchyard. They walked to the edge of the crowd, which was quiet and subdued — reverent even. The rain had stopped, but the grass was soaked.

Lila slowly surveyed the scene and took account of what was gone — the church where her parents had met at a social; the aisle she had walked down, first to marry her husband and then a second awful time to bury him; the baptistery where her precious son had professed his faith and his choice of a path to follow; the fellowship hall, scene of a million church dinners and homecomings and wedding receptions. John put his hand to her back and steadied her as she swayed a little at the thought of what had just happened.

"Daddy?" Dovey said, taking his hand. She had been walking around the church-yard with Pete, but Lila could understand why she would want her father now. "Will you help us? Will you help us build it back?"

Lila knew how much Dovey was asking. For John, who was so very private, the idea of working shoulder to shoulder with the people of the church — most of whom had never seen him before and were bound to be curious — had to be his idea of hell on earth. He was a man of faith but not of fellowship — not on this scale, anyway.

John looked around at all the church people, some of whom were already casting glances in his direction, then put his arms around his heartbroken daughter. "Whatever you want, my girl."

Lila finally caught a glimpse of the ring. "John, look!" she exclaimed. She gave Pete a big hug and then reached out to Dovey. "Come here, sweetheart, and let me see it on you."

"What's going on over there?" Geneva called, bringing a horde of church ladies with her.

As the women swarmed his daughter, John took a few steps back, and Pete walked over to offer his hand to his future father-in-law. John shook it and smiled. "Guess I better get down the road and check on everybody."

"Can I come with you, in case you need

some help?" Pete asked.

"Might be a good idea," John said, looking at the damage in the direction of the hollow.

Pete handed his keys to Dovey and kissed her on the cheek before climbing into John's truck. John and Lila settled for a distant wave before he had to go.

Car doors slammed and engines cranked as, one by one, church members left the scene of their shared loss. Walking among them was one who didn't belong, someone who was there not out of love and sorrow but out of curiosity. And something he heard on those church grounds had stopped him in his tracks. It was a voice — the voice of a tall, dark man standing with that loser McLean and his backwoods trash of a girlfriend. They were too busy whining over this old church — which didn't even have a pipe organ, by the way — to notice him standing in the background. But he had heard that voice — one he recognized from a night in the woods when he had tried to chase a ghost that didn't exist with friends he no longer had.

"Where you reckon everybody is?" Pete asked, standing on John's front porch and looking around. There were no signs of life in the hollow. Once they turned onto Hollow Road, they had found so many trees down that they had to cut their way through with two chainsaws John kept in his truck. They had stopped by Aunt Babe's on the way in. A single piece of tin had blown off her roof, but the house was standing, and she wasn't in it. Cyrus wasn't in the yard either. They could only hope that whatever house she had fled to somehow made it through. All the Picketts' houses looked undamaged, but the barn would need some repair.

"There's a cave where we go if the weather's bad enough," John said, pulling off the note Delphine had tacked to his front door. He looked worried.

"That big Indian cave?" Pete asked.

John nodded, pointing in the direction of a wide swath of mangled trees. The tornado had apparently hopped over the houses that the Picketts vacated and headed straight for the spot where they had taken shelter.

John oiled and gassed both of his chainsaws and handed one of them and a pair of gloves to Pete. Then the two of them set out for the cave. It wasn't far from the cluster of houses, but the damage to the woods was so great that their progress was slow. Soon it would be getting dark.

"Why are we stopping?" Pete asked.

John pointed to a pile of debris in front of them. "That's the cave. But even I wouldn't have recognized it without that chunk of limestone on top of it."

Pete looked up to see sort of a warped, upside-down triangle of limestone right on top of the cave. It was peeking up, like an arrow marking the spot, over all the tree limbs mounded up in front of the cave's mouth. They put on their gloves and started to crank the saws.

"Remember what I showed you, now," John said. "Be careful how you cut so it doesn't kick back on you — you can get hurt real quick with one of these things."

"Yes, sir."

They got the saws going and started cutting their way in. When they could finally make out the mouth, John motioned for Pete to shut off his saw. "Y'all in there?" he called into the last layer of tree limbs blocking the entrance.

"Help!" Ruby screamed. "They's a dead body in here! Get me out! Get me out!" Then her voice got muffled and Pete heard Miss Paul's voice.

"Son?"

"Mama, what's going on in there?"

"Ruby is overwrought. We are fine. We are safe."

"But she said —"

"I have everyone away from the cave mouth, so take your time, and mind you be careful with that saw."

Pete and John cranked their saws again and carefully cleared away a tangle of limbs and the trunk of one small tree that had fallen across the mouth of the cave. At last they could see all the Picketts standing against the back wall of the cave, which was lit with three big kerosene lamps.

Ruby shot out of there. "I'm a-callin' the sheriff!" she screamed as her husband ran after her.

"Glad to see you, brother," Adam said.

"Everybody okay?" John asked. His sisters looked serene, like his mother, but his sister-in-law Aleene was clearly shaken. John's brother Noah had his arms around her.

"We didn't think till it was too late that you're the one always brings the chainsaws," Noah said with a wry grin. "Sure glad to see you. You too, Pete."

"Anything left?" Adam asked.

"Houses are fine," John said. "Barn lost part of the roof. Looks like most of the damage was right here. Don't think it went toward the cotton, but I didn't get down there yet."

"We'd best go see to the fields," Adam said.

The Picketts gathered their supplies and their chicken coops and made their way out of the cave, leaving Pete and John alone with Miss Paul. Pete was dying to know what on earth Ruby was screaming about, but he knew better than to ask. You didn't ask Miss Paul for information. You waited for her to decide you ought to have it.

"Should Pete stay?" Miss Paul asked.

"Dovey wears his ring now, Mama," John said.

Miss Paul gave Pete an approving nod. "Well and good," she said. "Sit down, the both of you."

The three of them sat down in the folding chairs nearby. "How long before the sheriff gets here?" Miss Paul asked.

"Ruby ain't callin' nobody right now," John said. "All the lines are down. What's this all about?"

"A skeleton in the back room," Miss Paul said. "Not an animal."

Pete was about to explode with questions. Mercifully, John took pity on him and explained, "Cave's got a back room a lot smaller and tighter than this one. We don't go in there unless the wind starts throwing

things in here — or pulling us out. Probably been in there maybe three times my
whole life. Last time was . . ."

Miss Paul finished for her son. "The fall
your father died," she told Pete. "That was
the last time we had need of the cave at all.
Our root cellars have been sufficient for all
storms since."

She watched Pete as he put two and two
together. "If nobody's been in here since
before Daddy died, then that skeleton could
be . . ."

"Yes," Miss Paul said. "I divine the back
room holds Babe's grandson. Your Isaac."

Pete could barely breathe as Miss Paul
went on. "I've not yet divined how this
meanness came about, since no one outside
knows of our cave."

" 'Scuse me for contradictin' you, Miss
Paul, but that's not true." Pete's mouth was
moving and words were coming out, but he
wasn't looking at Miss Paul. He was walking slowly toward the small back room.
"Fellow from Auburn mapped all the Indian
caves in Alabama," he said absently with
each step. "They're in a book in the school
library — history teacher makes all of us
check it out and map the caves around
Glory."

"Who would allow such a thing?" Miss

Paul looked mortified, as if Pete had just told her the history teacher required his students to peek in her windows and report her activities. "To meddle so, to trespass —"

"I need to see him, Miss Paul," Pete said quietly.

"Carry the light." The old woman motioned toward a kerosene lamp.

"You sure, Pete?" John asked him.

Pete nodded as he picked up the lamp and stepped into the back room of the cave. He didn't see it at first, there in the pitch-black coolness, but then the lamp cast a glow on something white against the back wall, stretched out like a body at the funeral home. Standing over it, Pete thought it looked like whoever put these bones here had done it with care — like maybe they even stopped to say a few words.

Light from the lamp glinted off something silvery down in the skeleton, about where a person's belt would be. It was a buckle, rusted and half covered with dirt. And even though he couldn't see it, Pete was sure that somewhere underneath all that dirt and rust was a cloverleaf. *You can call me Lucky,* the buckle cried out in the darkness.

Pete felt a strong hand grip his shoulder as he fell to his knees and buried his face in his hands.

Paul poured her son's coffee and sat down across her kitchen table from him.

He had given Pete the keys to his truck and sent him to check on the women and to let Ned Ballard know what they had found in the cave. That was for the good. They would have time alone.

"You have secrets, John," she said.

He nodded.

"I divine it — you mean to leave."

"Yes, ma'am." He told her about the trips to Birmingham and about the store.

"But, son, to be so indebted — to a Ballard?"

"She doesn't see it as a debt, Mama. She sees it as sharing something . . . maybe . . . sharing a life."

Paul sat back in her chair, gaping in shock at her son. How had she missed this? How had she seen no signs? "So that is how it will be."

"I hope."

"She is not our kind, John. She has many possessions. What would become of you if you should put your trust in a Ballard only to have her desert you when you cannot keep her in finery?"

"I guess I'll have to take that chance," he said.

"Well then." They were quiet as Paul thought it over. "Did I fail you in some way, son?"

"No, never."

"But it's not enough for you, is it — this haven of family. It never has been."

"I'm sorry."

Paul no longer saw through a glass darkly. Always she had told herself that John, the son so dear to her heart, was different from her other children because Hinkey had allowed the boy his friendship with Jack McLean. Now she could see, plain as day, that it was the other way around. John had been drawn to Jack McLean because he was so different from all her other children. Her beloved Hinkey had known this, had seen what she was afraid to see.

Paul stared down at her worn and aged hands folded together on the table. She fingered the narrow gold band she still wore, missing her husband more at this moment than she had since the day he died. "You know you can always come home," she said.

John reached across the table and wrapped his hands around his mother's. "I'll always be your son. You'll always be my mother."

■ ■ ■ ■

By the time John returned home, Lila and Pete had dropped Dovey off. Father and daughter sat down together on the couch in their small front room.

John held up her left hand and looked at the ring. "Pretty big day, m'girl."

Dovey smiled. "I reckon so."

"You still gonna come by and see your ole daddy after you're married?"

"Pity anybody that tries to stop me — and you are *not* old. Want me to bring you anything from the kitchen before I go to bed?"

"No, baby, I'm fine."

Dovey hugged her father good night. "I'm really happy for you, Daddy," she said with a big smile.

"What for?"

"Because," she said as she kissed him on the cheek, "you smell like Chanel No. 5."

TWENTY-SEVEN

March 11, 1968

It was a miracle the bones had survived. Two days after the tornado, Ruby Pickett had badgered her husband into driving her to a pay phone in Childersburg to call the sheriff. Sheriff Harley Flowers was ecstatic. Nothing would please him more than to swoop in and solve a big murder case right about now. That would show old man Ballard, who had galled him no end by throwing money away on a private detective to find some colored boy gone missing for years. Harley knew he could've found that boy if he'd really wanted to. He just didn't think it was worth his time or the county's money. But what to do about those bones? No FBI, that was for sure. All they ever did was take over and take all the credit.

He sat down at his desk and dialed the number for the vet school at Auburn, where a befuddled department secretary trans-

ferred him to Dr. James Lishak, who specialized in large animal medicine.

"You're telling me you have human remains?" an incredulous Dr. Lishak asked.

"That's right — human as all get-out,"
Harley said.

"But why did you call us? This is a police
matter."

"I *am* the police," Harley said.

"Yes, I realize that, but what I meant was,
you need to call the FBI. They have forensic
specialists who —"

"No, no, no — no FBI. All they do is
meddle and boss. I just need me some
scientists to take a look at these here bones
to see if they's any clues on 'em. Want me
to box 'em up and mail 'em to you? What's
your address?"

"No! Don't mail them. Don't touch them.
Have you touched them already?"

"Naw, I ain't touched 'em. Just found out
about 'em a few minutes ago."

"And you say they're in a cave?" Dr.
Lishak asked.

"That's right."

"So they're not in a location where they're
likely to be disturbed?"

"Not unless them Picketts goes in there
a-messin' with 'em."

"What are picketts?"

352

"Not what — *who*," Harley said, wondering how on earth a man as slow-witted as this Lishak fellow ever got to be a college professor. "The Picketts live back in there near that cave. They the ones what found them bones."

"I see," Dr. Lishak said. "Sheriff, I'm glad you called us. Can you give me the exact location of the cave?"

Harley gave him directions.

"Here's what I need you to do," Dr. Lishak said. "Have one of your deputies cordon off the cave. Tell him not to go near the skeleton and to make sure no one disturbs the scene. I'll have a team of scientists there to help you within two hours. Is that clear?"

"Yessir, Dr. Lishak, that there's crystal clear. I'll get a coupla m'deputies out there right now. And I thank you for your help."

Dr. Lishak hung up the phone and called out to his department secretary, "Molly, would you please get me the number for the FBI in Birmingham?"

Twenty-Eight

March 12, 1968
Land alive, this old lady's spooky.

Harley sat across from Miss Paul at her kitchen table. Her face was expressionless. He would need to rattle her, get her nervous — that's how you got 'em talking.

"Do you have any idea what kind of trouble you're in?" he said in his sternest voice.

"No," Miss Paul said, staring him down.

"Well, you better believe — it's some trouble!"

The old lady was silent.

He would have to try again. "What we got us here is a dead body hid on your property. I guess you know what that means."

"I do not."

"Well, what it means is — it means it looks bad."

"And why is that?"

"Dead body on your land, looks like you

done the killin'."

"Your murderers usually hide the people they kill in their own storm shelters?"

"Well, naw, they usually —"

"Mr. Sheriff! Mr. Sheriff! Is that you?" A little firecracker came prissing into the kitchen, wearing gold sandals, tight red shorts, and a red-and-white-flowered halter top. She had that hair teased and that face painted up — whoo-ee, what you talkin' about!

Harley stood up to greet her.

"I'm the one called you," she said, smiling and smacking her gum. "I'm the one *reported* it."

"Well, now, we sure do thank you, Miss — Miss — ?"

"Oh, it's Mrs.," she said. "Mrs. Joseph Pickett." She winked at Harley. "But you can call me Ruby."

"Why are you here, Ruby?" the old woman asked.

"Just thought I'd come by and see if I could help," Ruby said, taking a seat and crossing her legs.

"You are not needed," the old lady said.

"Oh, now, she might be," Harley said, watching Ruby's scarlet toenails go up and down as she kicked her sandaled foot. Curvy one, that Ruby.

"You have questions for me, or should I be about my business and leave you to your lust?" the old woman asked.

Dang that old bag! Harley felt his face flush. This just wasn't going like it was supposed to. He was in charge. He was the sheriff. And this old lady was making him out to be an idiot.

"Now lookie here, ma'am, you are speaking to an officer of the law."

"That is the unfortunate truth."

He decided to try a new tack. He would pretend to be her friend — a little psychology.

"Now, ma'am, I'm a public servant, just tryin' to do my best to keep our community safe. I know it was a long, long time ago. And I completely understand that a lady such as yourself, what's got some years on her and all, might have trouble recollectin' things. But now, you just take your time and think it over. I need to know where you all was on the night in question."

"And what night was that?"

"The weekend before Easter — Saturday night, to be specific — 19 and 64. Take your time. I know it was a long time ago."

"The year matters not — the answer would be the same," she said. "The weekend before Easter is the annual Brush Arbor service downriver. It is held on Saturday afternoon and lasts into the evening. We camp there for the night. I have gone every year since my childhood, and my children honor me by going with me every year."

"All of you go?"

"I've said as much."

"Not John, Mama Paul — he hates that crowd, 'member?" Ruby smiled at Harley. "That's my husband's brother — John. He's a little different."

"Hush, Ruby," the old woman said.

"He live around here?" Harley asked.

"Right across yonder," Ruby said. "But he ain't home. He's down at the Baptist church helpin' out. Now *there's* a shocker — John down there covered up in them church people. He don't like people. Makes him a little hard to talk to on accounta you never can tell what on earth he's a-thinkin'."

The old woman abruptly stood up and said, "Ruby, you will cease your mindless chatter or reap what you sow."

"Uh . . . Sheriff Flowers, would you see me out?" a clearly rattled Ruby said.

"My pleasure," he said, grinning at her and tipping his hat. "I'll be in touch, ma'am," he said as he left with Ruby.

"Lila! Lila! Where are you?"

"Over here!" Lila called. "Neva, I need your help!"

Geneva rounded the corner, and Lila had never been so glad to see her. "Neva, thank goodness!" she cried.

The minute Dovey called in a panic to tell her what had happened at the church, Lila had phoned her father first and then her sister before sprinting to her car to get to John as quickly as possible. Harley Flowers and two of his deputies had pounced on the churchyard, where John was helping one of the work crews. With sirens blaring and guns blazing, the sheriff and his men had arrested him right there in front of everybody.

Lila had been pleading with one of the youngest deputies to let her into John's cell, but he was immovable. Or so she thought.

"I'm trying to persuade Dilbert here to let me in to see about John, but he just refuses, and I don't know what to do." Lila was so scared and frustrated that she was very near tears. She needed the comfort of her sister's arms, which Geneva immediately wrapped around her.

"Everything's gonna be fine, baby sis," Geneva said. "You just hold on. Neva's gonna fix it."

Lila stepped back and nodded her gratitude, unable to speak without crying.

Geneva glared at the chubby young deputy with his red cheeks and crew cut hair straight out of the 1950s. "Open that door," she said.

"I'm real sorry, Miz Masters," the deputy said. "Like I done explained to Miz McLean here, I'd let you ladies in if I could. I surely would. But the sheriff said nobody goes in nor out till he gets back from his press conference, and I'm afraid that's that."

"Press conference?" Geneva barked. "What *press* is there to conference *with* in this puny little burg, I'd love to know?"

"Aw, we're covered up with 'em," the deputy said. "They's newsmen from the *Shelby County Reporter* and the *Talladega Daily Home* and that colored paper in Birmingham. I wouldn't be a bit surprised if the *Alabama Baptist* was to send somebody."

"How'd they find out about this so fast?" she demanded.

"Well, uh, the sheriff, he found a minute to call 'em right after he got him a haircut and shave down at the barbershop. You know, before we raided the church and apprehended the killer — I mean the suspect."

"Oh, I'll just bet he did," a clearly disgusted Geneva said.

Lila had a feeling her sister was about to take charge of the jailhouse. When Geneva marched up to the deputy and got right in his face, Dilbert's bottom lip quivered slightly.

Geneva glanced down at his badge. "*Deputy* Greathouse," she read.

"Yes, ma'am." He beamed. "Bet you never guessed I'd make deputy back when you was teachin' me in Bible school."

If he was looking for a pat on the back from Geneva, he was looking in the wrong direction. "Open that door, Dilbert," she said. Lila could hear it in her voice — Dilbert was sorely taxing what little restraint Geneva had left.

"Now, Miz Masters," the deputy said as if he were speaking to a child, "I'll be happy to explain it to you like I done for Miz McLean here so's you ladies can understand —"

"Explain it to me? Explain it to *me*?" Geneva's voice was rising, right along with the color in her face. "Let me tell you something, Dilbert Greathouse!" she shouted. "I have personally changed your diaper and wiped your snotty nose in that church nursery more times than I care to count. Do you want me to call your mama on the telephone and tell her you're down here sassing me and my sister in the middle of the county jail?"

"N-n-no, ma'am," Dilbert said. Lila could see little beads of sweat popping out on his forehead, and if his cheeks got any redder they would surely catch fire.

"Well then, you get that door open before I turn you over my knee and blister your broad behind right here in front of God and everybody! Press conference, my — oh, just open that door!"

She had him so flustered that it was all he could do to get the key in the lock and hold the door open for the two women.

Lila and Geneva stepped inside the cell, which was hotter than it should be, even though the weather was unseasonably warm. "Why's it sweltering in here?" Geneva demanded.

It didn't take the sisters long to spot a small barred opening on the back wall. This part of the jail was at least sixty years old, and when the county had modernized and installed window-unit air conditioners in the offices, they hadn't thought to close off the openings in all the cells.

"Wonderful!" Geneva exclaimed, waving an arm impatiently at the window. She was pacing back and forth between the open cell door and the dumbfounded deputies outside. "You can't have an open window with air-conditioning!" she shouted. "I swear to my time! If this place is hot in the spring-time, I guess all your summer prisoners die of a heatstroke! Where do you hide the bodies?"

Lila took a seat next to John on a small cot, the only furniture in his cell. His face, hair, and shirt were all damp with sweat after just an hour in there. He and Lila were both watching Geneva.

"I *mean*!" she said to anybody listening. "Why couldn't Jimmy Hays and Eddie Thurgood be on duty today? Those two are smart as any agents at the FBI."

Lila watched as Geneva zeroed in on a frail-looking deputy who was trying not to make eye contact with her. "You there!" she called, pointing at him. "Yes, you — pale, skinny boy. Come here!"

Lila could see that he didn't think of disobeying her sister. Geneva took a twenty-dollar bill out of her purse and handed it to him. "Run across the street to the Western Auto and buy two or three box fans and an extension cord big enough to run them. And you might wanna take somebody with you because you don't look like you could carry much."

"But ma'am, I don't think I'm allowed to —"

"Move!"

The deputy took off running for the Western Auto as Geneva came back inside the cell. John stood up and offered her his seat.

"No thank you, honey," she said, smiling sweetly and patting him on the shoulder as he sat back down. "I can't be still when I'm all worked up." Anybody could see that Geneva wasn't anywhere close to simmering down. "I *mean*! This is just stupid piled on toppa stupid. First they arrest an innocent man. Then they stick him in this stuffy old cell like we haven't progressed a day since the surrender. And now I got snot-nosed deputies talking back to me in the county seat. Where's Daddy?"

"He's in the courthouse, trying to get hold of the district attorney," Lila said. "Why don't you go see what's keeping him, okay, Neva? Could you go do that for me and give us just a few minutes?"

"What? Oh. Sure." She left the cell and headed for a corridor connecting to the courthouse. "But I'll be back," she said, pointing her finger at the trembling deputies.

"Are you alright?" Lila quietly asked John.

363

He nodded but didn't answer. "Nobody believes there's a word of truth to this. You know that, don't you? We're all here to help you, and we're going to get you out of here."

Again he just nodded. Worst of all, he kept staring at the floor, as if he were too ashamed of his circumstances to even look at her.

"And don't you worry about Dovey. We'll help your family take good care of her until you come home, which can't be long. John —"

Just as she reached over to take his hand, he got up and walked to the corner of his cell. He stood with his back to her, his hands pressed against the walls.

After a long, uncomfortable silence, with Lila struggling to understand what was happening, he finally said, "I think part of me always knew I'd end up like this. No matter how much I worked. No matter how hard I tried."

"John, you haven't 'ended up' like this. You're in a bad, completely absurd situation, but it's temporary. And you certainly don't deserve it."

"Maybe not, but it was always comin'. I guess Mama was right. I shoulda just stayed in the hollow. I shoulda been content with my family instead of wantin' too much for

Dovey — and for me."

"But you and Dovey deserve —"

"Lila, I'm not sure I can . . . I mean, I think it would be best if you . . ."

"Please look at me. Please?"

He turned to face her but stayed as far away as his cell allowed.

"You have absolutely nothing to be ashamed of," she said.

"How can you say that?"

"Because it's true. You haven't done anything wrong."

"That doesn't mean there's no shame."

"I don't understand, John."

"I know you don't. Look, I think it would best from now on —"

Before he could finish, Geneva was back. "Y'all, I just talked to Daddy," she announced, breezing past three deputies who knew better than to try and stop her. "The good news is, Daddy talked to the DA, and he says this is all a load of you-know-what."

Geneva looked from Lila sitting on the cot to John standing in the corner. Lila could practically see her sister figuring out what had happened in her absence, but Geneva went on as if she hadn't noticed the painful space that had opened up between them.

"They've got nothing but your sister-in-law telling Harley that you were in the hollow the night Isaac was killed," Geneva explained to John. "Oh, and get this — that little snit Judd Highland told his parents that he's sure he heard your voice in the woods the night somebody pulled a gun on him and his hooligan friends. Never mind that those useless twerps were trespassing and needed their sorry little backsides whipped — 'scuse me, John . . ."

Geneva was so busy relaying the latest that she hadn't noticed the skinny deputy return with the box fans, plug them in, and retreat to a corner of the cell as if he were powerless to leave without orders from the fiery blonde now commanding the whole jailhouse.

As a breeze stirred from the fans, she whirled around and saw the deputy, who seemed to be trying to make himself invisible in the corner. "What are you still doing here?" she said calmly.

"I b-b-b-brought the f-f-f-fans," he said.

"So you did," she said. "And I thank you. But again, *what are you doing in here?*"

The deputy fled.

"Now that we can breathe," Geneva continued, "there's some bad news. The DA's at some stupid national conference in California and can't get back here to undo this mess till Thursday. Daddy's right now seeing if that FBI agent can talk some sense into Harley. John, honey, you could be looking at a couple of days in this hellhole. But you know what? I'm gonna make it all better." She marched over to the nearest telephone and dialed. "Willadean? I need you to rally the girls. We're gonna need covered dishes, an ice chest . . ."

"We'll get through this," Lila said as John closed his eyes, fighting hard, she knew, to shut out the walls closing in on him.

Hattie never ceased to amaze Ned. There was just no end to the kindness in her heart.

Once he had done all he could for John at the courthouse that morning, he had gone home to find Hattie at her usual work in his house. The two of them had sat down at the kitchen table, where he explained everything that had just happened.

"They think Paul's boy killed Isaac?" she asked incredulously.

"Not *they*, Hattie — *he*," Ned explained. "And I don't know if the sheriff himself actually believes it or if he's just gettin' back at me for hirin' that detective. But I guarantee you, John Pickett did not lay a hand on Isaac. I'd bet my life on it — and my land."

"Where is he? Oh, please take me to my boy!"

"Just as soon as I can, Hattie. The FBI says it will take some time to positively identify Isaac's remains, and we want to be sure. You've been disappointed enough."

Late that afternoon, when it was time for her to go home, she had come into the living room and asked him if he had time to drive her to the jailhouse. She had fixed a plate of supper for Paul's boy, she said, but those white men might not let her give it to him if Junie drove her. So Ned had driven her the ten miles to the courthouse and escorted her inside.

"Sheriff Flowers ain't here, Mr. Ballard," Deputy Greathouse said. "He's down at the café with a coupla reporters, but I expect he'll be back soon."

"That's alright, Dilbert," Ned said. "No need to take up the sheriff's valuable time. We just need to drop this plate off for Mr. Pickett. Geneva assured me that you could let Hattie inside just long enough to give it to him?"

"Y-yessir," Dilbert said, hurrying to unlock the cell door. Ned smiled to himself, knowing that Dilbert's nerves wouldn't take another run-in with his daughter.

John stood up when they came into his

cell. "John, how you holdin' up?" Ned asked, shaking his hand.

"I'm alright," he said. "And I thank you for your help."

"Wish I coulda done a lot more a lot faster, but it'll all be over soon." He looked at Hattie. "John, I've got somebody here wants a word with you. This is Hattie, Isaac's mother. Hattie, this is Paul's son John. I'll be right outside when you're ready to go. You take care now, John."

Ned left them alone and took a seat in front of one of the empty desks outside.

"I brung you some supper," Hattie said, offering John the plate. He took it from her, dumfounded that a woman would want to feed somebody accused of killing her child.

"You wanna sit down?" he asked.

She took a seat at one end of the cot, with John at the other. She looked at all the casserole dishes and Tupperware stacked against one wall. "I never seen the likes o' this in a jail cell," she said.

"Geneva," he said, and she nodded and smiled. They were silent for a moment before he said, "I didn't hurt your boy. I swear I didn't."

"I know that."

"How?"

"I know your people — not as good as my mama does, but I know 'em. You favor your daddy. He used to bring my mama figs ever' summer 'cause he know she got a sweet tooth. And precious Dovey — ain't no killin' man could raise a chile loves him like I know she loves you. Her and Pete, they forever stoppin' by to check on Mama and take her little things along. Even built her some new front steps with a hand railin' on accounta they was afraid she might hurt herself on them wobbly concrete blocks she been walkin' up and down. Ain't nobody can teach a chile love like that gonna turn around and kill my boy just for meanness."

"Thank you for the plate — and for comin'," he said.

"Don't look like you need my plate," she said, nodding toward Geneva's handiwork.

"I'll have it for my supper," he said. "I've looked under that tinfoil over there — don't quite recognize some of that food."

Hattie smiled. He stood as she got up to leave.

At the cell door, she turned and said, "White folks 'round here's quick to sweep up things they don't understand so they don't have to look at 'em and worry 'bout what they might mean. All this time I hear 'em spec'lating about what Isaac done to get *hisself* killed. Makes 'em uneasy to think about what one of them mighta done, so they tell theirselves he brung it on hisself on accounta him bein' colored. Now they done locked you up 'cause they don't understand your people neither. Don't you let 'em sweep you up. Don't you let 'em make you believe you belong in here. You the son of Christian people. You remember that."

"Yes, ma'am," he said, struggling now more than ever to maintain his composure.

The deputy opened the door, and John watched Hattie walk away. Then he uncovered her plate and had his supper in the county jail.

Twenty-Nine

March 13, 1968

Late Wednesday morning, Lila stood at the door of John's cell while the sheriff himself unlocked it. "Now, you be sure and tell Geneva for me, I am at the service of all you fine ladies," he said. "I've got some business to attend to, but I'll be back directly."

Sheriff Harley Flowers had been in Geneva's class in school, and like most of the other boys back then, he was crazy about her — terrified of her, but crazy about her. That was the funny thing about Geneva. The more she told men where to go, the more they trailed after her like a bunch of lovesick puppies.

"I'll tell her, Sheriff," Lila said, stepping inside the cell. She had been so preoccupied with just getting herself inside that she hadn't been paying attention to what was behind those bars. As she turned to face

John, her hand flew up to her mouth and she gasped in horror. "Oh, dear heaven — who did this to you?" she cried.

John just stared up at her from the cot like it was all he could do to keep from screaming.

Just then Geneva came in. "What in the . . . Who dropped the chintz bomb?"

Eager to please Geneva, the church ladies had gone overboard, covering John's cot with a floral quilt and tossing a matching seat cushion into the deputy's armchair, which they had dragged into a corner of the cell.

"Looks like the honeymoon suite at a two-bit motor court," Geneva said. "When did this happen?"

"Before breakfast," John said.

"John, honey, I apologize. Some women just don't know when to quit. Why on earth would you need a quilt in this heat? Is there anything you do need?"

"No — thank you."

"Well, I reckon I'll go tell Willadean there's such a thing as common sense."

"No, don't do that," John said. "I don't want 'em to think — they're Dovey's church now, and I don't want 'em to think she — just tell 'em thank you. Okay?"

Geneva smiled. "Okay. You know what,

John Pickett — you're good people. And I don't say that to just anybody." She looked at Lila. "Baby sis, I'm gonna go on home. You call me if there are any interesting developments — in the case, I mean." Geneva winked at her sister as she left the cell.

"You should go too," John said once Geneva was out the door.

Lila was startled. She had been waiting patiently for some time alone together so they could talk through whatever it was that had come between them. "But I —"

"I don't want you here, Lila. You don't belong here. Go on home to Pete and Dovey. They need you."

She felt her eyes begin to sting and knew she had no choice but to go. "Well . . . if that's what you want," was all she could say before hurrying away from his cell.

Lila left the jail feeling like something terrible had just happened, but she wasn't sure what or why. She wasn't crying, but she wasn't far from it either. All she could think about was getting home, so she quickly made her way down the street where she had parked in front of the town café. Just as she was about to get into her car, she spotted Celeste Highland and the sheriff, who were about to go into the café together.

"Harley, I can't believe it took you so long to invite me to lunch," Celeste was saying, her hand on his arm.

If Lila didn't know better, she'd swear that woman was actually flirting with Harley Flowers.

A truck horn caught Celeste's attention, and she looked up to see Lila staring at them. Her smile immediately faded.

"You go on in," Celeste said to the sheriff, "and I'll join you in just a second." She walked over to Lila's car. "Well, well, well. How's everything at the jail?"

Lila was reminded of what Geneva always said about her: "Douse a pit viper with Shalimar and you've got Celeste Highland." Her husband had a loud bark, but all the women in town knew that Celeste was the one who would bite — and laugh while you bled.

Lila didn't answer as she opened her car door.

"I guess now we know who taught that boy of yours his violent behavior," Celeste said with that cold sneer of hers.

Sometimes Lila wished she could be like Geneva, who would have known exactly what to say to take Celeste down a notch. But she didn't have the strength to get into it with her. Instead, she just drove away, leaving the most hateful woman in town sneering on the sidewalk.

"Thank you so much, Sheriff Flowers," Brother Jip said.

"No problem, preacher," the sheriff replied. "Maybe you could pose with me for some pictures later if any reporters happen to be around. Offered Pickett the chance, but he ain't very cooperative. Killer like him don't deserve the publicity no way."

Brother Jip smiled uneasily at the sheriff, who unlocked the cell door to let him in. It was almost five o'clock and he had meant to get to the jail a lot sooner, but with so many shut-ins to visit, it was hard to get to everybody.

"Brother John," the preacher said, "I am Brother Jip Beaugard, Dovey's pastor."

John nodded hello but said nothing. He was leaning against the back wall of the cell, his arms folded across his chest.

"May I?" Brother Jip asked, motioning toward the armchair in the corner.

John nodded again but remained silent.

Brother Jip took a seat and looked around. "I see our ladies have been here," he said. "They mean well, Brother John. It's just that they have a hard time understanding that a man don't need much pink in his surroundings."

Still the tall man with the dark stare said nothing, and Brother Jip was at a loss. His commitment to the Lord and devotion to his flock were genuine. But faced with a wall like John Pickett, he tended to sputter and spout, saying silly things he had to ask God to stop him from saying the next time around. Visiting the sick and shut-ins, preaching from the Word, working with other pastors in the community — these were all fulfilling duties, ones that assured him he had followed his calling. But thrown into more complex situations like this one, he often felt inadequate to the task. He would just have to pray a silent prayer and then say whatever God led him to, which was what he was doing right now.

"Brother John," he began, "I know I'm not your pastor. I imagine you look at me as just another meddlesome stranger come here for something to gossip about. But Dovey is a beloved member of our church family. So's Pete and his kinfolks. I want you to know that we believe you're innocent, and we want you to consider us *your* church family in any way you need us to be. I'm gonna leave my card with you, and I'm not gonna bother you, but just know that I'm here if you or Dovey needs me."

He waited for some sort of reply, some sign that he had handled this difficult situation as God intended, but he was met with silence. Probably best to go now and give Dovey's father his solitude.

Brother Jip tried to stand, but the chair was stuck to his wide rear end, and he had to push down on the arms of it to free himself. He looked up with a flushed face, embarrassed to death and certain John Pickett would be laughing at him, relishing the humiliation of an unwanted intruder.

Instead John walked over and extended his hand. They shook hands, and Brother Jip gave him his card. "Can I pray with you, brother?" the preacher asked.

John nodded, and Brother Jip reached up to lay a hand on his shoulder. "Almighty God . . ."

THIRTY

March 14, 1968

"Harley, I'm really trying to be fair here," the district attorney said. "But are you telling me that you arrested this man, who has absolutely no connection to Isaac Reynolds, just because he was home that night — and before the FBI even identified the remains?"

The minute the DA's plane had landed in Birmingham on Thursday morning, he had summoned Ned Ballard to the courthouse. The two of them, along with the sheriff, John, Lila, and Geneva, sat around a conference table in the DA's office, with Pete and Dovey waiting outside in the corridor.

"It just fits," Sheriff Flowers said, like any fool should be able to see it.

"What just fits?" the exasperated DA asked.

The sheriff sighed, as if he were growing impatient with slow people who couldn't keep pace with the lightning speed of his logic. "First off, Miz Highland made her boy come forward and tell me he's *sure* he recognized our suspect's voice from the churchyard. It was the very same voice that scared the daylights outta him and his buddies when they was out on a ghost hunt."

"It was my voice," John said. "The gun wasn't loaded — I just cocked it to scare them away. They were trespassing, and I told them to leave. They had no business there."

"He's right, Harley," the DA said. "What else you got?"

"What about them truck tires getting shot out of the Highlands' pickup?" the sheriff said. "What about *that*?"

"You mean the truck that was deliberately tearing up their cotton?" the DA countered.

"But still!" The sheriff was clearly getting worked up. "It shows he's a *violent* cuss."

"Can you even prove he was the shooter?" the DA asked.

"I would have if my deputies coulda found that gun."

"Mm-hmm," the DA said. "Next?"

Now the sheriff was obviously frustrated. "Reynolds was found in a cave in the *hollow*. That means he was murdered in the *hollow*. That means somebody who lives there did it. And the rest of the Picketts was away at that Brush Arbor. So that only leaves this one, who *had* to have killed him."

The DA just shook his head. "Mr. Pickett, you're free to go," he said. "And Harley, I intend to have your badge for this nonsense."

After the meeting, everybody stood around visiting on the courthouse steps — everybody except John. He had been quiet before they went into the DA's office, most likely because he was anxious, Lila told herself. But when it was all over, he walked silently through all of them and past her, like he couldn't even see her, then down the steps and around back to the parking lot, where Pete and Dovey had left his truck for him.

While Lila realized that the Picketts were intensely private people, she had yet to learn what her son already knew — that situations could hit John and Dovey in ways you wouldn't expect. Had she understood that, Lila might not have ducked out of the crowd and back into the courthouse so she could take the rear stairs and catch up with John in the parking lot.

"John!" she called, half running to his truck. "John, wait!" He already had his hand on the door handle. "You want to go get some lunch or —"

"No."

"Well, okay, I just thought you might want to —"

"Thank your daddy? I did that already."

"I didn't say anything about —"

"I just spent two miserable days and nights in a hot jailhouse getting treated like a criminal, and for what? For being home. And the only reason I'm not still in that jailhouse is because of you and your family. I'm not a free man because I deserve to be. I'm a free man because y'all say I should be. Why shouldn't my family's word be as good as yours?"

"I don't know what to —"

"Just go home. Go home to your people. We don't — make any sense. We're just too — I can't do this."

He got into the truck and drove away from her. Lila felt sick and thought she might die if she couldn't get away from the courthouse right this second. John had to know how much he had hurt her.

But it didn't stop him.

Pete and Dovey swam to the pier and climbed out of the water. Usually they were loyal to McAdoo's Lake, but neither one of them wanted to be around people they knew right now, so they had driven to a marina on the backwater, a little farther from town. On weekends it was packed, but on this Thursday afternoon, with the weatherman predicting rain, there wasn't a soul in sight, not even the usual weekday campers. They lay down on a quilt Pete had spread in a shady spot. In such a beautiful place and with this much privacy, they would ordinarily be struggling to remember the Remington right about now. But there was a wall between them. So they just lay on their backs, looking up at the sky.

"Something's wrong with them," Pete finally said.

Dovey nodded. "With Daddy and Miss Lila."

"What do you think it is?"

She sighed. "He put the walls up."

"When? Did you see it happen?"

"Didn't have to. I just know Daddy."

"Well, I knew he'd wanna get away from that courthouse crowd, but Mama's his . . . his . . . I don't know what exactly she is, but I do know she never did anything but try to help."

"I know."

"And if she hadn't . . . Dovey, I don't understand why Miss Paul and your uncles didn't come down to the jail."

"Why'd you keep *me* away?" she responded.

"Because your daddy didn't want —"

"Didn't want me to see him locked up in that cell, right? The rest of my family — they knew he couldn't stand for them to see it either. And they knew nobody at that courthouse would listen to anything they had to say. Since they couldn't help him get out, they did the only thing they could for him, which was stay away."

"Why'd you put clothes and food in your daddy's truck?"

"Because he'll want to get out of those dirty jail clothes as quick as he can, and he needs something to eat."

"But he could get that at home."

"He won't come home, not for a while. Daddy has to handle bad things on his own. And I'm pretty sure Miss Lila won't understand that. He doesn't mean to hurt you when he turns inside like that. He just can't help it."

"But still, Mama and Daddy Ballard — you'd think he'd want to thank — I mean, without them, he might still be in jail."

"That's sorta the problem."

"Dovey, I don't understand that at all."

"I know."

"Well, can you explain it to me?"

"It's hard."

"But would you try?"

"Well," she said, carefully considering her answer, "remember when you first learned how to ride a bicycle?"

"Yeah . . ." he said.

"Remember how your mother or your daddy would run alongside the bike to help you get your balance and keep you from getting hurt?"

"Yeah . . ."

"And you were so thankful they were there to keep you from falling, but at the same time, you wished more than anything that you didn't need them, because as long as they had to help you, that meant you weren't really riding on your own?" When Pete reached over and took her hand, she knew he understood. "Daddy just wishes he could ride on his own."

When he had driven a safe distance from the courthouse, John pulled over to the side of the road and opened the paper sack on the seat of his truck. Inside he found a change of clothes, a smaller sack filled with sandwiches in wax paper, and a thermos of coffee. *Thank you, my sweet girl.* He followed the highway to a narrow dirt road that led deep into the woods near the river. Even this rough trail would play out before he reached his destination, but he didn't care. He would gladly walk the rest of the way.

What he wanted was cleansing. From the shame and the stupidity. From the pain and embarrassment he knew this had caused his daughter. From the suffocating anger and resentment and humiliation. He had to get free of it.

When the trail ended, he stopped the truck, tucked the sack filled with clothes under one arm, and started hiking into the woods, which he knew like the back of his hand. It was a wonderful thing to know where he was going and how he meant to get there, without a single well-meaning do-gooder shoving him this way and that like he was nothing. The closer he got, the faster he walked, till at last he was running — running as fast as he could up hills and down, through the dense woods, his chest heaving, his heart racing, sweat flying off his face. At last he could see the familiar hillside where he would find a narrow opening. He climbed through it and into the darkness of a narrow cave, finding his way by pressing his free hand against the ceiling. Before long he could see light up ahead and knew he was almost there. He followed the light to a small grotto, where the sun beamed down over tall rock walls onto a sparkling pool of crystal-blue water.

Strangely enough, he had found this place by getting lost long ago when he was out rabbit hunting, so focused on his prey that he wasn't paying attention to where he was. Struggling to get his bearings, he had stumbled onto the tiny cave. Back then he wasn't tall enough to feel the ceiling the way he did now, but even as a kid he wasn't afraid of darkness. He liked it. And he had felt his way through it to the light of the grotto.

John was ashamed to admit he had never shared this place with Jack or Lottie. It wasn't such a bad thing keeping it from his wife, because she was skittish of deep water, which you wouldn't expect, given that she had grown up on a riverbank. Jack, though — he would've loved this place, and it was selfish to keep it from him. But the grotto was the only thing John had ever kept all his own, and he had never been able to bring himself to let anybody else in. He dropped the sack at the edge of the water, which rippled up from a natural spring somewhere far below. It was clear and deep and cold.

The pool wasn't very big — maybe thirty feet across. But it was a breathtaking shade of blue, and it made such a peaceful sound, just a faint gurgling from that underground spring. On a hot summer's day, it was pure bliss to dip down into those waters with the sun high above and the tall rock walls protecting you, and to know — or at least hope — that no one else could claim it or take it from you.

John pulled off his boots and socks, then unbuttoned his shirt and began peeling off the sticky, sweaty grime of the jailhouse. He stuffed his dirty clothes under a big rock and hoped they rotted fast, since he never meant to touch them again. Then he waded into the pool, feeling its floor with his bare feet. He knew the bottom would drop out near the center, and you could lose yourself in that depth. He treaded water for a little while but then relaxed, closed his eyes, and let the water take him down, down, down, till it covered his chest, his shoulders, his face — all the way down into the clear, cold water till he couldn't hear or think or feel. When he couldn't hold his breath anymore, he gave a powerful push with his arms and propelled himself up, breaking through the blue and back into the light.

Over and over he let the water take him down until the jail and the gawkers and that idiot sheriff were completely washed away, and the burning anger he had felt for days had faded to a flicker. When his last ounce of energy was spent, he relaxed in the warmth of the hot summer sun with the cool blue water wrapped around him. He could finally breathe again. And with the grime and the anger washed away, he had a clear, unobstructed view of one pure, beautiful image.

Lila sat in her front porch swing with her feet up in the seat and her head down on her knees. For a while she had tried her best to stop crying, but in the end, the pain and misery of losing John overtook her. At the courthouse that morning, she had managed to get hold of herself just long enough to beg off lunch with her father and sister and to assure Pete that she was okay so everybody would leave her alone. Then she had fled to the sanctuary of her farmhouse, which was the only place she could stand to be right now. It was probably going on four o'clock. No telling how long she had been sitting in this swing. She didn't even notice a vehicle pulling into her driveway, and when she heard the footsteps of a long stride crossing her porch and felt someone sit down beside her, she knew it had to be Pete, coming to check on her. She kept her head down so he wouldn't have to see her cry.

"Lila?" John had taken a seat as close as he could get to her in the swing, but she didn't move till he called her name. She looked at him, not with anger, which would've been easier for him to bear, but with the most profound hurt and sadness. He knew he had cut her to the bone. She looked like she might run away at any minute — like she might even be afraid of him. And he knew he deserved whatever she decided to put him through to make it right.

"I'm not . . . I mean, I don't . . . I wouldn't blame you . . . at all . . . if you told me to leave and never come back. I said some unforgivable things to you in that parking lot." He paused, hoping she would say something.

She just kept looking at him blankly, with those awful tears he had made her cry falling and falling and falling.

"None of my hard times is your fault or your family's," he went on. "I know that. But it's just . . . workin' so hard for so long and feelin' like you don't have nothin' to show for it . . . that's a wearin' thing. And I guess I didn't know how much it's been wearin' on me till you opened a door and showed me a way out, and I thought I could finally . . . steer my own boat and build something I could leave behind for Dovey. But then I got hauled down to that jail, and I knew I might never get out on my own. And that . . . well . . . it just reminded me that I still wasn't steerin'. So I loaded all that up and I fired it straight at you, which is without a doubt the meanest, sorriest thing I've ever done in my life. And there ain't no way to make up for it. Or take it back. All I can do is tell you I'm sorry. I'm just . . . so sorry, Lila."

They sat together, with only the squeaking of the porch swing breaking the silence, as he waited and hoped that she would say something — anything. Finally, when he thought he couldn't stand another minute of it, she looked at him with a puzzled frown, as if he were just now coming into focus.

"Your hair's wet," she said.

He nodded. "Went swimmin'."

"Where?"

He smiled. "Secret spot — way back in the woods."

"Oh."

"Want me to take you, Lila?"

"What?"

"Swimmin' — someplace nobody else can take you?"

She sighed. "I used to get a running start and dive into the deepest water I could find. Can you believe that? Now I'd probably drown."

"I wouldn't let that happen."

"You probably think I'm a wimpy pool girl, but I'll bet I could swim in the woods just like you do."

"*Just* like I do?"

"Just like."

He smiled at her.

"What?" she said.

"I was just thinkin' that's something I might like to see."

They were quiet for a little while before he said, "Don't you wanna . . . cuss me out or . . . hit me over the head with a skillet or something?"

"I really don't have the energy." She tried to laugh but looked too tired to manage it.

John gathered her in his arms and lifted her onto his lap. She put her arms around his neck and let him rock her in the swing for a little while. Mercifully, she had stopped crying, but he had a feeling she hadn't said everything she needed to.

"John," she finally said in a very small voice, "it's not what you said that hurt so bad — it's what you did."

He thought he had made it home, but now

he was lost again. He ran his hand over the tops of her bare feet propped in the seat of the swing. "Can you tell me what I did?" he asked, not at all sure he wanted to know.

"You let go. You let go — of me — and left me out there all alone."

It was true and he knew it. What's worse, he had done it on purpose, not out of meanness but out of fear. When he was growing up, if some good fortune had befallen his family, his father would joyfully exclaim, "Ain't we lucky?" To which his mother would respond, "Pride cometh before a fall." John had spent his whole life with those opposing voices doing battle in his head. And now here he was with this woman. If ever he had seen anything too good to be true, it was Lila. He knew, once he really let her in, that he couldn't bear losing her. But if he didn't break his old habits, if he couldn't find the courage to step out of the dense woods and show himself, he could lose her right now. So he closed his eyes, took a deep breath, and blurted it out.

"You scare the daylights out of me."

He felt her sit up and knew she must be looking at him. Unsure that he was ready for what was coming, he kept his eyes closed until she brushed her fingers feather-light across them, and his desire to be with her overcame his fear of losing her.

"You scare the daylights out of me, Lila," he said again.

"But why?"

"Ever lost something you wanted more than anything else?"

"You know I have."

"Well, I almost always do. And that's why you — I mean, it's why I couldn't — I just never wanted anything or anybody so much."

Lila was crying again, but she was smiling too — that smile he loved. "John," was all she said.

He kissed her eyelids, her cheeks, her beautiful mouth. She relaxed onto his shoulder as the swing rocked back and forth.

After a long while, she said something so softly that he could barely hear her. "I need to ask you something, John."

"I'm listening," he said, stroking her blonde hair.

"Did you and Jack — did he ever talk about — did he tell you that when Pete was born, I had some trouble?"

He tightened his arms around her. "I'm not a greedy man, Lila. You got Pete and I got Dovey, and I don't think ten more kids would make us one bit happier, do you?"

Lila didn't speak. She just shook her head and relaxed into him. They listened to the creaking of the porch swing and the early evening song of cicadas as the afternoon faded away.

THIRTY-ONE

March 16, 1968

Lila hung up the phone and shook her head. She and John hadn't had a minute alone since their moment of reckoning on her porch. He and Dovey were coming over for supper tonight, and since the kids would want to leave right after, she had hoped the two of them would have some time together. But her father had just called and said he needed to see all of them, so there was nothing to do but invite him to supper. Once she got over the disappointment, though, her curiosity kicked in. Why did he have to see all four of them today since they already planned to have Sunday dinner together tomorrow? What could be so important that it couldn't wait a day?

Hattie thought she heard a car in her driveway. Dear heaven, she didn't have time for company this afternoon. She had so many neighbors to look after.

She and her mother had ridden out the storm in Junie's brick house. It had a basement, which kept them safe. Sheer luck — no, God's guiding hand — had put them there. Junie had just bought a new living room suite and wanted her mother and grandmother to see it, so she had picked them both up and fixed them a nice lunch at her house. Cyrus was right there with them. Hattie's mother never brought him to Junie's, but on that particular morning she said she "had a funny feeling about the sky" and refused to leave him behind. They had just finished with their pound cake and coffee when the sky grew dark.

And now so much tragedy. Fifteen people in Glory had lost their lives — many of them members of Hattie's beloved Morning Star Baptist Church. One family — Lord Jesus, *one* family — had lost five. Reverend Patterson, whose sweet wife had died just six months ago, would be burying his sister and her husband because of that awful tornado. It got white folks too. That nice Mr. McAdoo that owned the lake, his mother-in-law was gone, and they said his poor wife near about had a nervous breakdown over it. At least Morning Star still stood, so those who were suffering had a beacon and a shelter.

Hattie was in the middle of fixing her part of supper for homeless neighbors sleeping at the church when she looked out her kitchen window to see Mister Ned getting out of his Cadillac. This wasn't like him. He never disturbed her on weekends. In all these years, he had never once asked her to work a weekend or a holiday. At Thanksgiving and Christmas he would pay her for the whole week, even though he only asked her to work one day, "just to knock through the house." Of course, Hattie didn't just knock through anything. Before she took off to be with her family, she got that house spic-and-span, washed all his clothes, cooked some food he could heat up, and let his girls know exactly what he had in the icebox so they could take turns inviting him over for the rest of his meals.

She heard him knock and met him at the front door. "Afternoon, Mister Ned. Come on in." She motioned for him to take a seat in her parlor. "Can I get you anything?"

"No, Hattie, thank you," he said as she sat down across from him. "I'm sorry to bother you on a Saturday, but I need to talk to you."

She listened and waited.

"Hattie," he went on, "the FBI just ar-

398

rested two white people for Isaac's death."

She stared at him in disbelief. "They . . . they done what?" she managed to say.

"They arrested two white people for Isaac's death," Ned repeated.

Hattie stood and walked to her front window. She clasped her hands together underneath her chin, almost as if she were praying. When she turned to face him, her eyes welled with tears, and her voice was trembling so that she could barely talk.

"Was it that awful Klan?" she asked.

"No, nothing like that," he said quietly. "Hattie, Isaac was killed in a hit-and-run accident. The driver was Celeste Highland."

Hattie frowned. "That hateful lady from Birmin'ham?"

Ned nodded. "She was with an insurance salesman from Childersburg, fellow by the name of Harv Akers. They were in his car when it happened."

"But how on earth did you find this out?" she asked, returning to her seat across from him.

"Well, turns out there was a witness. The FBI got her story the day of the storm, but they wanted time to gather more evidence, so they asked me not to say anything. But Hattie . . . they have positively identified Isaac's remains."

Her hands shaking violently, Hattie was trying to wipe the tears from her face.

Ned handed her a fine linen handkerchief from his pocket. "Right now he's at the FBI lab in Birmingham. But they've made a positive identification and gathered all the evidence they need. They tell me they can release him to you Monday morning."

"But how on earth did he end up in Paul's cave?"

"Here's what happened. Isaac was on his way home from his card game when he saw a white woman, Dolores Bobo — she works at the Tomahawk — he saw her broke down on the side of the road. Her and her husband live in that trailer park on 51. She had hit a pothole and knocked a hubcap off her car, and when she stopped to look for it, the car wouldn't crank again. Isaac happened by and stopped to jump her off. She was down in a ditch lookin' for that hubcap when he got hit. She overheard Celeste Highland and Akers talkin' — stayed hid in the ditch so they couldn't see her — and she heard how they were up to no good together and decided to hide Isaac so Celeste's husband wouldn't find out. They're the ones who hid him in that cave. What they didn't know was that the Picketts use it for a storm shelter. Paul's family hadn't been in there for years, but with the tornado . . . they found Isaac. That's why that crazy Sheriff Flowers arrested John Pickett — because Isaac was found in the hollow, and John was the only member of the family home the night he was killed — that and some mischief the Highlands cooked up."

Hattie was struggling to sort through it all. All these years and no answers. Now they were coming at her in a flood. "But if they found Isaac the night of the storm, that means —"

"Hattie, I don't blame you if you're mad at me for waitin' a week to tell you who did it. But the FBI had to run all kinds of tests — dental records and so forth — to make sure that was Isaac. And they wanted to gather all the evidence they needed before word got out."

"I'm not mad. Whatever you done, I know you was just tryin' to do right by me."

"And you need to prepare yourself for when you get Isaac. After all this time, well . . . there's only bones. Nothing you could recognize, except for his belt buckle. They found that in the — they found that with him."

"I wouldn't care if it was just one tiny bone of his little finger. I'd know. Somehow

I'd know my chile." She thought for a minute. "Them white people just dumped my boy in a dark cave and left him? People like that — was they even sure he was dead? Did they check to see could a doctor help him? Oh, Lord, if they left him lyin' in agony alone in that darkness —" Hattie broke into sobs.

Ned moved his chair closer to hers and put his hand on her shoulder. "Hattie, that did not happen. Isaac died the second that car hit him. He didn't suffer. I believe that with all my heart. I was there when the FBI questioned Dolores Bobo, and I was there when they questioned Harv Akers and Celeste Highland. I think Akers was actually relieved to get arrested and confess. He described in detail how he checked to see if there was any sign of life. And he said that when he carried Isaac into that cave, he checked again to make sure he was gone, and then Akers laid him out proper, like a funeral home would. Don't ask me how a man can be party to such a thing but still think it's important to lay the body out right, but I believed him when he said it. You can know that Isaac didn't suffer. I would never lie to you about something as important as that."

"What about that white woman you said

done the drivin' — what she have to say?"

"Mostly lies, far as I could tell."

"You think she's gonna pay for what she done?"

"I don't know. I wish I could say yes. But you know how things work around here well as I do. All I can tell you is that we've done all we can to get justice for Isaac. Now it's up to the law and the courts."

"Pete know all o' this?"

"Not all of it. He don't know they've made an arrest. Hattie, he saw Isaac in that cave. He helped John get the Picketts out of there the day of the tornado — the day they found Isaac. Pete's the reason I believed Akers when he said he'd laid Isaac out with respect — that's how Pete said Isaac looked to him. But he's gonna be pretty shocked when he finds out who did it. Don't quite know how to tell him, but I mean to do it soon as I leave here. I think he'll be a little put out with me for not tellin' him right away who killed Isaac. That's why I haven't seen much of him this week — stayin' away from him was the only way I could keep from tellin' him."

"And now he's got to find out that the woman what killed his friend's been sellin' pound cakes alongside his mama at the church." Hattie shook her head. "Got to

403

learn some hard lessons in this life."

"Never thought I'd see the day when I'd want a woman from my own community to go to jail," Ned said. "But that one deserves it. There's such a thing as evil in this world, Hattie."

"Yes, sir," she said, wiping her eyes with his fine handkerchief. "But they's righteousness too."

Everyone at the table was stunned. Ned had just delivered the shocking news about Celeste Highland.

Pete got up and stood at the screen door to his mother's kitchen, staring out at nothing in the backyard. "If y'all don't mind," he said flatly, "I think I need some air." He started outside but then stopped, turned, and held his hand out to Dovey. She hurried to him, leaving Ned sitting across from John and Lila at the kitchen table.

John knew that Lila was almost as distraught as Pete. It had to be a shock to find out somebody she actually knew was capable of killing a man and throwing him away like he was nothing. He could see her eyes filling with tears and knew she couldn't hold it in much longer. Underneath the table, he reached over to hold her hand.

He was relieved for Hattie, that sweet lady

who had been kind enough to come and see him at the jail. But he couldn't stop thinking about what had just happened between Pete and Dovey. John had never let anybody see him in the state that Pete was in now. His instinct was always to hide away in solitude until he had his emotions in check. But he had seen the look on Dovey's face when she thought she was going to be left at the table, and he had seen her relief when Pete came back for her. He remembered — much more vividly than he wanted to — Lila's stricken expression the day he had abandoned her at the courthouse. And he made a silent vow that he would die before he ever did that to her again.

Pete and Dovey sat together in a faded yellow glider in his mother's front yard. They silently rocked back and forth, with Dovey letting him think things through, until finally he said, "I feel like a really mean joke's been played on all of us."

"What do you mean?" she asked.

"Well . . . everybody in town knew Daddy Ballard had hired that detective and that we were lookin' everywhere to find Isaac. And all that time, Judd's mama and that insurance man — they're walkin' around, goin' about their business, knowin' exactly where he is. They don't care at all that he's got a mama and sisters wantin' to bury him or that Hattie's goin' half crazy, picturin' Isaac lost and hurt somewhere. And why'd they do it? So that awful woman can keep a husband she don't even love. It just makes me so . . . I don't know what I'm supposed to do now."

"I think you're supposed to do exactly what you're doing," Dovey said. "You're supposed to be so mad you can't see straight. And you're supposed to feel all of that anger till you're done with it. Then you can move on to the sadness. Because even though you knew in your head Isaac was gone, I imagine a tiny little part of you was still hoping for a miracle."

He put his arm around her. "Were you born like this," he said, smiling down at her, "or did it happen over time?"

Dovey and Lila were clearing the supper dishes when the telephone rang. "Oh, hello, Mr. Harwell," Dovey heard Lila say. "Yes, we heard. I guess you called to track Daddy down for the building committee . . . No? . . . Pete can *what*? . . . Are you sure that would be a good idea? . . . Well, I guess it's up to him . . . Yes, I'll send a note to school with him . . . Thank you so much.

Y'all have a good night."

Dovey had stopped washing the silverware and was watching Lila. "Something wrong?" she asked.

"Not exactly. C'mon, sweetheart. I think your daddy needs to hear this too."

Dovey followed Lila into the front parlor, where the men were watching a ball game. Lila walked over and turned off the sound.

"Pete," she said, "that was Mr. Harwell on the telephone. He says that, what with all the tornado damage to the school, they're short on space. So the school board held an emergency meeting and voted to give all the seniors whose grades are good enough the option of taking a high school equivalency test. If you pass, you get your diploma from the school this coming week. But now, before you even say it —"

Pete had already jumped up, grabbed Dovey, and twirled her across the parlor. "We can get married!" he exclaimed. "We don't have to wait anymore!"

"Now, Pete, just a minute," Lila said. "We have to talk about this. First you have to pass the test."

"I'll pass it!"

"And even then, we've always said the wedding would be in May." She looked to Dovey's father for reinforcements, but he appeared too blindsided to put a thought together.

"But Mama, we said May because that's when I was gonna graduate, right?"

"Well, yes, but —"

"And if we always agreed that me and Dovey could get married when I graduate, then we oughta be able to marry in March if I can graduate in March."

"Honey, there's no way we can plan a wedding in two weeks."

"Yes we can, Miss Lila," Dovey pleaded. "I promise we can."

"John Pickett, you open your mouth and say something right this minute or you and me are gonna have trouble!" Lila demanded.

"I'm thinkin', Lila, I'm thinkin'!" he said.

Lila's father was sitting quietly, taking it all in.

"Well," John said as quickly as he could gather his wits, "they've respected our wishes all this time. And now I guess we gotta honor our promise. Whether we like it or not."

Pete and Dovey squealed and jumped up and down.

"Mama?" Pete said. "We can't do this without your blessing."

She sighed and shook her head in defeat.

"You know you have it."

Pete and Dovey ran over and hugged her, then hugged everybody else in the room, then Lila again, then each other, and then they ran out the door and hopped into Pete's truck.

Lila's father stood up to go. "For what it's worth, honey," he said, putting an arm around her shoulders, "I think y'all made the right decision. A couple more months won't change a thing in the world but the date on the calendar."

John got up and shook Ned's hand as he left. As he and Lila watched the taillights of her father's Cadillac disappear in the distance, he turned to her and said, "You're feisty when you're all riled up."

"Oh, hush," she said with a laugh. "I guess you know we're going suit shopping tomorrow."

"I guess you know Pete and Dovey are on to us."

"No! What do they know?"

"Something — not sure how much."

"But how?"

He smiled and put his arms around her. "Dovey says I smell like Chanel No. 5."

THIRTY-TWO

March 17, 1968
Lila had just stepped into the kitchen to grab the tea pitcher when she heard a car in her driveway and looked out to see Junie pulling up. Junie waited in the car as Hattie came to the kitchen door. It was the first time Lila had seen her since Isaac had been found. She invited Hattie in, and for a minute the two mothers just looked at each other, not knowing what to say. Then Lila put her arms around Hattie and hugged her.

"I 'pologize for botherin' y'all durin' your Sunday dinner," Hattie said when they stepped apart.

"You're not bothering anybody. Won't Junie come in?"

"We can't stay. I just need to ask your men somethin', and I know they all here right now. Won't take but a second if you don't mind me interruptin'."

"They're all in the dining room. Come on in."

All the men stood up when Hattie came into the room. Pete hugged her, then pulled up a chair for her.

"I'm sorry to come durin' your dinner," Hattie said, "but Pete, Mister Ned, Mister John — I wanted to ask y'all a favor. We gonna bury Isaac on Wednesday — have his funeral at my church. I wanted to ask y'all if you would be honorary pallbearers."

"Why, Hattie, of course we —" Ned began.

"No," Pete said.

"Pete!" Lila was stunned.

"No, Hattie," Pete said again. "That ain't right. Everybody knows when Morning Star invites white men to be honorary pallbearers and follow behind the casket, it's a way for y'all to honor *us*. But we want to come to your church to honor *Isaac*. Let us help carry him, Hattie. I wanna help carry him."

"Hattie, it would be a privilege," Ned said. "But now, Pete, Hattie may have family members that she wants to do that."

"No," Hattie said, smiling at Pete. "Just my three girls' husbands. Nobody I'd rather have helpin' 'em than y'all." She stood up to go. "Well, now we got that settled. 'Scuse me again for interruptin' your dinner."

Ned walked Hattie to her car as Lila refilled Pete's tea glass and kissed him on the cheek.

THIRTY-THREE

March 20, 1968

Morning Star Baptist Church was packed,
with people standing all along the side aisles
and in back. The little church had never
hosted so many white people. Everybody
Hattie had ever worked for had at least one
family member there to represent them.

Pete's mother and Dovey sat together with
his Aunt Geneva and her family on the pew
just behind the section reserved for family.
Dovey's father and Daddy Ballard were
seated next to Pete on the front row with
the other pallbearers. A beautiful blanket of
red roses and white lilies covered Isaac's
closed casket. Hattie had placed a framed
picture of him on a little table near the head
of it. Pete had overheard his grandfather
call the florist and tell her to put a $150
balance on Hattie's account so she could
have whatever she wanted for Isaac's funeral
blanket. Isaac's youngest sister, Iris, had

413

bought two matching sprays. These had to be the prettiest flowers Morning Star had ever seen.

As the organist took her seat, the choir filed into the choir loft. They wore purple robes with gold satin stoles and swayed in time as the organist began a slow gospel swing. All over the church, one little cluster at a time, the congregation started clapping in time until everybody was keeping rhythm with the organ — everybody except some of the white people, who couldn't seem to land on the beat and struggled to find something to do with their hands. And then the choir sang out.

Glory, glory, hallelujah,
Since I laid my burden down.

On and on the music went, one great song right after another.

On Jordan's stormy banks I stand
And cast a wishful eye
To Canaan's fair and happy land,
Where my possessions lie.

The congregation stood as Reverend Patterson came down the aisle, leading a procession of Isaac's family. Hattie and Aunt Babe walked side by side, their arms linked. Though she wore her black funeral dress, Aunt Babe carried the bright red walking cane Isaac had made for her. The choir sang Hattie's favorite hymn.

Blessed assurance, Jesus is mine!
O what a foretaste of glory divine!
Heir of salvation, purchase of God,
Born of his Spirit, washed in his blood.

Once the family was seated, the rest of the congregation sat down, and Reverend Patterson motioned for Dovey to come forward. Hattie had spoken with her the day before and said she knew Dovey had a hard time singing by herself in front of people, but would she be willing to do it just this once? It would be so nice to hear that pretty voice singing Isaac's favorite song with his church choir. Dovey had agreed.

Now she stood at the podium, facing an overflowing church, with the Morning Star choir behind her. Isaac's favorite song was an old spiritual. They would sing it the old-time way, without the organ.

"Guide my feet," Dovey sang out, and the choir answered, "While I run this race . . ."

Pete was fighting hard to hold himself together. That song made him feel as if Isaac were sitting on the pew next to him. Knowing how hard it was for Dovey to do what she was doing, how much love she was showing Pete and Hattie and Aunt Babe — it was too much to feel all at one time. As much as he loved to hear her sing, he was relieved when she stopped and Reverend Patterson came to the podium.

"Before I begin my message," he said, "Miss Iris Reynolds would like to make an expression."

Pete hadn't seen Iris since he was a little boy. She was tall like Hattie and dressed in city clothes — an expensive-looking gray suit with a black-and-silver scarf tucked around her neck. When she spoke, she didn't sound like anybody around Glory. She sounded like the people who gave the news on TV.

"As most of you know, Isaac Reynolds was my older brother, and I am a blessed woman because of him. So many of the dreams that I held as a child have come true. But I would not have any of it were it not for my brother and the sacrifices he made on my behalf. I imagine he had some dreams of his own growing up. But when our father died, Isaac and Mama put their dreams aside and tended to ours — my sisters' and mine.

"When I was at Spelman, one of my

classmates from up north learned that I was raised in an Alabama farm town, and she wanted to know what that was like. As I began telling her about my home and my family, both of which I am very proud of, she said, 'You mean your brother is just a field hand and your mother is just a maid?' I never spoke to her again.

"Yes, my brother was just a field hand — just a field hand who worked hard every day of his life to feed his family. Just a field hand who found the good in everybody. Just a field hand who loved books and music, who had a fine mind and a sharp wit, but who, unlike me, never got the chance to realize his potential. Isaac could have done so many things if only he'd had a big brother looking out for him the way he looked out for me.

"And my mother — just a maid? I look out at this congregation, and I see many families who have never been inside this church before, but you are here today out of respect for my mother. You are here because you've seen in her God's goodness and grace. There is one very generous visitor here today whose name I will not call because he would not want me to. But he helped my family change my life. And I don't think he would mind my saying that he did it out of respect for the people I come from.

"I suppose what I'm trying to say is that you do not need money to leave a legacy. My brother has left one. It is a legacy of love and kindness and friendship and selfless devotion to family. That is a treasure I will carry in my heart always. And I will love Isaac Reynolds forever."

Iris sat down, and Reverend Patterson began his message. "Our Scripture this morning comes from the Gospel of John. 'Let not your heart be troubled . . .' "

When Reverend Patterson closed his message, the choir began to slowly sing.

Amazing grace, how sweet the sound
That saved a wretch like me;
I once was lost but now am found,
Was blind but now I see.

The pallbearers carried Isaac out of the church — Hattie's sons-in-law on one side, and Pete, his grandfather, and John on the other. Even on such a solemn occasion, Pete could hear some of the ladies of the church whispering to each other, and he knew why. They had seen honorary pallbearers before, but never had white men helped carry one of their church members to the burying ground.

418

At the church cemetery, with Hattie's whole congregation gathered around, the pallbearers laid Isaac in his grave.

Reverend Patterson read one more passage of Scripture before saying his final prayer. "Peace I leave with you, my peace I give unto you . . ."

Dovey stood beside Pete as he lingered at the graveside, even after most of the Morning Star congregation had left. She glanced over to where Hattie and Aunt Babe were standing just in time to see Reverend Patterson put his arm around Hattie. A familiar look passed between the two of them.

"We should invite Reverend Patterson to the wedding," Dovey said as she watched them.

Pete nodded but said nothing. He took off the red rose pinned to his lapel and laid it on Isaac's blanket of flowers. "Let's go home, Dovey. It's time to go home."

THIRTY-FOUR

March 23, 1968

"Wait a minute — I'm not ready!" Dovey said, stopping at the foot of Pete's front porch steps.

Pete grinned. "Ain't gonna get any easier."

"What do you think they'll do?" Dovey fretted.

"Well, I think Mama'll have a heart attack — hopefully a mild one — and your daddy'll strangle me with his bare hands and lock you in your room for the rest of your life. But then, I tend to look on the bright side."

"I'm serious!" Dovey cried.

Pete put his arms around her and kissed her. "I know. But you don't need to be. This is the fun part, Dovey. We've waited all this time. I passed that crazy test. And we dodged the dadgum tornado that got me outta school early. Your Aunt Lydia's been workin' on your dress ever since you showed her that ring. It's time to have ourselves a wedding! If it drives our parents batty, so be it!"

She started giggling, and he knew everything would be okay. They went inside the house, where their parents waited in the front parlor.

"Okay, you two, what's the big announcement?" Pete's mother asked.

"We know you've been wantin' us to settle on where to have the wedding," Pete began, "and you can put your mind at ease. We've found the place."

"At the Methodist church?" she asked. The Methodists had invited First Baptist to use their sanctuary for Sunday services while the Baptist church was being rebuilt.

"Uh . . . no, ma'am," Pete said.

"Surely not at the barn?" John asked.

"No, sir," Dovey said.

"Well?" Pete's mother asked.

"See, Miss Lila, we wanted to get married someplace that's special to the two of us," Dovey said. "And the way we figure it, we're bringing both our families to sort of a crossroads, you know?"

"So we've found a place that makes sense to us," Pete finished for her. "It just needs . . . a little spruce-up."

Dovey sat down next to John and took his hand. "Daddy, we're gonna need your help."

THIRTY-FIVE

April 6, 1968

John stepped back to have a look. He had just hammered the very last nail, with Pete coming behind him, painting as John built. One grueling day after another, they had worked from sunup till bedtime, taking their only break on Sunday, when the women wouldn't hear of allowing any carpentry work. John's brothers agreed to handle the crop for now so he and Pete could get everything done. Wonder of wonders, the two of them had finished. The paint might actually have time to dry before the wedding tomorrow. And he might get back to his store before Christmas.

As he came around front to search through a box of brushes on the porch and help Pete finish painting, he heard a car in the driveway and looked up to see Junie and Hattie helping Aunt Babe across the yard. Once the hammering started, she had abandoned her house and taken refuge at Hattie's, leaving Pete strict instructions on how to look after Cyrus while she was gone. This was the first time she had seen Pete and John's handiwork.

"Well?" Pete said, coming around the house with a paintbrush in his hand. Cyrus followed his every step. "What you think, Aunt Babe?"

She nodded. "It'll do."

Junie rolled her eyes. "Grandmama, you know it's beautiful!"

"Let's go," Aunt Babe said, starting back to the car.

"But we just got here!" Junie objected.

Aunt Babe would have none of it. "All this paintin' and sawin' gets on my last nerve."

Pete's clothes were covered with paint and wet with sweat. He grinned as he walked over to her with Cyrus at his heels. "Aw, c'mon, Aunt Babe," he said, scratching the hound behind his ears. "Give me and ole Cyrus some sugar."

"Get out from here, Pete McLean," she grumbled, shooing him away. "You filthy nasty. And you better not forget to feed Cyrus his supper!"

"Don't you worry 'bout Cyrus. He gets his supper before I get mine."

Hattie followed John around to the back

of the house. "Mama ain't one to let on," she said, "but I know what this means to her. Thank you."

He smiled. "You might not wanna thank me tomorrow, when you got half the town traipsin' over this yard."

"It'll be fine," Hattie said. "Brung you some fresh coffee." She set the thermos down beside him as she left to join Junie and Aunt Babe.

John understood why finding a wedding site had been a struggle for Pete and Dovey. His mother, they all knew, might refuse to set foot in any of the churches in town. And if they got married in the Picketts' barn, everybody from First Baptist would spend the whole wedding wondering where the snakes were. Lila had offered her house, but John and Dovey were afraid his mother would declare it "a Ballard wedding" and refuse to come. Finally, Pete and Dovey had come home from the Dairy Queen late one afternoon and announced that they had found the perfect place, halfway between both families and special to the two of them.

Dovey laughed when she told him how Aunt Babe planned to use their wedding to get her house redone. She had told them she couldn't think of it otherwise, what with her old place needing a coat of paint so bad and that sorry, piddling little porch she had to make do with. Naturally, she told Pete she wanted her house painted red, but Hattie had prevailed on her to consider her second-favorite color, yellow. John and Pete had completely repaired the house, painted it a soft, buttery shade, and added a white porch and trim. The old shotgun had never looked better.

With all the trim finished, Pete and John began loading scrap lumber into their trucks, packing up tools, and clearing away paint buckets. By the time they cleaned up the yard, it would be time for supper, which Dovey and Lila would have ready for them.

John couldn't believe how much he missed Lila. While he and Pete worked on Aunt Babe's house, Lila and Dovey had been busy calling caterers and ordering flowers and getting the wedding announcement out. They had barely gotten it into all the church bulletins the Sunday before the wedding. The only time John saw Lila was over supper, and somebody was always with them — Pete and Dovey or Lila's father. Every night, John and Pete would eat their supper and then go back to the house and hook up shop lights to work a few more hours before they went home and fell into bed. Right now John would give anything for just an hour alone with Lila when he wasn't too exhausted to hold his head up. But that would have to wait.

Thirty-Six

April 7, 1968

"Hattie, don't you even think about puttin' that apron on."

"But Mister Ned, look how them caterers got the coleslaw ahead of the barbecue! Everybody knows the barbecue comes first! Bet they put the sauce with the sweet tea and the lemons with the baked beans."

Hattie was clutching one of Aunt Babe's favorite aprons in her hands and watching in dismay as the caterers from Childersburg set up long buffet tables right on Hollow Road. Aunt Babe's yard was just big enough to hold all the folding chairs for the wedding guests, so the food had to be set up in the road. Cars could park on either end of the tables, but anybody wanting to drive past them would just have to wait till after the reception.

"Aunt Babe, can't you do anything with her?" Ned asked. He was standing at the foot of her front steps, looking up at the two women on the porch. They wore new Sunday dresses with matching hats and gloves, which he had bought for them — pale pink for Hattie and bright red for Aunt Babe.

Aunt Babe had been happy to go shopping with him in Birmingham and didn't pay one bit of attention to the price tags. Hattie, though, was another matter. Early in their shopping trip, Ned had to resort to threats. "Hattie, I swear if you don't get away from those sale racks, I'm gonna drive off and leave you in Birmingham. Just pick you out a pretty dress and quit frettin' over the price." Right now he could tell she was itching to take off her pearl-buttoned gloves, tie on her apron, and show those caterers how it was done.

Suddenly, though, Hattie was distracted from the buffet table and its ill-placed coleslaw. "Why, that looks like Reverend Patterson's car pullin' up," she said. "What's he doin' here?"

Ned smiled. "Pete and Dovey made me go over to his house and personally invite him. They said you're gonna make a fine preacher's wife."

Hattie shook her head. "I don't know what them young'uns think they know," she said.

"Looks to me like they know plenty." Ned chuckled, walking out to greet Reverend Patterson.

"Seems like yesterday I was helping you get ready for your first spring dance," Lila said as she fussed with Pete's tie and stepped back to look at him. "All grown up." Pete was wearing a new navy suit she and Dovey had picked out for him.

He smiled. "You planning to get all weepy on me?"

"You better believe it."

He hugged his mother and kissed her on the cheek. "I love you, Mama."

"I love you too, sweetheart. And I want you to be just . . . so, so happy."

"Same to you," he said with a grin.

"Now, Pete, I don't know what kind of notions you and Dovey have gotten into your heads, but I can explain —"

He stopped her with another hug. "Nothing to explain, Mama." He offered her his arm, just as she'd shown him the night of that first dance with Dovey. "May I escort you to your big ole Buick, ma'am?"

"You may." Lila laughed, taking his arm. The two of them left the farmhouse together, ready for a wedding.

■ ■ ■ ■

"Dovey, honey, you got any idea how to do this?" John was standing in front of Lottie's mirror, struggling with his necktie.

"Let me see," Dovey said. But when he turned and saw her standing there, he forgot all about the tie.

She was dressed for her wedding — his little girl, a bride. She must've looked at fifty dress patterns, but in the end she had asked her Aunt Lydia to re-create the dress she wore to that first dance with Pete — sleeveless, scooped neck and back, Empire waist. It looked completely different in white silk and antique lace. Dovey wore her hair down with a simple veil — just a single layer of very delicate lace that fell from the crown of her head all the way down her back. Pete had given her a strand of his grandmother's pearls as a wedding present. She wore them around her neck, along with his locket.

She smiled at her father. "Well, say something, Daddy."

He opened his mouth to tell her how beautiful she looked and how proud her mother would be and how much he loved her — but no words would come out. So he just put his arms around her and held her close.

Dovey kissed her father on the cheek, then stepped back, tied the Windsor knot, and straightened his collar.

John held his daughter one last time before he had to stand on a porch in front of all those people and give her away.

With all the guests in their seats, laughing and talking, the First Baptist choir gathered beside Aunt Babe's steps and began to sing.

Come, thou fount of ev'ry blessing,
Tune my heart to sing thy grace.

Lila's father escorted her to one of two empty chairs out in front of all the others and then took his place on the row a few feet behind her. Pete's grandparents on his father's side had died when he was a little boy, but his McLean aunts and uncles came. So did John's mother and her entire clan. Altogether, the family — including Aunt Babe, Hattie, and Reverend Patterson, at Pete and Dovey's request — filled six rows of chairs stretching all the way across Aunt Babe's yard.

The front railing and columns of the new porch John had built were covered with garlands of greenery and pink roses. Two white wicker baskets, brimming over with flowers, rested on pedestals on either side of the steps.

As Pete came out the front door with Brother Jip, Lila stood up, and everybody else followed her lead. John escorted Dovey down the side porch and around front, where Pete waited for her at the top of the steps. Cyrus trotted around from the backyard and took a respectful position at the foot of the steps.

"You all can be seated," Brother Jip said to the guests as the choir finished singing.

As bittersweet as this moment was for any father, John couldn't help smiling at the expression on Pete's face the first time he saw Dovey in her wedding dress. The preacher would have a time getting words to come out of the boy's mouth because he looked dumbstruck.

"Who gives this woman in marriage to this man?" Brother Jip said.

"I do," John answered almost in a whisper, kissing Dovey's hand before placing it in Pete's. He went down the steps and took his seat next to Lila.

"Dearly beloved . . ."

Lila was already starting to cry, and they hadn't even exchanged rings yet. John reached into his suit pocket and gave her the crisp white handkerchief Dovey had carefully ironed and folded for him, just like Lila showed her. Lila dabbed at her eyes but was clearly getting overwhelmed by the emotion of the moment, the tears flowing faster by the minute.

Their chairs were so close together that John was sure no one behind them could see — and if they could, well, they'd just have to see. He reached over and took Lila's hand. She looked up at him and smiled. The two chairs out front, placed so that the two of them could have a little privacy and see the wedding together, with their backs to the rest of the crowd — that was Dovey's idea, and now John knew why she had planned it so.

"Dovey, if you will take this ring and place it on Pete's finger," Brother Jip was saying.

John tightened his grip on Lila's hand ever so slightly.

". . . And now, by the powers vested in me by the state of Alabama, I pronounce you husband and wife. Pete, you may kiss your bride."

Before Lila and John had time to think about it, their children were married.

The crowd was thinning out now that

they'd had their fill of barbecue and wedding cake. Miss Paul and the Picketts were the first to leave. Aunt Babe's yard was strewn with rice, thrown at Pete and Dovey as they ran for Lila's Buick and drove away to their honeymoon. Reverend Patterson had offered to take Hattie home and was escorting her to his car as Geneva walked her father to his Cadillac, making him promise to come over to her house and stay for supper. Aunt Babe had gone inside to lie down. She even let Cyrus come in with her. Lila had heard her grumbling, "They's just so much of these white folks me and you can take — ain't that right, Cyrus?"

As car doors slammed and friends said goodbye, Lila walked down to the buffet tables to tell the caterers they could start cleaning up. She scanned the few small clusters of people left in the yard, looking for John. Just as she was beginning to panic for fear that he might have stolen away, she spotted him leaning against one of the pecan trees next to Aunt Babe's house. In the afternoon heat, he had taken off his jacket and tie, unbuttoned his collar, and rolled up the sleeves of his white dress shirt. He smiled at her like he had been waiting for her to find him.

They had picked out her dress together

the same day they bought his suit. At the first store, when she told the saleslady she was the mother of the groom, out had come a bunch of brocade dresses with satin-cuffed jackets and shimmery wraps and pearl buttons and rhinestones all over the place. But then they went to Loveman's, where John immediately spotted a dress of pale blue silk and chiffon, simply cut. It was sleeveless, with a V-necked front and back and a fitted waist. The skirt fell just below Lila's knees and floated around her legs.

"You don't need any ornamentation, Lila," he had said. "Anybody can see that."

John gave a little nod toward Aunt Babe's backyard, which was surrounded by tall cedar trees. Aunt Babe always said your front yard was for show, but your backyard was "for yo' own self," and she didn't want "no meddlesome noseys" snooping around hers. Years ago, Daddy Ballard had sent over field hands who planted those cedars to give Aunt Babe her privacy.

Lila followed John all the way into the strange-looking gazebo where he had waited with Dovey before the wedding. The seconds ticked by as they stood silently, facing each other. Their friendship had been so comfortable and easy, but now they had started down a riskier path. The two-week separation, coming just as they were taking those first tentative steps together, had made them unsure of their footing.

"Remember me?" he said.

She nodded. "You're that mysterious, exhausted man who's been showing up at my supper table every night and disappearing right after dessert."

There was something a little sad about his smile as he reached out to brush her hair away from her face. "I won't disappear anymore."

"Promise?"

"Promise."

He looked a little overwhelmed, so she let him take his time. "What *is* this thing anyway, Lila?" he asked, looking around at the gazebo.

"It's supposed to be a Chinese pagoda," she said. "Aunt Babe's been fascinated with China ever since a foreign missionary spoke at her church. When she found this in a catalog, she tore the page out and taped it to Daddy's windshield, so he took the hint."

He smiled at her. "Sounds about right."

"Want me to tell you more about mail-order architecture? Because I could go on and on. We could cover Sears, the Green Stamp store . . ."

He shook his head, taking her hands and

pulling her very close to him. "I missed you so much, Lila." He said it like it was a terrible thing to endure. "I don't . . . I don't ever wanna miss you again."

The way he was looking at her, all she could manage was a whispered, "You don't have to."

THIRTY-SEVEN

April 13, 1968

The log cabin was completely hidden away. From their front porch, Pete and Dovey could see the Smoky Mountains soaring into the sky. This time of year, the air was cool and crisp. Across the back of the cabin was a deep covered deck overlooking a waterfall that spilled into a gushing stream below. It had a chaise lounge for two, which had become the newlyweds' favorite spot after supper every night.

Aunt Geneva had rented the cabin for them. When she stopped by Aunt Babe's to see how the porch was coming along and discovered that Pete had forgotten to plan a honeymoon, she had thrown up her hands and said, "But that's the most important part!" Seeing Pete's dismay, she had given him a big hug and said, "Now, don't you give it another thought, honey. Aunt Geneva knows a thing or two about romance. Just leave it to me."

She had outdone herself. Tonight Pete and Dovey were snuggled under a blanket on the chaise lounge, listening to the waterfall.

"I think waterfalls might be my very favorite thing in the whole world — besides you, of course," Dovey said, smiling up at Pete. "Is this Friday night or Saturday night?"

"Sorry to say it's Saturday."

"A whole week has gone by?"

"I know." He sighed. "Hey, you know what we should do, Dovey? We oughta plan a special trip every year — someplace neither one of us has ever been."

"That won't be hard for me. I've never been anywhere."

"Ain't exactly a world traveler myself," he said. "Tell you what. Every time we take a trip, we'll spend the last night of it plannin' where to go the next year. That way we won't be sad when it's time to leave because we'll have something to look forward to."

"Can we really do that — go somewhere every year?"

"Sure. Maybe not this time of year, though. I'll be plantin' cotton."

"So what's a good time? Maybe August?"

"Sounds perfect. Where you wanna go?"

"I guess I'd like to see the ocean," she

said, "but you've already been to Florida."

"Just Panama City. How 'bout we start in Pensacola and drive all the way across Mississippi to New Orleans — follow the water the whole way. We could take two weeks if we wanted to."

"Are you serious?" Dovey sat up a little so she could see his face.

"Absolutely." He kissed her as she snuggled back onto his shoulder.

They were quiet for a minute before she said, "You're not done yet, are you?"

"With what?"

"With Isaac."

"What do you mean?"

"I mean, it's not finished. I can tell you've thought about him some this week."

"No I haven't —" He stopped. "I don't know why I still think I can hide anything from you. I'm sorry. I shouldn't have been thinking about anybody but you on our honeymoon."

"Don't be sorry. You feel what you feel. I think I can help, though. I was wrong before."

"When?"

"Way back in the beginning, when I said you were looking for a way to tell Isaac goodbye. That was only half of it. You need a way to remember him too."

"But how?"

"I don't know," she said. "But you'll find a way. You always do."

EPILOGUE

November 30, 1968

Daddy Ballard stood with Reverend Patterson and Hattie as half the town looked on, with Geneva's family, Pete, Dovey, John, and Lila at the front of the crowd.

"Mrs. Patterson, if you'll do the honors," Daddy Ballard said, handing Hattie a pair of scissors.

Hattie cut the big white ribbon stretched across the doorway of the new town library named for her son. The crowd applauded before lining up to file inside and have a look around. The county and the high school had libraries, and there were a couple of small ones in neighboring towns, but Glory had never had one all its own.

Pete and Dovey had come up with the idea on the way home from their honeymoon. Isaac loved books, they reasoned, and some of the other libraries weren't entirely welcoming if you didn't happen to be white. So a library that was open to everybody would be the perfect way to remember Pete's friend.

Daddy Ballard had been easier to convince than Hattie. "What about all the white people in town that wouldn't think of checking out the same books as us?" she had protested.

Daddy Ballard had a simple answer. "Why, Hattie, I reckon they can drive on down the road to a library I didn't pay for."

Hattie wasn't done, though. "How you gonna make sure the librarian don't turn people like me away when you're not lookin'?" she asked.

"Ain't Junie looking for a job?" Daddy Ballard countered. "She can be the librarian."

At last Hattie was satisfied. Daddy Ballard asked Principal Harwell to have the school librarian teach Junie the basics, and that was that.

It was a small but pretty brick building, with hardwood floors, tall windows, and two long wooden tables dotted with reading lamps and lined with comfortable chairs. Iris had chosen all the books and paid for half of them. The rest were donated by members of Hattie's church and the families she had worked for.

While most everybody roamed among the stacks to see what they had to choose from, Pete and Dovey lingered in the foyer. They stood hand in hand before a large portrait of Isaac painted by a Birmingham artist. Dovey's father had made the frame. The portrait hung above a simple but elegant entry table — also John's work — with Isaac's wingback chair next to it. At the base of the frame was a small engraved plate.

In loving memory of Isaac Reynolds,
a dear friend forever
Mr. and Mrs. Pete McLean

Pete ran his fingers across the plate as he gazed at the portrait. It was a wonderful likeness. Just as he felt himself drifting back, missing Isaac too much to truly celebrate his friend's memory, Dovey tugged him away from the portrait and led him inside the library. There, in a corner set aside especially for children, they spotted two of Isaac's young nephews huddled around an oversized, illustrated *Treasure Island* — Isaac's favorite book.

As Pete stood there watching their faces light up with each turn of the page, he slowly broke into a smile. For the first time in a long time, he felt connected to Isaac, not forever separated. He squeezed Dovey's hand and kissed it. Together they had lightened the burden of his sorrow to something he could carry, and there was room in his heart at last for happy memories of his friend.

As he and Dovey walked hand in hand out of the library and started home, Pete felt it deep down in his soul — he was free. And so was Isaac.

Both of them were finally free.

ACKNOWLEDGMENTS

Stories came out of the woodwork where I grew up — a farmhouse with a tin roof (rain never sounded better) and a big front porch (breezes never felt better) in Shelby County, Alabama. I'm so thankful to my parents, grandparents, aunts, uncles, and cousins for filling my childhood with stories.

Just as my parents made sacrifices I'll never even know about to educate me and give me the tools I needed to write, my husband, Dave, has stood by me through my abundant insecurities and moments of self-doubt. All three of them have offered nothing but love and support.

Special thanks and much love to Bill and Jeanetta Keller. I lost count of how many times they read my story because they read every version, always offering support and encouragement. Special thanks also to Tanner Latham, my storytelling friend, who edited the first draft of this book and helped

447

me shape characters over fried green tomatoes at a Birmingham cafeteria. And a big shout-out to Gary Wright for talking me up in the Big Apple and encouraging me.

I met Leslie Stoker of Stoker Literary when we both landed on the same nonfiction project, *Southern Living 50 Years*. Her editing skills amazed me daily, and when she agreed to represent me, I was on cloud nine. A few months later, when she told me Kelsey Bowen at Baker Publishing Group wanted to chat, I just about had to reach for the smelling salts. Kelsey, like Leslie, has been a real champion for my manuscript and an incredible editor and writing coach.

As this manuscript progressed, I had the opportunity to work with still more talented people at Revell. Jessica English is an insightful and sensitive editor who saved me from myself more than a few times. Cheryl Van Andel and the creative team produced a beautiful, evocative cover. Hannah Brinks Korns has guided me through the marketing plan so that someone might actually buy this book we've all worked so hard on. And publicist Karen Steele has put my little fictional Southern town on the map. Many thanks to the entire team at Revell.

Photographer Mark Sandlin has shot beautiful images of people and places from

Nepal to New Orleans, but I think his greatest challenge must have been dealing with a camera-shy writer in her own backyard. Thank you, Mark, for the portrait on this book (and the whole portfolio you shot, which my mother is busy framing).

I also owe a great debt to *Southern Living* magazine, where my former editor in chief, John Floyd, used to tell me, "Put your faith and your family first, and this magazine a distant second." Martha Johnston was a constant "you can do it" mentor there — and still is. When I was completely green, Dianne Young, John Logue, and other literary writers at the magazine taught me the difference between stringing together sentences and telling a story. Fast-forward about thirty years, and I'm still learning from Sid Evans, Krissy Tiglias, and an incredibly talented *Southern Living* staff, including Nellah McGough, who has pushed and prodded and nudged and cajoled me to make sure I never gave up on this book.

Through *Southern Living* and friends I made there, I met wonderful people who somehow made time to read and critique this book for Revell, serving as my "official" editorial board: authors J. I. Baker, Nancy Dorman-Hickson, and Michael Morris;

HGTV Magazine editor in chief Sara Peterson; a couple of straight-talking, free-thinking Southern lawyers, Sabrina Simon and Sally Reilly; my favorite literary scholar at the University of Alabama, Yolanda Manora; and my longtime friend Carole Cain, who has read every version of this manuscript (and who has such a sharp Southern wit that she daily says funnier things than I write).

If I try to name everyone who has read versions of this book — from magazine writers to my girl cousins to story-loving friends back home — I will surely leave someone out. And that would put me in hot water with Mama. I don't want to be in hot water with Mama. So to all the friends and family who spent some time in Glory and helped me on my journey, I count you among God's blessings to Dave and me.

One last word of thanks to my dear friend Jane Cain for her encouragement and enthusiasm for my book and for giving me one of Geneva's best lines: "I *mean!*"

ABOUT THE AUTHOR

Valerie Fraser Luesse is an Alabama native who has spent most of her life in the Deep South. She is best known for her work with *Southern Living* magazine, where she has specialized in stories about unique pockets of Southern culture — those places where the people and their landscape are intricately intertwined — such as the Gulf Coast, the Mississippi Delta, Acadian Louisiana, and the Outer Banks of North Carolina. The many years that she spent crisscrossing the South, meeting local people and listening to their stories, have lent her fiction its authentic color.

Luesse is a graduate of Auburn University and Baylor University. *Missing Isaac* is her first novel.